GRACE TO THE FINISH

JULIE HYZY

BERKLEY PRIME CRIME
New York

BERKLEY PRIME CRIME
Published by Berkley
An imprint of Penguin Random House LLC
375 Hudson Street, New York, New York 10014

Copyright © 2017 by Julie Hyzy
Penguin Random House supports copyright. Copyright fuels creativity, encourages
diverse voices, promotes free speech, and creates a vibrant culture. Thank you for buying
an authorized edition of this book and for complying with copyright laws by not
reproducing, scanning, or distributing any part of it in any form without permission.
You are supporting writers and allowing Penguin Random House to continue to
publish books for every reader.

BERKLEY is a registered trademark and BERKLEY PRIME CRIME and the B colophon
are trademarks of Penguin Random House LLC.

ISBN: 9780425281635

First Edition: July 2017

Printed in the United States of America
1 3 5 7 9 10 8 6 4 2

Cover art by Kimberly Schamber
Book design by Laura K. Corless

For Curt, who makes all my dreams come true.

Acknowledgments

My ever-delightful, fabulous editor, Michelle Vega, has been a joy to work with throughout my career at Berkley Prime Crime. Big hugs and heartfelt thanks to her and to the team who brings these books to life, especially Bethany Blair, Stacy Edwards, and Erica Horisk.

I'm forever grateful to you, my wonderful readers, who have come to love Grace almost as much as I do. Thank you all for allowing me to dream up new mysteries for Grace and the gang to solve.

And, of course, all my love to my family. You are my strength. You are my world.

Chapter I

"BEFORE WE GO IN"—I RAISED MY VOICE TO BE heard over the thunderous wind—"I think we should say a few words. It's an important day. Wouldn't it be nice to mark the occasion with a little ceremony?"

Four of us huddled in the doorway of the former Granite Building. My roommates, Bruce and Scott, positioned closest to the front door, turned to me with bemused expressions. Scott pointed out toward the street. "It'll pour buckets any minute and you want to conduct a ceremony?"

Anton Holcroft—the fourth member of our small party—nodded vigorously. My roommates and I had only recently come to know this sturdy, elderly man, but his vast experience in the hospitality industry had earned him a key position in our new venture.

"Our Grace is correct," Anton said, also raising his voice. "Today marks the beginning of a new life for this building and a new adventure for us all. Regardless of the elements, before we cross that threshold, it is fitting for us to say a few words."

Bruce jangled the building's keys. "Then I hereby call this meeting of Amethyst Cellars's board together. Do we have a quorum?" He glanced around, grinning. "Looks like all are present and accounted for. Grace, you have the floor. Make it quick."

With all eyes on me, I hesitated. I'd made the spontaneous suggestion without expecting to be called upon to deliver. Filled with the spirit of camaraderie, however, I spoke from the heart. "As Anton said, we're embarking on an exciting adventure. This is new for all of us. No doubt it will be challenging, but I hope we always remember to have fun. And as long as we work together, I'm sure we will." Wrapping a hand around Bruce's, I dragged the keys up high between us.

Scott and Anton raised their hands to join ours.

"Together?" I asked as we stood with our hands clamped above our heads.

"Together," they chorused.

A hard burst of thunder accompanied our declaration, shooting rumbling reverberations beneath our feet and encouraging a hasty retreat. Bruce pulled the keys back down and, fumbling, tried fitting one into the scuffed lock. He tried a second, then a third key, before one slid home.

"Whuh-oh," Scott said as the sky opened up and the predicted buckets came sluicing down.

Bruce turned the key, grasped the knob, and yanked open the antique door.

"Woof!" I said as we scurried in. Two seconds longer and we would have been drenched.

Anton closed the door behind us, shutting out the noisy storm. Rubbing his hands, he ran his gaze up and down the massive foyer. "Well, here we are," he said, his words bouncing hollowly against blank walls.

Dark and dank, the entryway featured an elongated oval

interior that narrowed at the far end. Like a teardrop without the sharp point. Our footsteps echoed as they scuffed along the fifties-era mosaic tile floor. The space smelled of damp metal and old dust. I shivered as a chill seeped in through my shoes.

"Wow." As my eyes adjusted, I reached out to run a gloved finger along the tiled wall. "The place that time forgot, isn't it? What color is this? Avocado?"

Bruce skirted past us. "Let me get the lights." He disappeared around the far corner.

"Midcentury at its finest," Scott said. "It's actually closer to sage, thank goodness. We can work with that if we have to."

The entryway flooded with light. Bruce called out to us, "Did I get it?"

"Yep. They're on," I called back.

Anton cupped a hand against the side of his face. "See if you can kick on the heat, too, while you're there," he shouted to Bruce. Turning to me and Scott, he added, "Who would expect such brisk temperatures this time of year?"

He was right. Emberstowne, and indeed most of the state, shivered in the midst of a prolonged cold spell. It was April, for goodness' sake. After teasing us with a few weeks of spring, Mother Nature had decided to shoot rainy, chilly weather our way. I'd lived through much worse growing up in Chicago, but here, April temperatures were expected to be mild, bordering on warm.

"This is your first visit to the building?" Anton asked me as I made a small tour of the sage-tiled teardrop. "I'm surprised."

"I had every intention of touring the place before we took possession," I said, continuing to examine the area. Scott was right. The glass tiles lining the walls from floor to ceiling were a good color to work with, given Amethyst Cellars's established color palette. The sage would serve as a lovely counterpoint to the cherrywood furniture and violet crystal accents. "Unfortunately, however, family matters ate up a good deal of my free time these past couple of weeks."

I didn't explain further. If Anton had heard anything about my sister's crimes and federal conviction, he'd been supremely tight-lipped. If he hadn't heard, I'd be obliged to tell him the unpleasant truth about Liza at some point.

More pressing, perhaps, was how I planned to deal with her going forward. I'd recently gotten word that she'd be released within thirty days. That call had come in almost a month ago and I still hadn't tied up all my loose ends. But I refused to allow any negativity to intrude on today's celebratory mood.

Bruce rejoined us. "What do you think, Grace?"

At the center of the teardrop, high above our heads, hung a multitiered chandelier so blanketed with dust it would have looked at home in Disney's Haunted Mansion. Although it practically begged for a good scrubbing, the place gave off a cool, kitschy vibe. Lots of potential here.

"I love it already, and I've only taken ten steps in," I said. "I can't wait to see the rest."

There were three doorways leading deeper into the building from the wide foyer. The ones to the right and left opened to identical musty rooms about fifteen feet square.

"We think this is where they invited guests and visitors to wait. Salespeople and the like," Scott said.

I poked my head into each one in turn. "Big rooms."

"Everything was bigger back then," Anton said. "Architecturally speaking, that is."

Opposite the front door, at the teardrop's narrow end, a tiny reception area boasted a dusty, waist-high countertop.

"Check this out," Scott said as he took up a position

behind it. "Is this a perfect place for our host stand, or what?"

"Perfect," I said with a smile.

"We'll have to spruce it up a little, of course," he said. "Make a few changes."

"A little?" Bruce cough-laughed. "How about a complete redo?"

"True." Scott didn't stop beaming. "And eliminate the crud, of course," he added as he ran the tips of two fingers along the countertop, then promptly sneezed from a kicked-up cloud of dust. "Too bad there wasn't a dirt discount."

I ran my fingers along the wall again, then glanced at my grimy glove. "If there was, the bank would have had to pay you to take this place off their hands. I've never seen dust this thick." I made a so-so motion. "On second thought, maybe I have in a few of Marshfield's forgotten rooms. But this really is something."

"How long has the building been abandoned?" Anton asked as we made our way, single file, past the reception area into the heart of the structure.

"Fifteen years, at least," Bruce said. "When the glass factory closed up shop."

"Wow." I cleared the threshold to find myself in an expansive industrial space that stretched the entire width of the building. "This place is huge."

Bruce stretched out both arms, walking backward. "Can you believe it?" he asked. Exposed brick walls, concrete floors, and high ceilings combined to soften the acoustics. "With a basement." Broadening his arms, he pointed toward two open stairways at the building's far ends.

"You'll change the lighting, I assume," I said, looking up.

Bruce frowned at the fluorescent fixtures. "Ya think?" He glanced around. "At least we have some natural light."

In addition to the multipaned windows that lined the three brick walls, four oversized, cobwebbed skylights dotted the beamed ceiling. I could imagine how lovely they'd be on a sunny day. Once they were clean, that is. "They seem to be watertight," I said as thunder shook the building again.

"They are," Bruce said. "According to the building inspector."

Scott and Anton had meandered away, heading toward the building's north end. They were too far for me to hear their conversation, but I could tell from their body language—pointing and nodding—that the two men were enjoying themselves.

"This is wonderful," I said to Bruce. "Have you decided where you'll locate the wine-tasting area, and where you want the restaurant?"

He shook his head. "We hope Anton will give us guidance there. He's managed so many successful venues, I know he'll have great suggestions to maximize space, efficiency, and atmosphere."

I tucked my hands into my hips. "This is even better than I imagined."

"I take it that you're not regretting investing with us?" Bruce asked.

"Not for a moment." Now that I was beginning to warm up, I tugged at my gloves to remove them. "Can I see the rest of the place?"

"Of course," Bruce said. "Wait for us," he called to Scott and Anton, who had stopped dead at the top of the stairs. Something in their body language sent a jolt of panic to my gut.

The two men didn't answer. There was no chance they hadn't heard Bruce's shout. A second later, still ignoring us,

Scott rushed down the stairs. Anton held a hand over his mouth and quickly followed behind.

Bruce and I looked at each other, then hurried to join them.

A woman lay at the basement landing. Face up, her arms were spread high and wide, looking as though she tried to signal a touchdown. With softly coiffed, thinning white hair, she appeared to be in her mid-sixties, perhaps older. Her eyes were closed, her expression mild, her lips faintly blue.

Bruce gasped, "It's Virginia," as he brushed past me.

She wore a red blazer with a mandarin collar. Scott reached in to feel for a pulse, but even from three steps up, I knew.

He sat back, shaking his head, and covering his mouth. When Bruce crouched next to him, Scott's eyes were wide. "She's dead," he said.

Anton, looking shocked, turned to me. "Who is Virginia?"

Though I'd never met the woman in person, my roommates had talked about her often enough. "Virginia Frisbie," I said. "She works at the bank."

The older man frowned. "A terrible accident."

I'd already pulled out my phone. "I'll call Rodriguez." I had the detective's number on speed dial.

"Rodriguez?" Bruce asked as I started up the stairs to get a better signal. "But he's homicide."

Anton, glancing between us, chimed in. "You can't believe someone killed her," he said. "It is obvious she fell down the stairs."

"I'm sure you're right." I pressed the phone to my ear. "But I'd rather have Rodriguez make that determination."

Chapter 2

RODRIGUEZ SNAPPED PHOTOS OF THE SCENE while we waited for Flynn, his partner, and the police forensic team to arrive. Rodriguez had stationed two uniformed officers at the Granite Building's front door and had asked Bruce, Scott, Anton, and me to step back from the immediate area while he took pictures and scribbled notes. Anton kept the farthest distance.

While we watched, Rodriguez peppered us with questions. He jotted down specifics about the time we'd arrived and how long we'd been in the building before we'd found her. "And you're certain of her identity?" he asked.

Bruce and Scott said that they were.

"We will confirm, of course, but for now, I'd like to know as much about her as you can tell me. Any idea how long Ms. Frisbie worked at the bank?" he asked.

Bruce turned to Scott. "What did she say? Thirty years? Thirty-five? I can't remember."

"Thirty-eight, poor thing." Scott tilted his head to look at

her. "She was about to retire, too. At the end of the month."
Facing Bruce, he said, "She was twenty-seven when she started
work there as a teller. She was very excited to have finally
turned sixty-five."

Bruce nodded. "That's right. One afternoon while we were
stuck waiting for her boss to get out of a meeting, she told us
her entire life history. Didn't she plan to move to Oklahoma
to be with her daughter and new grandchild?"

"Grandchildren," Scott corrected. "There's another one
on the way."

"Virginia married?" Rodriguez asked.

"She's widowed," the guys answered together.

Anton withdrew deeper into the basement even though
we'd widened our perimeter around the base of the stairs to
give Rodriguez room to move. The detective didn't seem to
mind us sticking around as long as we didn't interfere.

This lower level stretched the full length and width of
the building, but lacked the high ceilings and industrial pa-
nache the main floor offered. This was a stout, damp-
smelling space chock-full of heavy equipment. Aisles of
piles. Like a grocery store of junk. All covered in thick dust.

I tried to imagine how Virginia had fallen and landed face
up. Perhaps she twisted in a vain attempt to right herself as she
tumbled. Sixty-five years old seemed about right. She had on
a silky blouse beneath her red jacket. Wandering a little closer,
I noticed that her sleeve cuffs were slightly frayed. Her black
polyester pants looked as though she'd hemmed them herself.
Both of her soft-soled, sensible shoes were still on her feet.

Behind me, in the shadows, Anton dragged a wooden
crate out from beneath a cluttered table. He offered a seat.

"I'm fine," I said. "I'd rather watch."

He sat down and mopped his head with a plaid handker-
chief.

Scott shot me a worried look before sitting next to the elderly man. "Are you okay?" he asked.

Anton offered a weak smile. "I am what you call squeamish." He held the patterned cloth near his eyes as though to block his view. "I prefer not to see."

"Maybe it would be better for you to wait upstairs," I said, pointing to the second stairway at the basement's south end. "Would that be all right, Detective?"

Rodriguez was crouched near Virginia's head, one hand gripping his phone, the other hanging limp by his knee. There would have been a time when the middle-aged detective wouldn't have been able to lower himself to the floor without risking injury. After a near-fatal heart attack, the once-portly cop—though he would never be slim—had lost at least half his weight.

"Go ahead," he said without looking up. "I may have questions for you later, though, so don't leave."

When Anton's shoulders slumped in relief, Scott took him by the arm. "I'll go with you," he said, leading the older man to the far staircase. My roommates exchanged a look of such helpless despair that my heart broke for them. This was a terrible way to begin our new venture. The worst way.

In the chilly belowground space, I'd been holding my arms close, hugging myself for warmth as I paced behind Rodriguez, stealing glances at the deceased Virginia.

Rodriguez rose. "I agree it looks like a fall," he said, "but I called the coroner to come, too, just to be sure. You remember him, don't you? Joe Bradley?"

I fixed the homicide detective with a glare. "Ha-ha."

"Whatever happened between you two? I thought you guys were going to get together."

Behind Rodriguez, Bruce held up both hands as if to say: "Don't look at me. I didn't tell him."

"We were," I admitted. "We had a date set up right after . . ."

"Right after the business with Frances?" Rodriguez asked.

I caught my lower lip with my teeth, astonished to realize how little time had passed between then and now. "Was that only three weeks ago?" I asked.

"Give or take." Rodriguez made a so-so motion with his hand.

"Not that I don't enjoy your company, Detective," I said, "but I could go without these impromptu meetings for longer periods of time."

"You do keep us busy." He scratched his chin as he walked around Virginia's prone form again. "But you're avoiding the question. What happened? Change your mind?"

I glanced over at Bruce, who shrugged as if to remind me that one broken date did not mean complete failure to connect.

"He got called out of town," I said. "No explanation, except to say that it involved family."

Rodriguez studied Virginia for a moment, then frowned up the staircase. "And you haven't rescheduled?" he asked.

"Between his weekends on call and my issues with my sister, no," I said. "We haven't." I waited a beat, then asked, "Do you know anything about these family issues Joe talked about?"

Rodriguez faced me. His deep brown eyes were warm but held a hint of sadness. "Have you told him about your sister? Does he know that Liza is due back here any day now?"

I shook my head. "I figured there was time for that."

He nodded. "Just as there's time for him to tell you his story."

"You're being very cryptic," I said.

Bruce broke in. "If you know something important about the guy, shouldn't you tell Grace?"

Rodriguez turned to my roommate with a wry grin. "I can tell you that he isn't a serial killer, if that's what you're worried about. He doesn't have a criminal record of any kind. But if Grace and Joe are really interested in a relationship, they ought to peel away the layers of their lives at a pace that works for them."

Bruce frowned, giving me a look that said that he would much rather I be provided a full dossier first.

Rodriguez crouched again, this time a few feet beyond Virginia's head. He closed one eye and squinted up the steps. "You Googled him, I assume," he said.

"Joe?" I asked. Of course he meant Joe. "I did. There's not much there, other than the fact that he's a doctor. He doesn't seem to participate in social media. Unless he does so under a pseudonym. Which I think is unlikely."

"Me too." As Rodriguez stood again, Flynn and the forensic team made their way down the far staircase. The wiry young detective led two professionals, both of whom I'd met before, across the basement's expanse.

"Another murder, Grace?" Flynn asked. "How many does this make for you?"

"Not this time," I said. "Looks like she fell."

Behind me, Rodriguez said, "Maybe."

I spun. "You don't think so?"

"Let's wait for Joe to arrive," the older detective said mildly. "He'll let us know if we need to do an autopsy."

"If?" Bruce asked. "Aren't autopsies standard procedure in situations like this?"

Flynn rolled his eyes. "That's what everybody thinks. You watch too much TV."

Bruce shot me a look of exasperation, but held his tongue.

Rodriguez waved the air between them. "Autopsies aren't always required," he said, affecting a teacher-like tone. "If our victim's injuries are consistent with a fall and we determine she had reason to be here alone, her death will be ruled an accident."

"And that's what you think happened," I said.

He ran his gaze up and down the steps again. "Maybe."

Less than five minutes later, Joe arrived. Though he still used a cane, he seemed to be walking with a less-pronounced limp.

"Hi, Grace. Good to see you," he said as he donned latex gloves and stretchy blue booties. I barely managed to return the greeting when he addressed Rodriguez. "What do we have here?"

As the detectives brought Joe up to speed on the situation, he made a slow circuit around Virginia's body, calling out observations to an aide to record as he did so. With brisk efficiency, the assistants set up three bright floodlights and fixed their beams on Virginia, making the scene a surreal death tableau.

Joe was about six feet tall with wavy hair, an almost constant five o'clock shadow, and eyes that crinkled merrily when he smiled. I watched for a while impressed, though not surprised, by his thoroughness.

Bruce sidled up. "How long do these things take?"

"No idea." I shrugged. "I'm not usually present for this part."

"Mind if I walk around a bit?" he asked. "Even a space this big starts to feel claustrophobic when there's a dead body lying nearby."

I still wore my trench coat and had my arms crossed for warmth. "Claustrophobic and cold," I said. "I'll join you."

Rodriguez glanced up, giving us a nod of encouragement. He'd find us when he needed us.

Although the basement was chilly and smelled of wet

wood, it was well illuminated. Fluorescent fixtures, like bright stripes in the ceiling, cast their cold, sterile light on the detritus below.

Bruce and I strolled past piles of equipment, supplies, and machinery that had been crammed into makeshift rows. "What is all this stuff?" I asked.

He laughed. "Ours now." Running a finger along the lip of a metallic apparatus that resembled a giant vise turned sideways, he said, "The dust is so heavy down here we'll need hazmat suits to clean this place out."

"I think we should hire professionals to do that. What if there are toxic substances down here? Those who do this for a living will know what to look for far better than you or I or Scott would."

"True, but the cost may be prohibitive."

I didn't say anything. Although Bruce and Scott were the new owners of record of the building, I was the silent partner who had put up funds to enable the purchase. We'd settled on a system that I completely agreed with: They'd solicit my opinion before making any major decisions, but Amethyst Cellars's day-to-day business dealings were all theirs. Our new friend Anton served as a paid consultant.

I wanted to offer to cover the costs of a professional cleaning company, but knew better than to undermine their power by setting myself up as the controller of the purse strings who made things happen whenever I felt like it. Let them come to a decision on their own. If I constantly stepped in to affect outcomes, it wouldn't be long before they started to resent my influence. Bruce and Scott had run the original Amethyst Cellars successfully—without any help from me—for a number of years. Despite the fact that this new location involved a considerable level of complexity, my roommates needed to have the freedom to run it on their own. I pulled in my lips and said nothing.

We made our way down one row and up the second, emerging near where we'd started. Before turning left to start down the next aisle, I glanced over at Rodriguez and Flynn. The younger detective had begun to pace. Joe continued his assessment, oblivious to everything but Virginia's prone form. It didn't look as though we would be missed anytime soon.

I stopped to examine an eight-foot folding table that sat at the mouth of the next row. "What do you think was here?" I asked.

Bruce, having gotten a few steps ahead of me, turned to look. "I have no idea."

As he ambled back, I tilted my head to study the tabletop, far less dusty than most of the rest of the horizontal surfaces. Not only that, there were large, roughly rectangular patches that were practically dust-free. "I thought you said you haven't removed anything from down here." I bent down to look under the table, thinking that perhaps items had been relocated below but the floor beneath the collapsible countertop was clear.

"We haven't." Bruce blinked his puzzlement.

"Clearly, whatever had been on this table has been moved. Fairly recently, too."

Bruce reached to touch one of the clear areas, but I stopped him.

"Hang on a second. Let's not disturb this yet."

He shot me a look of concern. "What are you thinking?"

I wasn't sure precisely. "All those agreements you signed gave you and Scott ownership of the building and all its contents." Though the gesture was unnecessary, I pointed.

"If neither of you removed the items that were here as recently as"—I guessed, based on the dust variations—"yesterday, then who took them?"

Bruce shrugged. "There's no indication of a break-in," he said. "And even if there were, nothing else seems disturbed." He perched his hands on his hips and did a slow rotation. "Not that I can tell anyway."

"Do you think that perhaps there was a break-in, and Virginia walked in on the thieves while they were stealing these . . . whatevers?"

"You mean that maybe she didn't fall down the stairs? That she may have been pushed?"

I tapped a knuckle against my chin. "This could all be crazy speculation. There's probably a rational explanation. But I do think it's worth mentioning to Rodriguez."

As though he'd heard us, the detective lifted his head and turned our way.

I beckoned to him. "Do you have a minute, Detective?"

He mumbled something to Flynn then came over to where we were standing. He listened as we recounted the details of the baffling dust patterns.

"It looks to me as though several sizable items were taken away recently," I said. "And from what Virginia told Bruce and Scott, no one except bank officers had access to the building."

"Oh, and the inspector," Bruce piped in. "I'd forgotten about her."

"Village inspector?" Rodriguez asked. "I thought they were all male."

"No, the one we hired when we bid on the building," he said, turning to me. "You remember, Grace. We had her take a look at the structure to make sure it was sound before we moved forward. She found a few things we'll need to address—termites, for one—but otherwise pronounced this a good deal."

I expected Rodriguez to dismiss our dust discovery as unimportant, but he'd begun scribbling in his notebook again. "How long ago did she come through? It sounds as though it was some time ago. Not recently."

"Her first inspection was days after we decided to move forward on the deal," Bruce said. "But she provided a second, final inspection two days ago. To make sure nothing material had changed."

Rodriguez grunted. "She got a name?"

Bruce nodded. "Hang on." He pulled out his phone and began scrolling through his contacts. "I can't remember it at the moment. Cynthia something. Wait. Here it is." He rattled off the woman's information while Rodriguez took it all down.

The detective pursed his lips as he wrote, shooting wary glances back where Joe was finishing up his examination.

Bruce and I exchanged a glance. "What is it?" I asked Rodriguez. "What aren't you telling us?"

I watched indecision roll across the detective's face. He pursed his lips again, then lowered his head and spoke quietly. "Joe believes the some of the injuries that Ms. Frisbie sustained are inconsistent with a fall down the stairs."

Bruce's eyes went wide. "She didn't fall?"

"Oh, she fell all right," Rodriguez said. "But Joe's preliminary examination leads him to suspect she may have fought off an attacker and been hit by something heavy first. He believes that blow, along with the fall, contributed to her death. He won't go on record until he's had a closer look, though."

"Do you think Virginia surprised a thief and he killed her?" I asked.

"I wouldn't rule it out. Good going, Grace," he said.

At that moment, Flynn came bounding over. "Looks like our victim is headed to the carving table after all." He rubbed his hands together. Maybe he was trying to warm them, I told myself, but a glint in his eyes suggested otherwise. "And this time, the investigation is all ours, right, Rodriguez?"

"Not so fast, amigo," he said.

Catching a clue from our expressions, Flynn glanced down at the empty table, then back up at me. "You just can't stay out of our business, can you, Grace?"

Chapter 3

RODRIGUEZ AND FLYNN ASKED THE EVIDENCE techs to photograph the dust patterns, then pulled out their phones to snap a few shots of their own. The two detectives decided to spend time examining the rest of the basement, looking for anything else that might provide a clue to how Virginia died.

"There are two individuals upstairs," Rodriguez said to a pair of uniformed cops. "Scott and Anton. Please ask them to wait for us. We'll have a few questions for them. Also, try to keep them from wandering around. The scene has already been trampled on. Let's not make it worse."

When they started for the stairs, Bruce said, "I'll go up with them."

Rodriguez nodded. He and Flynn started down the first aisle, exactly the way Bruce and I had.

With everyone else gone, I wandered back to where Joe worked alone, squinting in the bright artificial light as he knelt next to the body. He noticed me watching.

"Crouching is a little hard for me, still," he said as he placed one gloved hand on Virginia's shoulder, the other on her hip, ready to turn her over.

"Is it okay if I watch?" I asked. "I promise not to get too close."

He glanced up, taking a moment to focus, then smiled. "That seems to be our problem, doesn't it? Not being able to get close?"

Pleased that he'd opened the door to a bit of an awkward subject, I decided to push it a little further. "How did your family issue work out? Is everything okay?"

"Long story," he said, retuning his attention to the matters at hand. "One of these days, when you and I have a chance to have a real conversation . . ." He let the thought hang as he eased Virginia's body onto its side. "Hello, what's this?"

Instinctively, I stepped forward. "What is it?"

Using the back of his wrist to scratch the side of his head, he frowned. "A credit card?"

"You don't sound so sure." Maintaining my distance, I came around to see better as he pulled out what resembled giant plastic tweezers.

"Hang on," he said. Using the tool, he lifted a maroon rectangle of plastic off the floor, which did, indeed, resemble a credit card. A second, similar card lay below it.

"What are they?" I asked.

He held the first card up, making it easier for me to see. "I'd say it is a credit card, or was supposed to be."

The small rectangle featured a familiar credit company logo but lacked any numbers or name. "It's a blank," I said unnecessarily.

"What would she be doing with unidentified credit cards?"

"She works—worked—at the bank," I said. "That's probably where they came from. Maybe she brought them with her."

"Hmph," he said. "Then why were they found beneath her body? If she had them on her person, they'd be in a pocket or her purse, not under her shoulder."

"Where is her purse, by the way?"

"Detective Flynn had one of the uniforms take it into evidence." He pointed about four feet away. "It landed there, some distance away from Virginia."

"What are you thinking?" I asked.

He looked up at me. "Nothing yet. Just asking questions."

"Do you think she may have been carrying more of these blanks?" I asked. "And that whoever killed her did it because he wanted them? Maybe when he shoved her down the stairs, he didn't realize that two cards went down with her."

Joe got to his feet as he peeled off his latex gloves. "Solid reasoning," he said. "Of course, we don't know for certain that she was pushed. My preliminary observations are just that: preliminary. I'll know more when I get her on the table."

"Is there any chance you'll let me know what you find out?"

"As long as Rodriguez doesn't mind." His gaze was warm. "Maybe we could discuss updates over dinner, or drinks."

"Or both." I smiled. "Speaking of Rodriguez—and Flynn—we should probably call them over to show them what you found."

"Detectives?" Joe called loudly. "If you have a moment?"

"Be right there," Flynn shouted back from the basement's far corner.

While we waited, Joe came to stand next to me. "Unfortunately, if our illustrious detectives order me to keep the matter confidential, I won't be able to share any information at all."

I wrinkled my nose. "That's a definite possibility."

Staring down at the dead body before us, he shrugged with the utmost nonchalance. "If that's the case, I'd understand if you wouldn't want to go for dinner or drinks. Or both." He turned to meet my eyes.

"I think we can restrain ourselves sufficiently to avoid discussing the investigation. If we have to, that is."

"Then I'm game if you are," he said.

"Especially since you promised to share your long story when we do get a chance to talk."

"That, too. And as long as we avoid Tuesday nights," he said. "My family practice office hours start in the afternoon and run late on Tuesdays. Patients can't always make it in to see me during the day."

"That's really nice of you."

"Patients are my life," he said. "It's a small inconvenience for me to avoid a huge inconvenience for them."

"Okay. Any night but Tuesday."

He smiled. "How about—"

"What's up?" Flynn asked as he loped over. Rodriguez followed behind. "You find something?"

"Maybe." Joe had slipped the two blank credit cards into separate evidence bags. He held them up. "What do you make of these?"

"Give them here." Flynn yanked the bags away from Joe and handed one to Rodriguez. "Where were they?"

Unfazed by Flynn's rudeness, Joe said, "Under our victim."

Rodriguez and Flynn wore identical expressions of puzzlement as they turned the bags over and studied the maroon cards contained inside.

"Under," Rodriguez repeated. "Could she have had them in her hand when she fell?"

Joe made a so-so motion with his head. "Of course it's possible, but I think a more likely scenario was that the cards fell to the bottom of the stairs before she did."

"What makes you say that?" Flynn asked.

"If, as I theorize, our victim was indeed struck by a heavy object prior to her fall, whatever items she'd been holding would have been launched from her hands. Her purse, as we documented, landed farther away from her body than it should have, had it fallen with her."

Rodriguez rubbed his forehead, then shot a glance at his partner as though asking a silent question.

Flynn shrugged. "She'll find out soon enough," he said. "You know how she is. Go ahead."

Rodriguez stepped closer. "We have a team down at the far end taking pictures and collecting evidence."

I bounced my attention between the two detectives. "Of?"

One end of Flynn's mouth curled up. "Looks like a squatter has had the run of this place for some time."

"A squatter?" I said.

"A homeless person. A bum," Flynn said. "You don't know what a squatter is?"

I resisted the urge to roll my eyes. "Of course I know what a squatter is. I was expressing surprise. Are you sure?"

"Of course we're sure." He gesticulated wildly. "We found a pile of junk over there. A grungy makeshift campsite. Most people would look at it and see a pile of garbage. But we've seen this sort of thing before. And geez, the smell." He shook his head, then turned to Rodriguez for support. "We just wait for the bum to return and we'll have our killer."

Rodriguez blinked slowly. "One step at a time, amigo. Let's let the good doctor present his findings first, okay?"

Joe and I exchanged a glance. "I'll get started as soon as she's brought to the morgue," he said.

"In the meantime, maybe we should try to figure out what's missing from that dusty table," I said. "Do you think the squatter is also the thief?"

"How about you leave the speculation to us?" Flynn said.

I looked up as a group made their way over to us from the far staircase. Bruce, Scott, and Anton followed two men rolling a gurney. "Doctor?" one of the men asked, addressing Joe. "Okay to take her?"

Joe trotted over to where they waited. While he spoke to them, I made my way over to my friends. "How are you, Anton? Feeling any stronger?"

He kept his eyes averted from Virginia's lonely form. "How are you unaffected by such sadness?" he asked.

"I'm not unaffected." It was the truth. Every time I caught sight of Virginia lying there, my heart clenched a little bit. But sadly, because of all the situations I'd been involved in these past few years, I'd begun to develop a protective shell that allowed me to compartmentalize. An accident would have been bad enough, but the idea that she may have been killed here shattered me. "Although I can't mourn Virginia personally because I didn't know her, I'm terrifically sad for those who did."

"You are able to keep your equanimity. Your balance," he said. "This is what allowed you to be able to help discover what happened to my friend Gus, is it not?"

He was referring to the situation involving Frances that had occurred a little more than three weeks ago.

I nodded. "Though whether that's a blessing or a curse, I can't tell for sure."

"It's a curse all right," Flynn said from behind me. I hadn't even realized he'd been listening in. "Everywhere Grace goes, murder follows."

Anton raised a thick hand to his forehead. "I should like to remain elsewhere."

Scott shrugged and followed the older man as he shuffled back toward the far stairs.

"Hold up there a minute," Flynn said, motioning to Rodriguez. "We have questions."

"Is it all right if I head back to Marshfield?" I asked Rodriguez. "I told Frances I'd be late, but I'm sure she's starting to wonder."

"Go ahead, Miz Wheaton. We'll be in touch."

As the attendants transferred Virginia's body to the rolling stretcher, I made my way over to Joe, who was packing up his examination kit. Time for me to take the initiative.

"You're heading straight to the morgue from here?" I asked him.

He paused and looked up. "I am. Even though I have office hours this morning, my colleagues will cover my patients until I get in. I'm lucky to be part of such an understanding group."

I waited a beat, then said, "Any chance you'll be free for drinks tonight? Or dinner?"

He smiled. "Or both?"

"Or both."

The smile faded. "I'd like that, but I don't know what the rest of the day holds. Let me get back to you."

Though his reasoning was completely understandable, I still felt a tiny sting of disappointment. "No problem," I said with a smile. "Talk to you soon."

Joe started to say something else, but Flynn stepped between us. "We're going to need to fingerprint you," he said.

"All of you. That way we can eliminate any familiar prints as suspects."

"You have my prints on file," I said. "But you may want to mention that to the guys before they take off."

"Yeah," Flynn said, though I didn't know why. Despite his earlier comment about questioning Bruce, Scott, and Anton, Flynn didn't appear inclined to move anytime soon, so I said good-bye and left for Marshfield.

Outside, though the rain had let up, the morning was still chilled. Gusty, dreary. I pulled my jacket tight and tucked my head down. But when I turned the corner toward my car in the adjacent parking lot, I stopped short.

A strange man stood behind my car, taking pictures with his phone. Wearing a nondescript windbreaker, sunglasses—on an overcast day, no less—and a baseball cap pulled low on his face, he was ever so slightly turned away.

"Hey," I shouted. "What are you doing?"

The man spun to face me, snapped another photo, then—in one smooth move—pocketed the phone and took off fast into the alley. I started after him, but by the time I got to the back of the parking lot, he'd disappeared.

Pulling up my phone, I called Rodriguez and told him what had just transpired.

He gave a thoughtful grunt. "Stay put. I'll be up there in a minute."

Moments later, three cops burst from the building, two of them running into the alley, the other down the street. Sirens echoed in the distance. I hoped that my vague description helped the police find the guy. Who was he?

When Rodriguez arrived in the parking lot, I explained the man's actions again. Provided his description again.

"How old would you say?" he asked.

"Hard to tell because I didn't get a good look at his face,"

I said, "but something in the way he moved makes me believe he's not a youngster. I'd guess over forty." I closed my eyes to picture him again. "He wore brown pants and gym shoes. And a plain, baggy windbreaker. Not particularly fashionable. That's not much help, is it?"

"Could be an ambulance chaser," he said. "Or in this case, a coroner's van chaser. Or a wannabe journalist. Don't know."

"Or the murderer?" I asked.

"If this was a murder," Rodriguez said. "Let's hope, this time, it isn't."

Chapter 4

FRANCES ROSE FROM HER CHAIR AND CAME around her desk when I walked in. "The Mister has been looking for you," she said by way of greeting.

"Good morning, Frances," I said. "Nice to see you. How did everything go this weekend?"

She waved the air between us as I slid my umbrella into the nearby stand and shrugged out of my trench coat. "You and your social niceties. Waste of time when there's business to be done. You don't really care about my weekend, so why bother asking?"

"But I do care," I said. "How's Percy settling in?"

Frances grimaced. I could only imagine the level of frustration she must have endured this past weekend as she supervised her ex-husband's relocation to Emberstowne. Recent events had encouraged Frances to move Percy—who had been housed in an assisted-living facility for about ten years—closer to home. My offers to help my steadfastly independent assistant during the move had been rebuffed. No surprise there.

"That man must believe he sits on a throne instead of in a wheelchair. You should have heard him ordering me around. And that young kid, Kyle, was no better. The two of them are a couple of lazy laggards."

Kyle, who also required a wheelchair for mobility, had been one of Percy's roommates before circumstances threw their lives into chaos.

"What's the new house like?" I asked. "I know you were concerned about accessibility."

"It already had ramps installed. Just had to make a few repairs on them before moving the guys in. And luckily, all the doorways are plenty wide. It's not Buckingham Palace but it'll do." She shook her head. "But boy, the kid's parents are a couple of whack jobs, if you ask me."

"Oh?" I said, knowing that was all the encouragement she'd need to spill the story.

"You wouldn't believe his mother," she began.

"Grace!" Bennett boomed as he walked in. "How did it go this morning?"

Frances made a face. "Oh yeah," she said, clearly annoyed by the interruption. "How's the new building?"

I let out a sigh of frustration.

Bennett's expression immediately shifted from excitement to concern. "What's wrong?"

"How much time do you have?" I gestured to the chairs at Frances's desk and we all took a seat.

I drew in a deep breath. How often had the three of us found ourselves here, discussing a local murder? Too often. I hated to have to break the news to them once again.

"What is it, Grace?" Bennett asked. "Was there a problem

taking possession? Are there structural difficulties the in-spector missed?"

It was unfair to allow tension to build. "We found some-one at the building. A woman. She's dead."

Bennett's and Frances's eyes widened. Frances drew in a sharp breath. "Who was it?"

"Until the police notify her next of kin—whoever they are—please don't let any of this get out. Her name was Virginia Frisbie. She worked at the bank."

Frances frowned as though concentrating. "I think I know her. Or at least know of her. Older woman? Sixties or seventies, maybe? White hair?"

"That's her," I said.

Frances nodded. "She's got a daughter, I think. Lives out of town. Oklahoma?"

Bennett regarded me warily. "How did she die?"

"Unclear," I said. "Rodriguez and Flynn—"

Startled, Bennett sat up. "Rodriguez and Flynn? Are you telling me this is a homicide?" he asked. "Another murder?"

"She may have died from a fall down the stairs," I ex-plained. "That's how we found her."

"But there's doubt," Bennett said, not even bothering to phrase it as a question. "Was she pushed?"

I explained everything that had transpired that morning. When I finished, Frances gave one of her customary grunts. "No wonder you were so late."

Bennett massaged his forehead. "You can't get involved in this, Gracie. Don't get involved in this. Please."

"I never intend to," I said. "But as Bruce's and Scott's business partner now, I'm already involved."

"Will this keep your roommates from moving forward with their plans to renovate?" Frances. Always the pragmatist.

"We'll see. Joe will be performing the autopsy today. We should have answers soon."

"You two haven't had your date yet, have you?" Bennett asked even though he knew the answer.

"I'm sure we will soon." I hoped to put an end to that line of questioning.

"Hmph," Frances said.

"What?" I asked.

"What about one of her coworkers? You never know who there may benefit from her death."

I'd already told them both about the theory that Virginia had walked in on a thief caught in the act of stealing, and I'd mentioned the detectives finding evidence of a squatter. But I hadn't considered the possibility of her being killed for any other reason. And I'd certainly not considered a premeditated murder.

"Thanks, Frances. Keep in mind, though, that she may have simply fallen on her own."

"Is that what you think?" she asked.

I gave a rueful smile. "No."

"Well then, we have to think outside the box. That approach hasn't let us down yet, has it?"

"Let's change the subject to something a little less morbid, okay?" Turning to Bennett, I asked, "Frances said you were looking for me earlier. What's up?"

Bennett's expression darkened. "I'm sorry to disappoint you. This morning I received several updates on your sister's release and wanted to know if you'd seen them yet."

I felt my shoulders slump. Ever since familial ties had been established proving that Bennett and I were related by blood, he and I had agreed to face the Liza problem together. I copied him on all correspondence, and the authorities in charge of her imminent release were authorized to contact him if they couldn't reach me.

With a sigh of frustration, I dug into my purse and pulled out my phone. "Yep, here they are. A missed phone call from Liza's advocate and"—I scrolled—"two missed e-mails."

Forcing a benign expression, I met Bennett's eyes. "What's the news? Have they firmed up her release date?"

I could tell it pained him to answer. "She gets out a week from tomorrow."

I gave myself a moment to digest that. "Okay," I said, working hard to appear unruffled. "We've put our plans in place, and even though it's cutting things close, we shouldn't have any worries, right?"

Frances snorted. "We've met your sister, remember?"

"I can't keep her from getting into trouble," I said. "All I can do is try to keep her from making trouble for those I care about. The two of you. Bruce and Scott. Tooney. Everyone at Marshfield."

Frances started to make another snarky comment, but Bennett cut her off. "When does your aunt arrive?"

"Saturday," I said. "She's not happy about it." That was an understatement. I'd enlisted Aunt Belinda's help. For as long as I'd known her, my mother's sister—her half sister, actually—had hammered at me nonstop to be kinder to my estranged sister.

Widowed now for many years, Aunt Belinda, retired and living in Florida, had reluctantly agreed to come to Emberstowne to help Liza get settled in. My sister's legal advocate had strongly suggested that, in order to provide the best chance for success, Liza live with or near a responsible adult. I wanted no part of her. She'd proved herself untrustworthy and disloyal too many times in the past.

But Aunt Belinda and I were the only family Liza had. I

suspected she had no friends. At least none willing to assume responsibility for her.

Liza's advocate had offered my sister a choice: move to Florida with Aunt Belinda or come to Emberstowne, near me. For reasons I could never fathom, Liza had chosen me.

For all her squawking about how poorly I treated Liza, Aunt Belinda hadn't been keen on my sister moving in with her, either. After a great deal of back-and-forth, however, our bellyaching aunt had reluctantly agreed to a show of support. She would temporarily relocate to Emberstowne to help Liza get settled.

I had no regrets about strong-arming my aunt into this agreement. She'd berated me almost all my life—telling me that I'd been the favored child—that poor Liza never had the opportunities that had been granted me. But I'd lived with my parents and lived with Liza. I knew the truth. Our parents had done everything in their power to help my sister find her way, but she hadn't been interested in school, family ties, or taking responsibility for her actions.

In order to help Liza achieve her potential, our parents had been through years of therapy, with and without my baby sister. All the while, Aunt Belinda had played Monday-morning quarterback from the sidelines, criticizing Mom and Dad on their parenting skills.

For all her bluster, however, our aunt had rarely visited us while we were growing up. Mom had told me it was because her husband was a skinflint and wouldn't give her the money to travel. But even after her husband died, Aunt Belinda still didn't come. She wasn't there to comfort our mom when our father died. Didn't come when Mom was diagnosed with cancer. Didn't visit while she lay dying. Didn't come to her funeral. Her own sister's funeral. She'd sent a card and piled on excuses.

I once asked Mom why Aunt Belinda complained so much. She said that it was because their parents had treated them differently. "I was the favored child, exactly the way Belinda thinks you are. Even though you're the older sister like Belinda is and I'm the younger, it's true that my parents treated us differently. I don't know why. I don't know why Belinda believes that about Liza, but it sticks in her craw."

In any case, I felt no shame in forcing our aunt to come up here and help with my ex-con sister. Maybe once Aunt Belinda got to know adult Liza, up close and personal, she'd lay off guilt-tripping me.

"I understand Mr. Tooney has found Liza an appropriate place to live," Bennett said.

I nodded. "It's a nice apartment within walking distance of Main Street, but far enough from my house to make her think twice before surprising me with a visit. At this point, I'm not sure if Liza knows that she's rooming with Aunt Belinda." I shrugged. "But beggars can't be choosers, I suppose. The sooner my sister straightens herself out, the quicker she can be on her own."

Frances crossed her arms. "She doesn't know about you and the Mister, does she? That she's a Marshfield, too, by blood?"

"Not as far as I'm aware." I fought the panic in my gut that hit every time I thought about how Liza would react when she discovered I was now co-owner of the Marshfield fortune.

Bennett leaned forward to pat my arm. "Whatever she knows or suspects doesn't matter. You and I will talk with her as soon as you deem appropriate. We will tell her of our familial relationship while making it clear that the reason you are my partner and heir has little to do with blood ties but everything to do with trust."

I smiled at him, wishing it would be that easy. Bennett and Frances had interacted with Liza enough to know not to trust her, but I'd lived with her treachery and duplicitousness all my life. If she'd turned her cunning and wily talent toward more productive endeavors—school, a trade, or starting a business, to name a few—she could have been extremely successful in her own right.

As it was, she was penniless, jobless, and homeless, with a federal conviction on her record. Entirely dependent on others for everything in her life, she resented me. Probably even more than I resented her. Once she discovered our relationship to Bennett, she'd want it all. She'd demand it. And she'd do her best to make our lives miserable until we acquiesced.

I gave a sad laugh. "So much for happier subjects."

Chapter 5

WHEN MY OFFICE PHONE RANG LATER THAT afternoon, Frances shouted, "It's the bank calling. I bet it's about poor Virginia," before I even had a chance to glance at the caller ID myself.

"Thanks, Frances. I'll let you know," I said before picking up.

Neal Davenport introduced himself as the bank's president before moving directly to the reason for his call. "As you may imagine, I was shocked to hear of Virginia's accident this morning. Everyone at the bank is heartbroken. She was beloved by all her coworkers."

He'd used the word "accident." Apparently Rodriguez and Flynn hadn't floated the homicide idea out to the masses yet. I murmured a nicety or two.

"Did you know she was nearing retirement?" Davenport asked.

"I did," I said. "My roomma—er—business partners, Bruce

and Scott, mentioned that. She'd worked at the bank for thirty-eight years, I understand."

"Started as a teller and worked her way up to senior vice president. She had quite a knack for business."

"So I've heard."

"You didn't get to know her?" he asked. "I thought you were one of the Granite Building's new owners. Virginia handled that transaction herself."

"Right, with Bruce and Scott," I said. "I'm the silent partner."

"Oh," he said in a way that led me to believe this came as news. "Hmm."

"Is there something I can help you with? In addition to offering my condolences, that is?"

He cough-laughed. "Looks like I jumped the gun here. I'd heard your name associated with the sale of the Granite Building and future plans to expand the Amethyst Cellars wine shop, and I made an erroneous assumption."

Frances hovered in the doorway, straining to listen in. I waved her into one of the chairs across from me.

"That's fine," I said to Davenport. "Do you need my roomma—er—Bruce's or Scott's contact information?" I'd have to get used to referring to them as partners rather than roommates. At least where business transactions were concerned.

"No, no. I have all that here." He cough-laughed again. "I suppose I just wanted the chance to talk with you a little bit," he said. "With the sudden change in your circumstances—with Mr. Marshfield, I mean—I'd been hoping to find a reason to connect."

I didn't know how to respond to that.

Didn't matter. He kept talking. "I'd like to invite you to

reach out if you ever needed assistance or financial advice. If there are any banking needs you have that aren't being serviced . . ."

Davenport continued, providing even more reasons to explain why he wanted to talk with me.

I decided to put him out of his misery and attempt a little fact-finding for myself. "I do have a question for you."

"Anything." I could practically hear his relief whoosh over the phone.

"How long ago did your bank take possession of the old Granite Building?"

"Oh. Hmm," he said again. "I would have to look that up to be sure because the foreclosure took place before I started working here. I want to say it's been more than five years. Maybe even as long as ten."

I thought about the evidence Rodriguez and Flynn had found suggesting a squatter had been living there.

"Other than Virginia, how many people from your bank had access to the Granite Building?" I asked.

Frances nodded approval.

"I couldn't say for sure. But I can certainly find out for you, if you think that's important information."

I not only was known in Emberstowne as being Bennett's niece, I'd also established myself as something of an amateur sleuth. Still, I didn't want to give Davenport the impression I was digging, or to tip the homicide detectives' hands before they were ready.

"Just curious," I said.

"I'll find that out for you," he said. "Is there anything else you'd like to know?"

Before I could form an answer, he jumped in to continue. "I'd be happy to schedule a meeting, either here at the bank, or out of the office. We could go for coffee and discuss whatever questions you may have. About the Granite Building or even about your financial needs."

Frances could hear every word. Her brows leaped upward and she smirked. Pointing at the phone, she nodded vigorously.

"Sure, that sounds great," I said, trying to boost my half-hearted tone.

We settled on lunch the following day.

"Just what I need," I said to Frances when I hung up. "Another financial guru who wants to get his paws on Bennett's fortune."

"Your fortune," Frances corrected. "And I don't think he's as interested in establishing a new account as he is in establishing a little one-on-one with you."

"No, he's a gold digger. For sure. Didn't you hear him asking about my financial needs?"

"Merely an excuse," she said. "He's interested in you."

"You got all that from eavesdropping on my phone call?" I pointed to the instrument on my desk. "I know you have superhuman powers, Frances, but I think this one is beyond your reach."

She shook her head, very slowly.

"Then why did you encourage me to meet with him? I'm not looking for a relationship right now." I tried not to think about Joe Bradley.

"And do you have some swamp land to sell me, too?" she asked with a snort. "Doctor-boy isn't moving fast enough, if you ask me."

So much for keeping that issue under Frances's radar.

"It can't hurt for you to spread your wings a little bit," she said. "See what else—who else—is out there. So you go for lunch with this banker guy. What's the worst that can happen? You find out that he really is only interested in your bottom line. That I'm wrong about his intentions." One end of her mouth curled up. "But I'm not."

BRUCE, SCOTT, AND I HAD KEPT IN TOUCH, UP-dating each other on the situation throughout the day, so when I returned home that evening, we didn't have a lot of new information to share.

"I did talk with Rodriguez again," I said as we sat down to dinner in the kitchen. Scott had whipped up one of his easy weeknight favorites: huevos rancheros. I dug into the cilantro-sprinkled egg, cheese, and bean combination, making sure to spear some avocado before popping the delectable forkful into my mouth.

"To tell him you plan to meet with Davenport?" Bruce asked.

I nodded and made affirmative noises. "And to ask if they found the guy who was snapping pictures outside."

"Did they?"

"Mm-mm." I shook my head as I chewed. "Wow. This is wonderful."

"Thanks," Scott said. "What did he say about the blank credit cards?"

"He e-mailed me a picture of one of the cards they found beneath Virginia so I have it for my records. He said that he and Flynn have already started talking to bank personnel, but they're coming up empty. If I want to mention it to Davenport, it's fine with him."

"If Frances is right," Bruce said, "you should probably stop calling him by his surname. That's not very romantic."

"Please. I haven't even met him yet." I dug into my dinner again. "Don't you two start matching me up with strangers now."

"What's going on with Joe Bradley?" Scott asked.

I shrugged. "Who knows? He and I seemed close to arranging a date, but we got interrupted."

Bruce waved his fork. "Always an excuse."

I gave them both a wry smile. "We're in the middle of a death investigation, remember?"

Scott made a show of looking around. "Where's your phone?" he asked. "He may be trying to text you right now."

"I'm not the president of the United States. I don't need to keep my phone by my side every moment of the day." I'd left it upstairs when I'd changed clothes. "But you're right. I'll go get it after dinner."

We talked awhile longer about our plans for resurrecting Amethyst Cellars. While the Granite Building would be cordoned off for another couple of days until the detectives cleared it, Rodriguez had assured us that—unless new information regarding Virginia's case came to light—it was unlikely we'd be delayed much longer than that.

"Don't get me wrong, I'm very happy we aren't facing huge delays," Bruce said as we finished up. "But I can't help feeling guilty about it."

I knew what my roommates were going through. "And yet changing our plans won't do Virginia any good. Not now."

"But it still feels wrong," Scott said. "We get to keep moving forward. Virginia doesn't."

"Remember how she fought us on buying the building at first?" Bruce asked. "It's almost like this is her final stake in keeping us from moving forward."

"Wait, I thought you told me she was a dream to work with."

"She was. Later," Scott said. "But at first, not so much. I thought it was us." Scott pointed to himself and Bruce. "You know. Unwilling to help because she didn't care for 'our lifestyle.' But she was warm otherwise. We eventually gave up trying to figure out why she didn't want us to buy the building."

"Was there a defect? Some problem she was afraid you'd discover?" I asked.

"That's why we brought in Cynthia Quinn, the inspector." Bruce made a funny face. "You don't think Virginia's hesitation to sell could have had anything to do with her death, do you?"

Scott shook his head. "I don't see how it could have. She eventually came around when she realized we were serious. That is," he said as he pointed to me, "once she realized we had the financial backing."

"What makes you think that, Bruce?" I asked.

He ran a hand through his dark blond hair. "I don't know," he said with a puzzled look. "Maybe we've been hanging around you long enough to start seeing clues. Even where none exist. What if there was something about the building that she didn't want us to find out?"

Scott sat up straighter. "Or a treasure hidden there that she didn't want us to find."

"Now you both are sounding too much like me." I picked up my empty plate to rinse it off in the sink.

The front doorbell rang.

The three of us exchanged a glance. "I'll get it," Scott said.

"Are you guys expecting anyone?" I asked.

Bruce started to clean up the rest of the table. "Nope."

A few seconds later, Scott returned with Bronson Tooney behind him. "Guess who's coming to dinner?" he said with a grin.

Tooney's cheeks reddened. "I don't mean to bother you,

but I saw all your lights on and thought you might want to hear what I found out about Virginia Frisbie."

"Have you eaten?" I asked.

The big man shook his head. "But that's okay. You guys are done. I won't be long."

"Have a seat," Scott said. "I've got plenty, and the three of us are all ears."

Chapter 6

"WHAT'S INTERESTING ABOUT VIRGINIA FRIS-bie," Tooney said once we were settled around the table, "is that she was the only bank officer with regular access to the Granite Building."

"Why is that important?" Scott asked. "The place was vacant for a number of years. I can't imagine the bank needing more than one employee to keep an eye on it."

Tooney had taken the opportunity to shovel a tall pile of eggs, beans, and tortilla into his mouth while Scott spoke. As he chewed, he pointed his fork for emphasis and a delicate string of orange-white cheese whipped around the utensil's tines.

"First of all," Tooney said after he swallowed, "it makes her a target. She had a habit of visiting the Granite Building at least once a week to ensure that nothing was amiss: no broken water pipes, no smashed windows, no rodent infestations."

"Eeyoo," I said.

Tooney waved his cheese-strung fork again. "Even though Virginia varied the days of the week when she took her tour of the building, she usually visited there immediately after the bank closed at night. A person with intent to do her harm may have waited for her to show up."

"But the detectives speculate that she walked in on a thief, surprising him," I said.

Tooney resumed eating.

"Unless there was no thief," Scott said, picking up on the flaw in the argument. "What if the killer took those items from the dusty table to make it look like a robbery? What if the killer had it in for Virginia the whole time?"

"But she was such a lovely woman," Bruce said. "Why would anyone want to kill her?"

"Who knows?" I asked. "Maybe she led a secret life as a criminal."

"I doubt that," Tooney said.

Bruce waved an index finger. "Remember, there may be no killer," he said. "This is all wild speculation. It could turn out to have been a terrible accident."

"I'd like to know what role, if any, the squatter played in this scene," I said. "I hope we can find him."

"Or her," Scott said.

"Or her," I agreed.

"The other thing about banks," Tooney said, "is that they are obsessive about dual control. What that means is that no single employee has full, unfettered control over any account. Like checks and balances, it keeps people honest. Most of the time, that is. There's still opportunity for collusion. That happens more than it should." He dug back into his meal. "But I'm getting ahead of myself."

I picked up the thought. "You're saying that you find it suspicious that Virginia handled the Granite Building on her own? And you think that may have had something to do with her death?"

Tooney, eating with gusto, made a so-so motion with his head. He tapped his napkin to his lips. We waited until he was able to talk again.

"Not necessarily. People are people. They take shortcuts. Bank presidents included."

I thought about Davenport. I'd have to ask him about this tomorrow.

"This situation," Tooney went on, "isn't like a bag of cash that needs to be watched constantly so that none of it goes missing. The Granite Building was a big, fat, vacant piece of property that no one much cared about until you two"— he pointed to Bruce and Scott—"expressed interest."

"In other words, no one would be able to sneak up to the Granite Building and steal it without someone noticing?" Bruce asked.

"Exactly," Tooney said. "The place required minimal maintenance, so—like Scott said—why would the bank devote more resources to its upkeep than necessary?" He again made the so-so motion. "But I don't want to dismiss it either. Virginia was the longest-serving employee at the bank. She held a lot of power. She controlled many assets. What if a person there wanted her out of the way? What better way to eliminate her than to wait until she was alone at the Granite Building to ensure she never came back out?"

I frowned. "That's sad."

"It is," Tooney said as he finished up his dinner.

We were all silent for a moment.

"The thing is," I said, "she was within weeks of retirement. If a coworker did, indeed, target her, why not wait for her to leave?"

"Very good question," Tooney said. "Which means maybe it wasn't anyone at the bank after all."

"What about family?" I asked.

Scott grimaced. "That's a terrible thought. Can you imagine anything worse than someone in your family wanting you dead?"

"Just gathering information," I said. "You mentioned that she's widowed?"

"Right," Bruce said. "And now she'll never get that chance to go live with her daughter in Oklahoma."

I turned to Tooney. "Other than the daughter, was there anyone else she was close to? Anyone in Emberstowne, I mean?"

"She had a few girlfriends, other widows mostly, but none of them are likely subjects." Tooney shrugged.

"And the daughter is completely in the clear?" I asked.

"Oh my gosh, Grace. What a horrible idea," Scott said.

"Grace is right," Tooney said. "We have to consider everything. Even stuff that can make you sick if you think about it." Returning to the question, he said, "I haven't had a chance to check the daughter out. Not completely. I'll follow up."

"Thanks, Tooney." I patted his arm. "I have faith in you."

His cheeks flushed.

BECAUSE OF TOONEY'S UNEXPECTED VISIT, I didn't remember that I'd left my cell phone upstairs until I got ready for bed that night. Two missed texts from Joe. Darn it.

They'd both come in during our talk with the private investigator, which, while helpful, was probably not nearly as informative as what Joe would have had to say. His first text: Rodriguez OK sharing results. You up for dinner? Drinks? Both?

Coming in an hour later, his second text read: Catch up tomorrow.

I shook the little phone as though doing so would make a difference. For about three seconds, I considered calling Joe for an update, but the finality in his second text kept me from making what could be a foolish move. He may have gone to bed already—even though it wasn't all that late. He may be winding down with a book or watching television. He could be catching up on paperwork or conversing with a friend. Who knew?

Tamping down my curiosity, I fought the temptation to text back. I really wanted to know everything about the autopsy results, but in all honesty, I mostly wanted to connect with Joe. Get to know him better.

Plenty of time tomorrow.

I sighed. Right.

"WHY DID YOU WEAR THAT?" FRANCES ASKED the minute I stepped into the office the next morning.

I glanced down at my cream-colored blouse, dark blue skirt, and navy flats. "It's supposed to be warm today," I said. "What's wrong with this?"

She shook her head, tsking as she took me in from head to toe. "You look like a nun."

I shrugged. "There are worse things in life."

"But today's your date with Neal Davenport," she said. "You're never going to reel in a man wearing an outfit like that."

I laughed as I made my way to my office. "Frances, you crack me up."

She grumbled.

An hour or so later, once I thought it was late enough in the morning to call, I phoned Joe at his office. His receptionist answered and let me know that Dr. Bradley was doing rounds at the hospital this morning. She assured me he'd return my call at his earliest convenience. I thanked her and hung up.

The minute I did, Frances came bustling in. "You have plans tonight?" she asked.

Taken aback, I needed a moment to reply. "Not yet."

"Good." She slapped a little pink note on the middle of my desk. "You do now."

"What's this?" I asked as I picked it up. First thing I noticed was Neal Davenport's name scribbled at the top of the sheet along with his phone number and the name of an Emberstowne restaurant below it.

"While you were on the phone, Mr. Banker called. Wanted to see if you were free for dinner instead of lunch. I told him you were."

"But I'm not."

"You said you didn't have any plans tonight." She pointed to the pink note as though that was sufficient. "What's the problem?"

"The problem is"—I caught myself sputtering—"I don't want to go on a date with Neal Davenport."

She raised both eyebrows, and although I couldn't see her feet, I knew she was tapping one of them. "Because of Dr. Bradley, I presume? You need to quit waiting around for him to show up. He's leaving you dangling on a string, that one. Time for you to take your love life into your own hands and pump some energy into it."

"Frances," I began, doing my best to keep my annoyance in check, "none of this has to do with my relationship status. Joe's been given the okay to share Virginia's autopsy results with me. Don't you think that maybe that's what's uppermost in my mind?"

"That's the problem," she said. "You keep worrying about murders instead of finding a man."

"I don't need one," I said. While that was true, it didn't necessarily mean that I was against the idea entirely. But I wasn't about to let Frances dictate my dating life. "And if it's a choice between talking with Davenport about Virginia's work at the bank, or finding out whether the poor woman died of an accident or was murdered, I'll take the cause of death conversation." I tilted my head. "If you don't mind."

"Hmph," she said, but I could tell I'd gotten through to her.

I reached for the desk phone. "I'll call Davenport now and let him know that I won't be able to make dinner tonight." I pulled my calendar over. "And since he's apparently busy for lunch today, we'll have to come up with a different arrangement."

"No, you won't." She whipped the pink sheet out from under me. "He can still do lunch today, but was hoping to start a little earlier. I told him you'd be in meetings most of the morning and couldn't get out any sooner. I'll call him back and let him know lunch is still on."

"He may have made alternate plans," I said. "We may still have to come up with another option."

"Pheh," she said. "Alternate plans. Give me a break. He'll make time for you."

I shook my head as she made her way out of my office. Just as she cleared the doorway, a thought occurred to me. "Frances," I called.

She stopped and turned.

"You didn't instigate all this, did you?" I made a circle with my index finger. "Did he really call you? Or did you try to wrangle things by turning this business meeting into something bigger because you thought having dinner was more romantic than lunch?"

"Me? Do something like that?" She pressed a hand to her chest. "How could you even suggest it?"

Alone in my office once more, I reached out and laid a hand on my desk phone. I wanted to leave the line open in case Joe called with the autopsy results, but I had another important task to face first. I should have made this call yesterday, but after our gruesome discovery in the Granite Building, it had slipped my mind.

Lifting the receiver, I dialed a number I'd come to memorize over the past couple of weeks. I didn't worry that the door to Frances's office was open. Her eavesdropping simply meant that I wouldn't have to fill her in later.

"Tessa Lundquist," the woman said when she answered. She sounded weary today, not that she'd ever been particularly chipper. I could only imagine how tough her job had to be. And how many such calls she fielded every single day.

"Good morning, Tessa," I said. "This is Grace Wheaton. We spoke a couple of times about—"

"Your sister, Liza," Tessa said. She sighed heavily. "Give me a second, I have her file right here."

I waited.

"Yep. Release coming up a week from today, right?" she asked. "You sure you're ready?"

Her question threw me off. "Is there any reason I shouldn't be?"

She gave a quick, breathy laugh. "I probably don't need to warn you about your sister, do I?"

I stared down at my desk blotter and massaged my forehead with my free hand. "I thought she was being released early due to good behavior."

Okay, so it wasn't exactly a question. But Tessa was kind enough to supply an answer. "'Good behavior' is a relative term," she said. "As long as someone like your sister doesn't get caught fighting with other inmates or smuggling contraband—transgressions that are documented—she's considered a model inmate. Makes it easy on the administration especially when a prison is overcrowded. Which hers is."

"'Doesn't get caught,'" I repeated. "That's the key phrase, isn't it?"

"Yep."

"There aren't any other places for her? Less crowded institutions?"

This time Tessa barked a laugh. "I'm no clairvoyant but I can already predict that this doesn't promise to be a happy family reunion. Sure, there are other places we could send her, but when you come down to it, this is Liza's first offense, she's not a violent criminal, and she poses no threat to society. So why not kick her out and give her the opportunity to reboot her own life?"

"And if she doesn't?"

"Then I suppose we'll see her again." Though I couldn't see Tessa, I swore I could hear her shrug. "I know it isn't easy and I don't like giving advice, but I can tell you that the recidivism rate of ex-convicts is high. The offenders with the best success rates are those with plenty of support from family."

I couldn't stop the tiny groan from escaping.

"I'm sorry," Tessa said, and I got the sense that she really was. "After all these years on the job, you'd think I'd know the secret to turning these women's lives around. But I don't. I can give you a list of mistakes that will send them back here, but there's no single answer for what keeps them out. I wish there were."

"Thanks," I said. And although I knew I'd be sorry later, I added, "I'll do my best for her."

"Good. She's a smart cookie, your sister. I'd like to see her put those brains to good use."

I bit my cheeks. "So would I."

Chapter 7

AFTER HANGING UP, I WAS TEMPTED TO TRY Joe's cell when Frances appeared in the doorway. "You finally off the phone?" she asked even though she clearly knew the answer. "I've got something to show you." With a tilt of her head, she gestured into her office and spun away, expecting me to follow.

I got to my feet.

Although it had taken some time for me to realize—for all her bluster and scorn— Frances had my best interests at heart. She'd reluctantly come to my defense early on in our relationship, and now that she knew I appreciated her, she'd become a bit of a mother hen. An opinionated, abrasive, chastising, pecking-at-me-constantly mother hen. But protective, always.

"I assume you overheard my conversation with Tessa," I said as I approached her desk.

"Only your end of it. But it was enough to get the gist." She clucked her disappointment. "You're setting yourself up again."

I started to sit across from her.

"No, no," she said. "Over here." She rolled her desk chair sideways to indicate where she wanted me to stand. "It's on the computer."

I came around the desk and took a look at her monitor. Nothing but her preferred wallpaper: a sun-drenched field of purple flowers.

"Something wrong with your desktop?" I asked.

She rolled her eyes. "Hold your horses, missy. I'm waiting until I have your full attention."

"You've got it."

"No, I don't," she said. "You're setting yourself up again."

"And you're repeating yourself."

"Wasn't sure you heard me the first time."

I leaned a hip against the side of her desk and folded my arms, staring down at my assistant. Seated, she folded her arms and stared up.

"What am I supposed to do?" I asked. "Pretend Liza doesn't exist? I've tried that. Doesn't work."

"You told that woman you'll do the best you can for your sister."

"What was I supposed to say? Sure, let her go free, but don't ask me to watch out for her?"

"Why not?" Frances asked. "She's an adult. There's no reason you need to feel responsible for her."

"I don't," I said. "Not really. I definitely don't feel responsible for her choices. But it's not like I can wipe the memory of her from my brain, you know."

Frances continued to frown up at me.

"All I want to do is get her settled," I said. "Make it clear she's got to fend for herself. Then I can walk away."

"And the minute she gets wind of your family ties? You think she's going to let you simply walk away?"

"I know she won't," I said. "But this time, I'm prepared. Most important, I'm not alone. I have you, and Bennett, and Bruce, and Scott. She caught me unawares when she showed up last time. This time, I'm ready for whatever she throws at me."

Frances's tadpole eyebrows eased upward as I spoke. "Maybe you are," she said. "I just don't want her to guilt you into trouble."

"Not going to happen," I said. "Not this time. That's partly why I insisted on bringing Aunt Belinda here. She's the queen of bestowing guilt. For the first time in my life, I handed it right back to her. And lo and behold. She's coming to take care of my prodigal sister." I gave a self-satisfied laugh. "They deserve each other."

When Frances said, "Hmph," I got the impression that the lecture was over for now. Not that I blamed my assistant for her words of warning. I'd been duped in the past and I knew she, Bennett, and my roommates all worried. But sad as it was, I'd finally learned the hard lesson that my sister couldn't be trusted. And I'd grown a little more callous, a little more cynical, because of it.

"What did you want to show me?" I asked.

She brightened. "Today's your lucky day."

"Uh-oh."

Spinning to face her monitor, she grabbed the mouse and navigated her cursor to a minimized window. I marveled at Frances's turnaround with the computer. When I'd first arrived at Marshfield, she'd been adamantly opposed to any type of automation. In short order, however, she'd become a whiz at finding and manipulating information. She loved the Internet, possibly even more than I did.

"Here you go," she said triumphantly.

I leaned down to look. The page she'd loaded was a photo

of a man—a very handsome man. About forty years old, he had a full head of dark hair, a square jaw, and the hint of dimples. The picture was one of those official shots taken from the shoulders up, the kind featured on political mailers designed to make a candidate look sincere. He wore a navy blue suit, a white shirt, and a red tie. His mild expression with its whisper of a smile made him look serious yet approachable.

I was about to ask why Frances wanted me to see this when I caught a glance at the page title.

As comprehension dawned on me, she jumped in to explain. "What do you think? Not bad, right?"

I straightened. "All right," I said, deadpan. "Good to know what he looks like. It'll make it easier when we meet later. Thanks, Frances."

I started back for my office.

"He's single," she said after me. "Divorced. Don't know if there are any kids. You're not going to be picky about a man having kids, are you?"

I didn't break stride.

"Your clock is ticking. You know that, right?"

I crossed the threshold into my own office with both hands fisted and my jaw clenched. A second later, Frances's outer door opened, and Rodriguez walked in.

"Good morning, Frances," the detective boomed. He held up his palm in greeting. "How are we today?" He noticed me in the doorway. "Glad you're here, too, Grace. We have a few updates for you on Virginia Frisbie."

Flynn loped in behind his partner looking as though he'd prefer to be anywhere but here. "Not my idea," he said to my unasked question. He jerked a thumb at Rodriguez. "He's the one who insists on keeping you informed. If it were up to me, neither of you would hear a word until this case was completely wrapped up. By us."

"Then I guess it's a good thing it isn't up to you," my assistant said.

I swallowed my pique about her pushing Davenport on me and smiled sweetly at her. "Let's not antagonize our detective friends, okay, Frances?" To them: "Good to see you. Both."

Flynn grunted. "You got coffee?"

If there was one thing that kept Flynn coming back to Marshfield, it was the promise of steaming coffee and fresh pastries. Frances made a phone call. Whatever it took to keep our local law enforcement happy.

"Have a seat, gentlemen," I said, indicating the two chairs in front of Frances's desk. "Let me grab one more from my office."

Moments later, when I returned pushing a wheeled seat to join the detectives, I realized that they and Frances were already in the midst of discussion.

Flynn leaned forward from the edge of his chair. "We've already talked with him. What more does she think she's going to get?"

"That's not the point." Frances folded her arms and turned her attention to Rodriguez. "You know what I'm saying."

Rodriguez scratched his head. "I don't see any harm." He shrugged, sending a baleful look at his partner. "He wasn't much help. Didn't tell us anything we didn't already know. Maybe Grace will have better luck."

"What are you talking about?" I asked as I positioned myself next to Flynn.

"You," he said. "And your lunch date with the bank president."

I shot a scathing look at Frances, who responded with a Cheshire cat smile.

"First of all, it's not a date," I said.

"Yes, it is," she said.

I ignored her. "He called because of my partnership with Bruce and Scott."

"Here you go. Coffee and treats." One of our Birdcage Room attendants arrived wheeling in a tray of coffee and breakfast pastries. As soon as she saw that we didn't require anything further, she left, and we all helped ourselves to a second breakfast. I opted for a fresh cup of coffee, but it was getting too late for more. Lunch with Davenport would probably turn out to be a terrible waste of time. I should have gotten the information I needed from him over the phone.

"So why are you going to lunch with him?" Flynn asked when we resettled ourselves. "Davenport, I mean."

Had Flynn read my mind? It sure seemed as though he had. "I asked him a couple of questions about Virginia and the Granite Building that he couldn't answer. He said he'd look into it and let me know. I assume he'll bring information to share."

Rodriguez had dark, hooded eyes. He studied me now, blinking slowly. "Is that all you're interested in?"

"What? Yes. What is wrong with all of you?" I asked.

"Just want to make sure I'm not leading my friend Joe astray," Rodriguez said. "I don't want him to get hurt."

"What about Grace?" Frances asked indignantly. "Don't you think the good doctor has had more than enough time to make his intentions known? Grace is perfectly within her rights to start seeing other men."

"Whoa," I said, holding up both hands. "I'm right here, have any of you noticed? For your information, I'm not technically seeing anyone. So there are no 'other men' at this juncture. And right about now I'd appreciate it if you would all take a big step out of my personal life."

The twin looks on Rodriguez's and Frances's faces let me know that they hadn't had anything in mind beyond my best interests. But their ideas and mine with regard to my love life were apparently miles apart.

Still, these were my friends. I softened my outburst. "If anything comes of anything, you will all be the first to know. But in the meantime, how about you let me navigate by myself. Is that fair?"

Frances harrumphed. Rodriguez pulled his lips to one side and chewed on a cheek. "Maybe Joe has a good reason for taking his time," he said.

Flynn scowled. "I thought we were here to talk about the murder."

"So it's definitely a murder?" I turned to Rodriguez. "Let's hear those updates you mentioned."

He made a show of digging out his notebook, flipping it open, and squinting at his notes. "According to the autopsy, Ms. Virginia Frisbie died of internal injuries sustained from a blow to her head and subsequent fall down the stairs. She had defensive wounds on both arms and traces of skin and blood under her fingernails." He put his notebook down. "Coroner's conclusion: homicide."

"Poor Virginia." I tried to imagine her last moments alive. I shuddered to think. "Was Joe—Dr. Bradley—able to tell if she suffered?"

Part of me wished I could ask Joe these questions myself—and not solely for the answers he could provide. All this talk about my upcoming lunch with Neal Davenport had me thinking, again, about Joe and whether he and I were on a path to a relationship or if I'd read signals wrong.

No. I hadn't read anything incorrectly.

"I'm sorry," I said, shaking my head when I realized Rodriguez had answered me. "What did you say?"

"Dr. Bradley is convinced she died almost instantly after she hit the basement floor. But based on his observations, he believes she was repositioned shortly after her death."

"The killer moved her?" I asked.

Flynn rolled his eyes. "Who else could it have been?"

"I don't know. Maybe the squatter? Haven't you found anything about the person living there?"

Flynn scowled again.

"Not yet, Miz Wheaton," Rodriguez said. "But we're following up."

"Of course you are," I said in a kindlier tone. I knew the two men were doing their very best. I just wasn't in the mood to handle Flynn's attitude at the moment. I decided to change tactics. "Have you spoken with the building inspector?" I asked. "From what I understand, Cynthia Quinn came highly recommended."

Flynn snorted. "Yeah? By who? She's a flake, that one."

Rodriguez shot him a pained look, then answered me. "We spoke with her on the phone but haven't interviewed her yet. She's been a little difficult to pin down."

"Oh?" I said.

Frances sat up straighter. "Do you think she could have killed Virginia? Is she a suspect? She'd have had the means and opportunity, right?"

Rodriguez waved a hand. "Let's not get ahead of ourselves, okay? We have no reason to suspect Ms. Quinn at this point."

"No reason to assume she's innocent, either," Frances said.

"Except—I don't know—because everyone is innocent until proven guilty under the law maybe?" Flynn said. He gestured with his mug, which fortunately he'd almost drained.

Frances gave an indignant head waggle. "Since when has that ever stopped you?"

"That's enough," I said as I got to my feet. "Frances, the detectives came here to update us of their own free will. Let's not make them sorry they included us, all right?" I tapped my wrist where a watch would be if I'd been wearing one. "As for me, I'd love to stay and chat, but I have a bank president to meet."

"Rodriguez could be right. Davenport may open up to you," Flynn said. "Let us know if he has anything important to say."

"Of course I will," I said as I hurried into my office to grab my purse.

Rodriguez had gotten to his feet by the time I came back. "Don't do anything I wouldn't do," he said with a mischievous twinkle in his eye.

Frances folded her arms and grunted. "You go right ahead and do whatever you like. Time to leave the slowpoke behind."

Because they meant well, I bit back a snarky reply. Instead, I opened the door, turned back, and winked. "Don't wait up."

Chapter 8

THANK GOODNESS FOR BLUETOOTH. ON MY drive to meet Neal Davenport, I had the car dial Joe's cell. My call was immediately routed to voicemail and I reasoned that he must still be busy with hospital rounds or patients. I left a quick message asking him to call me whenever convenient. Even though Rodriguez and Flynn had already delivered the news that Virginia's death was now a homicide, I wanted to hear Joe's insights.

The restaurant Neal Davenport and I had agreed on was a spacious yet homey place. A fixture in Emberstowne since my grandmother had lived here, Myrtille sat less than a block away from the Granite Building. Myrtille was a two-story corner structure with bright red awnings lining both street-facing sides. Its upper level featured a steep roof, pitched gables, and a half-timbered construction, reminding me of the picturesque homes at Marie Antoinette's Versailles farm. I had no problem finding a parking spot on

Main Street because we were still a few weeks ahead of our tourist season and it was a bit early for lunch.

With its high tin ceilings and black-and-white patterned tile floor, the restaurant gave off a lovely empty and cool vibe. The air inside carried the faintest whiff of garlic. A mahogany bar ran the length of one wall. Two men sat at it, three seats apart. They both glanced up at my entrance, watching me via the bar's mirror.

The sixty-something bartender came around from behind to welcome me. I'd met her before, several times, but couldn't remember if her name was Barb or Deb. All I knew was that I hoped to look as good when I got to her age.

"Good morning, Grace. Nice to see you again," she said as she pulled up a tall, black-edged menu from the hostess stand. "One for lunch today? Would you like a seat at the bar or would you prefer a table in the back room?"

"I'm meeting someone," I said. "I'm a little early."

"That's fine. Feel free to sit at the bar while you wait."

"Ms. Wheaton?"

At the whoosh of air and the sound of my name from behind me, I turned.

"Yes." I extended my hand. "You must be Neal Davenport."

Though there was no doubt in my mind, I wasn't about to let on that I recognized him from Frances's online Google ogling. I did my best to tamp down a blush of surprise that threatened to warm my cheeks. Wearing a trim, charcoal gray suit and a warm smile, he was even better looking in person than he had been on my assistant's screen.

"Wonderful to meet you," he said as we shook hands. To the bartender/hostess, he said, "Nice to see you again, Deb. We have reservations."

"Of course, Mr. Davenport," she said with a smile as she grabbed a second menu. "Follow me."

When Deb seated us, she shot me a surreptitious eyebrow waggle that needed no translation. "Ooh-la-la," it said. "This one's a hottie."

And he was. Frances would be licking her chops if she could see him. I shuddered to think about how she might commandeer the conversation had I brought her along.

"Looks like we have the place to ourselves," Neal said when Deb left. "Mostly."

Chianti bottle candles sat at the center of each table in this dining area. I wondered what stories their tall, multi-colored layers had heard over the decades.

Except for a middle-aged man sitting alone at a far corner table, we were the only ones here. At our arrival, he'd glanced up disinterestedly, then returned his attention to his newspaper and coffee.

Leaning toward Davenport, I indicated the man with my eyes. "I don't want anyone to hear details about Virginia's death investigation that they shouldn't be privy to."

"Good thought," he said. He gave a small, wry smile, smoothly acknowledging my point without making light of the subject. He leaned forward. "And I have those answers you wanted."

"That's great," I said. "I'm looking forward to whatever information you can share with me."

After a few social niceties where we agreed to call each other by our first names, we made small talk about the restaurant and about how often we each visited here. I learned that this was one of his favorite haunts. Deb came back to check on the man in the corner before taking our orders. When she left again, Davenport told me that Deb had been a fixture here since he first started working at the bank.

"She's the best," he said. "I moved here after I got

divorced and Deb was one of the many folks in town who made me feel welcome. It's tough to start over."

"I know what you mean," I said. "I relocated here from Chicago a few years ago, too."

"So I've heard. But life is better now, I'd imagine."

And here we were again. Ever since my blood relationship with Bennett had been established, people in Emberstowne had learned far more about me than I knew about them. Not only did it put me at an immediate disadvantage when I encountered these folks, it made me feel as though I were living in a fishbowl. Everything on display.

"Much better now," I said. "After my mother died, I was afraid I'd never have family. But for the first time in a long time, I feel as though I belong."

"I'm glad to hear it." He smiled.

It was a perfectly lovely smile. Nothing strange, nothing wrong, yet I fought the odd sense that I didn't belong here with him right now. I couldn't explain why I felt a rush of discomfort, but I did. And the oddest thing was, the feeling didn't emanate from him, but from within me. It was as though I felt the need to be somewhere else. I had no idea where.

"So tell me about Virginia," I said. "She was obviously already employed there when you started. But you were her boss, is that right?"

He broke a breadstick and used one of the halves to gesture. "Virginia basically ran the place. I'm going to be lost without her."

"I'm very sorry," I said. "I imagine this is hitting everyone hard."

"It is." He tapped the two broken ends of the breadstick together, causing a faint crumb shower. "She was the heart and soul of the bank."

I didn't like having to ask, but I plunged forward. "Was there anyone at the bank—a coworker or customer perhaps— who didn't like Virginia? Who may have wanted to do her harm?"

"The police asked me that, too." Neal sat back and took a big bite out of one of the breadstick ends. He shook his head as he made short work of the snack. "But no. Virginia was like everyone's favorite aunt. If anyone had a problem, they came to her and she fixed it. She knew everything about the banking industry. Even though she was close to retirement, she stayed on top of updated regulations and new trends."

"I understand she was the only bank employee with access to the Granite Building," I said. "Is that right?"

"Technically, I had access, too. Banks need to maintain dual control over everything, even something big and bulky, like a building."

That squared with what Tooney had told us.

He leaned both elbows on the table. "But Virginia never needed me to do anything. Now that all this has happened, I wish she had. Maybe if I'd been more involved with the building, the killer wouldn't have gotten to know her schedule and she'd still be alive today."

"You think this was a robbery gone bad, then?" I asked.

"What else could it be? The problem is that there was almost nothing worth stealing there." He finished off the half-eaten breadstick and chewed thoughtfully.

"Did the detectives ask you about the missing equipment?" I asked. "I assume you saw the dust markings. Do you know what may have been stolen?"

He shook his head. "The bank did an inventory when it first took possession of the property and removed items that could be sold or otherwise utilized by our location.

Whatever was left was sold to your partners as part of the deal. The police and a staff member are comparing notes right now to see if they can identify what's missing, but to answer your question directly: no. The police showed me photos of the dust markings, but I have no idea what's missing."

Deb returned with our lunch choices. BLT for him, turkey and avocado on garlic bread for me. House-made kettle chips and slaw on the side. Before she left again, she shot me an inquisitive glance that seemed to ask, "How's it going?"

I smiled back blandly.

"Back to the Granite Building," I said. "Was there anyone else at the bank who could have gained access? Is there a spare key? Was there any mechanism in place to keep track of who came and went?"

He'd taken a healthy bite of his sandwich, but downed it quickly. "To be truthful, I don't know. We should have had tighter controls, I suppose, but one never expects this sort of thing. It was a vacant building and Virginia seemed happy to check on it herself two or three times a week."

"Two or three times a week?" I repeated. "Doesn't that seem excessive?"

His brow furrowed. "It didn't at the time. Maybe I should have asked her about it. Virginia said that she liked to check regularly so that she stayed on top of potential problems. She worried about vandals mostly."

"Did she mention a squatter?"

He finished off the first half of his sandwich as he shook his head. "The police suggested that someone may have been living there, but Virginia never said a word. I wonder if she simply missed the evidence."

I chewed on that as I ate my turkey sandwich.

"The building went into foreclosure about seven years

ago," he said between bites. "I know you wanted that information."

"Thanks." Not that there was much to do with it. "And Virginia was in charge of the building the entire time?"

"As far as I know, yes. She worked with the utility companies to maintain it at the barest minimum. Heat, electricity, water, et cetera. She said that we needed to keep the lights on so that the building would be ready to show if an interested buyer ever materialized." He smiled at me. "And now someone has."

"My partners mentioned that the bank was initially reluctant to sell, though. Why is that?"

He wiped his mouth with a napkin. "We've always been eager to get that monster off our books."

"Bruce and Scott were told that your corporate office wanted to open a new location there. To consolidate a couple of branches."

"That's news to me," he said.

I detected nothing that suggested Neal was lying. He seemed genuinely puzzled. "I was thrilled when your partners made an offer to buy the place."

"I think they'd originally hoped to rent."

He shook his head as he nabbed a few kettle chips. "Banks are happy to liquidate our assets, not to get into the landlord business."

"Makes sense," I said.

"Speaking of banking," he said, and I wondered what other subjects he thought we'd covered, "I want you to know that I would be happy to serve as a personal adviser if you ever have need of one. I have extensive experience and worked as an investment adviser before I came to Emberstowne."

"That seems like a significant change," I said. Knowing

what I did about investment advisers and bankers, Neal Davenport likely lost a big chunk of income with that shift.

"Yes, it was." He wiped his mouth again and sat back. "It is." He gave another engaging smile. "I was a hedge fund manager during the market crash in oh-eight."

"Ouch," I said.

"That doesn't begin to describe it." He stared away. "I had corporate clients screaming at me morning and night. Worse, I had individual clients weeping in my office. Most of the time, I wept along with them. I'd let them down." He pulled in his lips and took in a sharp breath before turning to me. "Long story short, I realized I couldn't do the job anymore. Every piece of advice I'd given these people had made perfect sense when I advised them. But then the bottom fell out."

"I take it you lost money, too."

"Of course. I'd invested in the very same things I'd recommended to my clients. It was the worst time in my life. I felt responsible." He tried to smile but it fell flat. "I was responsible."

"But the market came back," I said. "Later."

He nodded. "But I no longer had the stomach for it." He leaned forward. "I couldn't stand the fact that 'poof'"—he lifted both hands and extended his fingers in emphasis—"people's lives could be ruined so completely."

I didn't know what to say except, "I'm sorry."

"Switching to banking made sense." He hesitated for a moment before continuing. "To me, that is. My wife didn't agree. She's an attorney, by the way. She thought I was running scared—which I suppose I was—and she didn't like the idea of being married to a mere bank president when she'd said 'I do' to a high-powered hedge fund manager."

"I'm sorry," I said again.

"So am I." He flashed a quick smile. "But she has the right to the life she wants just as I have a right to the life I want. She hasn't spoken to me since the divorce was final. I suppose the fact that we never had kids makes the break easier on both of us."

No kids. I'd have to let Frances know.

A couple of other tables had been seated while he was talking. Deb had come by to clear away our plates. Neal wore a sheepish expression. "I didn't mean for this lunch to turn into the story of my life. I was hoping to learn more about you. But there you have it. How I came to Emberstowne."

That sounded a lot like an invitation to share a similar summary of my life. I pondered my response. As I lifted my napkin to pat my lips, my attention was caught by Deb leading another couple in. I sucked in a quick breath of surprise. Not because the red-haired woman behind Deb was such a stunner, but because Joe Bradley—leaning heavily on his cane—followed behind.

Blood rushed to my face as surprise and dismay quickened my heartbeat. I averted my gaze. Now I knew why he hadn't answered his phone. Was he on a date with this gorgeous woman? More to the point: Was it any of my business? He could simply be conducting a business lunch the same way I was.

"How about you?" Neal asked when I was slow to reply. "Word is you're single, but are you seeing anyone?" A moment later, he seemed to notice my sudden discomfort. "I'm sorry. Have I talked too much about myself?"

"No, it's fine." In the few seconds that had transpired since I'd spotted Joe, the logical part of my brain advised me that saying a quick hello now could help avoid an awkward situation later. I dropped my napkin onto the table and pointed vaguely. "Give me a second. I just saw someone I know."

By the time I started to rise, however, Joe had turned away and—to the extent that he could, considering that his cane usage impeded his progress—was now hurrying his companion back out. Deb followed behind looking puzzled.

So he'd spotted me, too.

I blew out a breath as I sat back down. "Sorry. I must have been mistaken."

Neal wisely didn't press for details. Resting his elbows on the table, he folded his hands in front of his chin. "How about I slow down a little bit," he said. "What else did you need to know about Virginia?"

Chapter 9

"AND?" FRANCES ASKED THE MOMENT I RE-
turned to the office. "How did it go? Was he a dreamboat?"

"You should have come along, Frances," I said lightly.
"He was charming and self-deprecating. He seems like a
great guy."

She followed me into my office. "When are you seeing
him again?"

"What do you mean?" Feigning innocence, I shook my
head. "Wasn't I auditioning him for you?"

She made an impertinent noise. "Can't you be serious
for once?"

"Are you kidding me?" I found myself more annoyed by
the question than I ought to be. "I haven't been anything but
serious these past few years." As the words tumbled from
my mouth, I realized their truth. I hadn't quite thought about
my life in those terms before. "When we aren't investigating
a murder, I'm dealing with my sister. Or helping friends stay

out of bankruptcy. Or working with Bennett's financial guru to master Marshfield family business."

I waved the air. "Okay, that one I don't mind so much."

She sat down without invitation. "What happened?"

I lowered myself into my desk chair. "Nothing terrible. As I said, Neal is a nice guy."

She gave an encouraging nod.

"Better looking in person than in his picture, believe it or not."

"Really?"

"Really." I faced the window and frowned. "I had a nice time with him. And yes, I definitely got the impression that he'd be interested in seeing me socially."

He'd suggested meeting for lunch again next week, in fact, though I didn't mention that to Frances. I also chose not to mention that I'd tentatively agreed. "Sure," I'd said to him. "I'll check my schedule and get back to you." Part of me wondered if I was willing to see Neal again because I was actually attracted to him or if Joe's unexpected appearance and hasty departure was fueling my need for an ego boost.

"And?" she asked.

"Nothing set, but I haven't closed the door."

"Hmph," she said right on cue. "You talk about always being serious. Why don't you stop worrying if a guy is the right one and just get out and enjoy yourself once in a while?"

About to dismiss her, I stopped myself. "Good point, Frances."

Her tadpole brows shot upward.

"Don't act so surprised. You know I take your advice more often than I let on."

"'Bout time you admitted to that."

My office phone rang and I glanced at the caller ID.

"It's the hotel's front desk," I said.

Although the staff in charge of the Marshfield Inn, our on-site resort, technically reported to me, the hotel was so efficiently run that I rarely needed to involve myself in their day-to-day activities.

"Double-checking Saturday?" Frances asked.

"Probably." I picked up the phone. Aunt Belinda was due to arrive Saturday. I'd arranged for her to stay at the Marshfield Inn until Liza was released. No doubt the front desk was calling to confirm preparations.

Ranielle's voice came through cheerful, if slightly strained. "Good afternoon, Ms. Wheaton," she said. "I'm sorry to bother you, but we have a situation here that requires your assistance."

"Oh?" I sat up straighter. Frances did the same. She leaned forward, eager to listen in.

"A Belinda Zicker is here, attempting to check in but—"

"Wait. She's there now? She isn't supposed to arrive until Saturday."

Ranielle's relief whooshed across the phone line. "That's what our records indicate. Yes, she's here at the desk. Fortunately, we have rooms available and we're happy to get her settled. But we needed to check with you. And she seems particularly eager to speak with you in person."

That sounded a lot like polite-speak. Aunt Belinda must be getting ornery.

"I'll be right there," I said. "And I'm sorry for any confusion."

"These things happen," she said before we hung up.

Frances had clearly heard both sides of the conversation. "Tell me if you need any help."

I nodded as I got to my feet and grabbed my purse. "And so it begins."

* * *

EVEN THOUGH IT HAD BEEN AT LEAST TWENTY-five years since I'd seen Aunt Belinda, I recognized her at once. Back then she'd been petite, yet willowy, with shoulder-length brown hair. A very pretty woman, except for her ever-present scowl.

Now, all these years later, she seemed so much shorter. Her long, dark mane had been replaced by a messy cap of white.

"Aunt Belinda," I called out to her. "So wonderful to see you."

As I drew closer, I realized she not only was shorter, but looked so much older than I'd expected, too. Her eyelids drooped heavily, her skin was oatmeal colored, and there were deep groove lines around her mouth. She wore burgundy sweatpants, scuffed white cross-trainers, a hot pink sweatshirt with patches of shiny embroidery, and a grimace that warped me back to childhood.

In the seconds it took me to cross the lobby's marble floor, she raked me over with sharp scrutiny. "Grace?" She fairly barked my name. "Well, you've sure grown up."

I gave her an abbreviated hug. "I'll take that as a compliment," I said even though I wasn't sure that's how it had been meant.

Aunt Belinda had been talking with one of Ranielle's assistants, a young man who gave a quick nod of acknowledgment before turning away to assist another guest. My aunt had piled her purse, giant tote bag, and rumpled jacket onto the front desk. At her feet was a rolling suitcase the size of my bathtub. I resisted the temptation to comment. The more she brought meant the longer she could stay. When it came to corralling my sister, I was happy to have our aunt here for as long as possible.

"These people don't have my reservation," she growled. And with Aunt Belinda, it was most definitely a growl. "What kind of place do you run here, anyway? I thought you said these people were professionals."

Reminding myself I was no longer a youngster and that correcting another adult wasn't "talking back," I said, "They are professionals, and the Marshfield Inn is one of the finest hotels you'll ever encounter. The reason they don't have your reservation is because you weren't due to arrive until Saturday."

"No." She gave a vehement shake of her head. "You told me to be here today."

I drew in a sharp breath. If Aunt Belinda and I had corresponded via e-mail, I'd have a paper trail with all the dates spelled out in pixel and white. Unfortunately, my aunt claimed to not like computers. Everything we'd discussed had been over the phone.

"Today's Tuesday," I said.

"I know that."

"Last time we spoke, we talked about when you were arriving." I kept my tone light. "You mentioned not wanting to miss your senior lunch on Wednesday, remember?"

Awareness flashed in her eyes. She remembered saying that, all right. A split second later, she grimaced again, this time letting me know she planned to hold tight to her original assertion, no matter what. "I heard you say Tuesday. That's why I'm here. And nobody seems to know what to do with me."

I glanced up to see Ranielle waiting to speak with us. "I'm happy to get your aunt settled."

Ranielle speedily, but very politely, walked my aunt through the welcome process. She handed her a tiny folded packet. "Your keys. I've given you two. If you require more, please let me know. Your room number is written inside."

Aunt Belinda harrumphed. For the briefest second she reminded me of Frances, and it made me realize how much more I preferred spending time with my acerbic assistant than with my aunt.

"You're going to help me get settled, right?" she asked me. "There are a few things I need to clear up with you."

"Of course," I said as I handed my aunt's luggage to one of the porters. He disappeared around the corner with it as she grabbed her purse. I hoisted her tote bag and coat, then directed her toward the elevators.

"That bellboy isn't getting a tip from me," she said. "Doesn't take much effort to manage a rolling suitcase."

I said nothing.

We rode to her floor without speaking. The tension rising off her made the silence as vivid as a scream.

I took a good deal of pleasure from her gasp of surprise when we stepped into her room. On the side of the hotel that offered sweeping views of the estate grounds, it featured a sitting room, bedroom, and luxury bath. Although it wasn't the largest suite we offered, it was spacious and airy, decorated in yellow, soft white, and gold, with royal purple accents.

She ran her hand along the bedspread, ivory with gold glints. "Look at the size of this thing."

After dropping her tote onto the gold velvet sofa, I hung up her coat in the wide closet. "I didn't know what you preferred, so I opted for king sized. I hope that's all right."

From the look on her face, I knew it was. I waited as she took a slow tour around the room, checking out the view, the desk, the lighting, and finally the bathroom. "This place is fit for a queen," she said.

"I'm glad you like it."

The bellboy arrived with my aunt's case. I tipped him, thanked him, and closed the door when he left.

My aunt stood between the hallway and the bathroom. Wagging a finger, she said, "Don't think that all these fancy trappings will make me less angry with you. Marshfield. Of course. I should have known. Why didn't you tell me the truth?"

"As I said before," I said as I held up both hands, "I was waiting to tell you in person."

Crossing the room again, she took a seat in one of the wing chairs by the window. "Sit down, girl. You and I need to have an important chat."

I pointed vaguely toward the door. "I really ought to get back to work."

"That's exactly what I want to talk with you about." She indicated the chair across from her. "Is Bennett Marshfield such a tightwad that he still makes you work full time? Isn't he willing to share his fortune with you now—you being family and all? That isn't right."

When Aunt Belinda had found out about my blood relation to Bennett, she'd been furious. Not because I was now the apparent heir to his estate, but because she'd hadn't heard it from me.

I decided that now was as good a time as any to clear the air. I sat. "The situation is a lot more complicated than it looks to the outside."

"What's complicated is why you kept all this a secret. I've known you since you were born. I used to change your diapers, young lady. I've practically been a second mother to you and your sister. This is the thanks I get?"

My aunt had never been like a second mother to me. Or to Liza, for that matter.

"I'm sorry you feel that way," I said. "I thought the news would be better delivered in person."

"You're lucky I found out on my own. Otherwise I would never have agreed to come." She waved an index finger in emphasis. "Here, I mean. With you all busy with your 'job'"—she made air quotes—"I knew your poor sister would be left alone. She deserves better."

Belinda had delivered that final line with enough of a pointed look that I decided now was the best time to raise an important topic.

"I think it would be best," I began carefully, "if I told Liza about my relationship with Bennett myself."

Belinda's expression morphed from wary to shocked. "You weren't planning to tell her at all, were you?"

"I definitely intend to make her aware," I said. "But Bennett and I want to approach her together. For a lot of reasons." None of which were my aunt's business.

"Oh, you planned that, did you?" She shook her head. "I see what you're doing. You want to keep your sister from sharing in your windfall. You want to keep it all for yourself. You want to deny your sister her birthright."

"It's not her birthright."

Her exaggerated shocked expression intensified. "Seems to me that's exactly what it is. The way I hear it, you worked here for a few years and your precious boss never changed a word of his will. But right after you got the results proving you were related, he started making changes. That says birthright to me."

I ran a hand up through my hair. While what she said was absolutely accurate, anyone who knew Bennett and me knew the deeper truth.

"Liza needs to understand that Bennett chose to make me his heir for many reasons. Not simply because we're uncle and niece."

She folded her arms, wiggling deeper into her chair. "I always thought our mother was too enamored with the Marshfields. Little did I know that she'd gone off and had an affair with one of them." She shook her head. "No wonder my sister, your mother"—she glanced up unnecessarily, as though to remind me—"was our mother's favorite. She was Marshfield's love child." She frowned. "Your grandmother hated her husband, by the way. Did you know that?"

"I didn't," I said, even though I'd suspected as much.

Belinda pointed hard into her own chest. "My father. She hated him. That's why she never really liked me. I look just like my dad, you know. Your mother doesn't, naturally. I should have put that together a long time ago, but I didn't. I had my suspicions, of course, but never any proof."

"I'm sorry." I could only imagine how hard it must have been for both my aunt and my mother to grow up in a family where the husband and wife couldn't stand each other and where one daughter was favored so much over the other.

"Yeah, you look like you're sorry. Easy to say when you're sitting on millions of dollars."

Inwardly, I winced. Billions, actually.

She grimaced. "Well, I should say, when you expect to inherit those millions of dollars. Obviously, you have to wait until the old guy kicks off before you see any of it. Otherwise, why would you still be working for him?"

I bit back a retort. Though elderly, Bennett hardly deserved to be referred to as "the old guy." My aunt's statement epitomized how poorly she understood the situation. I chose not to correct her.

"Back to the matter at hand," I said. "I would appreciate

it if you'd allow me to talk with Liza about all this first. I know that it's difficult to keep such a big issue under wraps, but I think it would be best for her to hear the news from me and Bennett directly."

"Too late."

Startled, I could do no more than repeat. "Too late? What do you mean?"

She shrugged as though it was nothing. "I already told her. Sent her a letter as soon as I found out."

I found it almost impossible to draw breath. My heart, even, seemed to stop beating. "No, you can't have."

The glint in her eyes was both triumphant and fearful. "Why shouldn't she know? Why shouldn't she be able to lay claim to half of Marshfield's money?"

"Because . . ." I fought to calm myself. "Because it is Bennett's money. Who he shares it with is up to him. She has no claim to it. Neither do I, for that matter. The fact that Bennett has chosen to name me in his will does not mean that he must name Liza. That's not how it works."

She twisted her mouth to one side. "I knew you'd be selfish. You're just like your mother. It's a good thing I expected this. That's why I have a meeting set up with an attorney just as soon as Liza gets out."

Chapter 10

I CALLED FRANCES ON MY WAY BACK TO THE office. "Where's Bennett?" I asked. "No, forget that. Find him and ask him to meet me in my office as soon as possible." Remembering my manners, I added, "Please."

"Done," she said and hung up.

I drove back to the mansion in half the time it usually took, ruminating all the while about my aunt's disastrous disclosure. Of course she'd told Liza. Of course she had.

I slammed my steering wheel in frustration. I'd acted as conduit between the two for so long that I'd lost sight of the idea of them communicating directly. Liza had played me well in that regard. She'd begged me to handle everything with Aunt Belinda, telling me that it was too hard for her to gain access to the phone while in prison. Too difficult to deal with our aunt's constant badgering when they finally did connect. Liza swore she hadn't had any direct communication with our aunt since her incarceration.

What was wrong with me? I'd dropped my guard—
again—and been bitten. By both of them this time.

Gripping handfuls of skirt, I took the back stairs two at
a time up to our offices. Frances and Bennett turned to face
me when I burst through the door.

"She told Liza," I said.

Out of breath from my sprint to the third floor, flushed
from my fury—at myself, truth be told—I threw my body
into the open chair next to Bennett's.

"She told Liza," I said again.

Neither of them needed further explanation.

"How long has your sister known?" Frances asked.

Tiny beads of sweat gathered at my hairline. Most people
would think they were a result of exertion. I knew better.
Anger boiled so furiously within me that it needed to blister
out as a means of escape.

"She 'can't remember.'" Making air quotes, I huffed.
"Long enough to hire an attorney, though. The two of them
already have an appointment set up."

Bennett listened without reaction, his hands folded in his
lap, his sharp blue gaze steady.

"The Mister doesn't have to share a penny with anyone
he doesn't want to," Frances said with the same level of rage
I was feeling. "No attorney in his right mind will take on
such a frivolous case."

"You want to bet?" I asked.

Bennett remained quiet. He nodded briefly, looking less
concerned than I thought he ought to be.

Frances picked up a pen. "Which attorney are they meeting?" she asked. "I'll find out what I can about him. Or her."

"Yet another thing my aunt conveniently couldn't remember," I said.

"Maybe we need to get your friend Tooney involved," Frances said. "I bet he could follow her and find out who they're meeting with."

Bennett leaned forward. "We'll find out soon enough," he said. "No need to meet trouble halfway. Let it find its own way to our doorstep."

Frustration got the best of me. "But it's here. Right now. Don't you think we need to mount a defense? Shouldn't we call in Marshfield's lawyers?"

Bennett nodded. "I'll make them aware, but let's not get ahead of ourselves." He leaned forward to pat my hand. "In some ways, I'm almost glad this has happened."

A noise in my head—the sound of my brain exploding perhaps—drowned out what he said next.

"Can you repeat that?" I asked.

Bennett seemed more amused than annoyed. He patted my hand again. "You are wise and wonderful, Gracie, and you've seen far more than your share of criminal activity these past few years, but what you haven't had to deal with yet are the many lawsuits we face here at Marshfield every day."

"I've worked with you on at least four," I said. "Maybe five. I think that last one—the man who broke his arm when he jumped off a garden wall—was the only one that went to trial. And then it was dismissed. If I recall correctly, the rest got tossed out on summary judgments."

"Those are the ones you've seen. There were some fairly disagreeable lawsuits we faced before your time. This one, involving your sister, will be good practice for what's to come. For what you must learn to expect. As the future head of Marshfield Manor, you'll face the wrath of hundreds—maybe even thousands—of people who despise you simply because you have more than they do. They believe their only recourse is to attack you and the estate and then swoop in and claim the spoils of war."

That was probably the most cynical sentiment I'd ever heard Bennett utter. But he wasn't finished.

"It's never-ending, Gracie. The attacks, I mean. They don't stop. They won't stop. You'll cut your teeth on this situation with your sister. With any luck it will be the toughest challenge you'll face. This certainly won't be a pleasant experience, but you will learn."

"How have you stayed so positive," I asked, "after all these years of constant bombardment?"

"I remind myself that the attacks aren't personal. That it's the people in the world who have lost hope in themselves who come at me. I feel sorry for them." He winced. "Unfortunately this time, it is personal. And that will make it so much harder."

I nodded.

Frances frowned. "So what do we do?"

As if in answer, the phone rang in my office. Frances glanced at the caller ID from the console at her desk. "Dr. Bradley's office," she said as she reached for the receiver. "Are you in?"

I wasn't ready. "Not now."

Frances briskly answered the phone, told Joe that I was unavailable, and asked if there was message.

"He said to call him later. But only if you want to," she said when she hung up. "Hmph. What kind of attitude is that? He expects you to call him. I have half a mind to tell him you had lunch with Neal Davenport this afternoon."

I waved the air, weary beyond words over this situation with Liza. "Don't bother. He already knows."

"Neal Davenport?" Bennett arched a brow. "The banker?"

"All business. I promise," I said.

"Got it." He smiled as he stood. "Let's not get too worried about your sister yet, all right? I'm sure that when you and I have a chance to talk with her, we'll persuade her to see reason."

Unconvinced, I got up, too. "I wish I shared your optimism."

BEFORE LEAVING WORK FOR THE DAY, I CALLED Scott to ask about progress at the Granite Building. I made a mental note to start thinking of the place as the new Amethyst Cellars. "How's it going?" I asked when he answered.

"Better than we expected, given the tragic start to our new venture," he said. "The police gave us the okay to move forward. They've removed all the evidence they need and we have full access to the building again. Bruce and I have been here all afternoon, cleaning. And we're setting up a schedule for fumigation. For the termites."

"That's wonderful news. Except for the termites, that is. Do you need any help?"

"Only moral support at this point. We're taking our time, trying to assess all that needs to be done before we finalize remodeling decisions. We'd love it if you'd stop by. We'll even bring in dinner if you're game for fast food tonight."

"I can't imagine anything I'd like better," I said. "I have to drop by the hotel and check on my aunt before I head out, though. Is that okay?"

"Your aunt?" he asked. "I thought she wasn't due until Saturday."

"Yeah. Long story. I'll tell you when I get there."

"Text when you arrive so we can let you in."

Frances popped in when I hung up. "I forgot to tell you that Detective Rodriguez called while you were at the hotel. Said he had an update to share but didn't tell me what it was."

I dropped my head back to stare at the ceiling. "There's not a moment to breathe anymore, is there?" I asked rhetorically.

"Why not let the police figure this one out by themselves this time?" she asked. "Except for the fact that you were there when Virginia's body was found, you really aren't involved at all."

"True," I said, bringing my gaze to meet hers. "Unless, of course, you count the fact that the murder site is where my partners and I intend to open a wine shop and restaurant, and the sooner the murder is solved, the better for business."

"Weak argument," she said as she sat down across from me. "The truth is that you can't let it go, can you?"

I shook my head, embarrassed to admit it. "I can't. You and I have been intimately involved in so many investigations that it feels wrong to turn away from this one. Plus, Rodriguez and Flynn have practically invited us in."

"Correction." She pursed her lips. "Invited you in."

"We're a team, Frances," I said. "And they know it."

She blinked twice. Her face brightened. One second later, she scowled again. "They'd better."

MY SECOND VISIT WITH AUNT BELINDA TURNED out to be blessedly brief. Once she understood that I'd arranged for everything to be paid for—including room service—she shooed me off, insisting she was exhausted from her long day of travel. I didn't argue. Twenty minutes later, I pulled up to the new Amethyst Cellars.

Back before gentrification had hit this part of town, giving us our lovely, tourist-friendly Main Street and surrounding quaint shops, this location had been the site of a successful manufacturing company. I had no idea how many workers had been employed here when the Granite Building had housed a busy glass factory, but there was a sizable paved parking lot immediately adjacent to the building's south wall. Perfect for future customers eager to wine and dine.

I parked next to Bruce's car and prepared to get out, thinking about the oddity of granite versus glass. According to town history, the building had been named well before the glass company moved in, but the original moniker had stuck. I hoped my roommates would have better luck in getting the town to recognize it as Amethyst Cellars, reborn.

Movement in the alley behind the building caught my eye when I stepped out of my car. Definitely human-sized. My first thought was that it was either Bruce or Scott taking trash out to the Dumpster.

"Hello?" I called.

A breeze kicked up, making my hair twist around my face. I brushed it back. "Hello, who's there?"

No answer.

The next closest building to my left across the wide lot was a low-rise brick structure that housed a coffee and pastry shop, open mornings only. No one there. There was nothing across the alley except a tall, prefabricated concrete wall that had been constructed as a barrier between the unattractive backs of these buildings and the leafy family park beyond.

Even though it would stay light out for another couple of hours, I wasn't about to investigate the stranger in the alleyway by myself.

Acting quickly, I dialed Scott. "Hey, I'm in the parking

lot," I said very quietly. "Can you and Bruce make some noise outside the building's rear door? Make it sound as though you're coming out. I have a hunch."

"What kind of hunch?"

"I'll explain in a bit. After you make your ruckus, meet me here, okay?"

"You got it, Grace."

I dropped my phone into my purse and dug quickly for cash.

"Hey," I called again, this time louder. "You look like you could use some money. I've got ten dollars here, if you want it."

This time I heard a little scuffling.

I reopened my driver's-side door as a precautionary move in case I needed to leap back inside in a hurry.

"Ten dollars. All yours," I shouted. "All you have to do is talk with me for a couple of minutes. I promise not to hurt you."

A screeching creak drowned out my last words as Bruce and Scott pushed the heavy metal back door open. Banging and clanging—hard objects being moved and dropped— followed. A second later, my roommates' voices over the din.

The shadowy figure I'd spotted earlier slunk around the building's corner. Keeping low to the ground as though to make himself invisible, he stared at me. More accurately, he stared at the money I held aloft.

Filthy, except for around his wide eyes, he had brown, matted hair, a braided beard, and a fearful expression. Wearing a dirty coat that had once been either beige or light gray, he seemed to be torn, deciding whether to run or to take his chances with the stranger waving a ten-dollar bill in the air.

"I'm not going to hurt you. I'm not going to call the

police." Well, not right away, at least. A lot would depend on what happened next.

Bruce and Scott completed their noisy ministrations and came around the back of the building moving resolutely until they spotted the man crouching against the wall. They stopped at once, taking only a moment to comprehend the situation.

The man twisted his head frantically between me and my roommates. He was frighteningly skinny—bony-faced with deep-set eyes. From the dull gray streaking his hair and beard, I guessed him to be in his sixties, maybe even a little bit older.

"I'll make it twenty," I said. "A few minutes of your time. I promise."

Bruce took a tentative step forward. "We're not angry with you. We just want to talk," he said as he arced slowly around to take up a position between me and Scott, while giving the man a wide berth. Bruce held his hands up, as though in surrender.

"Yeah, we were about to order dinner, in fact," Scott said. "Would you like us to get you something? Are you hungry?"

Surrounded now, with his back to the wall and the three of us evenly spaced before him, he crouched lower.

I took a small step forward. "We know you've been living here," I said softly. "And we know you must be worried now that the building has been sold. You're scared, aren't you?"

The tip of his tongue poked out. Bright pink and possibly the only clean spot on the poor man's body, it slid over his crusty lower lip. His brows were wiry, so thick as to almost obscure his dark eyes. "You're the ones that bought the building?" he asked.

I gestured to include Bruce and Scott. "We did," Bruce said.

"And you want me out of here, pronto. Is that it?"

"We'd like to talk with you first." Even though I knew we may have cornered Virginia's killer, I doubted that this terrified, weak-looking creature could have done the deed. This guy didn't have the body weight for that kind of leverage.

He sucked in his lips in a way that made me believe he had few or no teeth. Everything about him screamed no health care and minimal nourishment. Yet his eyes were clear. And clearly filled with terror. Like a trapped animal, he glanced back and forth and up and down as though desperate to escape.

If we let him go, we may not ever see him again.

"Twenty dollars," I repeated. "Plus dinner."

He snapped to face me.

"And there could be more in it for you," I said. "If only you'll talk with us a little bit. Answer a few questions. That's all we want. That isn't too difficult, is it?"

He worked his flexible lips again, clearly considering the offer.

"Think of it this way," I said. "If we wanted to call the police, we would have done so already. But it's just us. The three of us." I pointed toward Bruce and Scott again. "We're partners and this is our building now."

His wild eyes took in everything I had to say in a way that let me know he understood.

After a moment, he held out a filthy hand. "Money first, then talk." His deep, rich voice was surprisingly steady.

Right. And the minute he had my twenty, he'd be gone.

"Nice try." I smiled to take the sting out of my words.

"Food first," I said. "Then talk. Then money. What do you want for dinner?"

He narrowed his eyes, one brow arched as though surprised to find out I wasn't a pushover. "If I got to wait, then you better make it fifty."

Chapter II

SCOTT OFFERED TO DO A FOOD RUN. "WHAT should I get?" he asked me.

I turned to the scruffy stranger. "What would you like?"

He seemed bewildered by the question. "Can't remember last time I got to pick what I wanted to eat. I don't even remember what I like." As Scott walked away, the man rallied. "Hot, though. Gotta be something hot or no deal."

Scott shot me a look that asked if I knew what I was doing. I shrugged. Not really. A moment later, he was off.

Bruce led the way inside through the squeaky back door. The bearded man followed and I brought up the rear. We made our way into the high-ceilinged brick-walled space, toward a small, better lit area where Bruce and Scott had set up an ersatz command post. Three chairs around a folding table. Paperwork and boxes and dust. Lots of dust.

"Let me get another chair," Bruce said.

I nodded, keeping a tight hold on my breath. I'd encountered many homeless people in my life, but I'd never spent this much time in one's wake. The hot, sour tang of body odor made me want to turn away. I blew out a breath as I pulled my chair farther out of the circle, hoping to keep my eyes from watering.

I introduced myself and Bruce. "Scott will be back shortly, I'm sure," I said. "What's your name?"

He sucked in his lips again. I was wrong. He did have teeth. Few, though. Widely spaced, and dark yellow. "Let me see the fifty bucks first."

I dug into my purse, pulled out two twenties and a ten, and laid them in my lap. "All yours as long as you answer us truthfully."

His eyes narrowed at that, but he bobbed his head. A tiny leaf dislodged from the back of his hair. It fluttered to the floor. "Oscar."

"Oscar, what?" I asked.

"You don't need my last name."

"Fair enough." I crossed my hands atop the money. "You've lived here for a while, haven't you? Inside this building, I mean."

"On and off," he said. "Five years maybe."

"Whoa," Bruce said. "How did the inspector miss that bit of information?"

Oscar shrugged. "People don't find what they're not looking for, do they? And that inspector woman can't tell her"— he glanced at me and coughed—"can't tell her right hand from her left. She wasn't never going to notice me. Anyway, even if I thought she might, I got ways of disappearing and making myself scarce." He sat up a little straighter. "Plus, this here isn't the only spot I have, you know. I got two more safe places nobody knows about. And I ain't going to tell you about where they are, so don't even ask."

"We're not interested in rousting you from your homes,"

I said, keeping my tone modulated. "What can you tell us about an elderly woman who used to come here to check on the building from time to time? You've seen her, haven't you?"

"Virginia," Oscar said.

My face no doubt broadcasted my surprise. "You know her name?"

"Kinda hard not to," he said reasonably. "She came here all the time."

I hesitated, but needed to ask, "You know she died, right?"

"I didn't do it. You gotta believe me. I wasn't even here."

"So you've heard about it?"

"Who hasn't?" he asked. "It's all what people's talking about. It's in the newspaper. That's why I came back here today, to clear out my stuff before somebody comes sniffing after me, thinking I had something to do with killing her."

"She knew you lived here?" Bruce asked.

"Never said that." Oscar gave a robust head shake. Another leaf tumbled. "She maybe suspected that vandals broke in from time to time, but I never did no damage. I just stayed in to keep warm and dry and store my stuff, you know."

Bruce and I exchanged a puzzled glance. "How did you know Virginia's name?" I asked. "Did you know her from somewhere else? Were you a customer of the bank?"

Oscar laughed hard. I got a quick view of his mouth before he brought up a filthy hand to cover it.

"You crazy?" As though ashamed of his discolored teeth, he continued to hold his hand in front of his face while he chuckled. "Yeah, I'm a real wheeler-dealer."

Okay, so the question had been ludicrous, given the man's appearance. But the moment of levity seemed to cut the tension in the room.

"Hey," I said. "You never know. I've heard plenty of stories of frugal folks with stashed-away fortunes discovered only after their deaths."

"Not me."

"Then how did you know Virginia?" Bruce asked, taking the question right out of my mouth.

"Because that's what her boyfriend called her."

"Boyfriend?" Jolted, Bruce and I both sat up straight. "She brought a boyfriend here?" I asked. This was completely unexpected.

Oscar waved the space between us, sending a swirl of foul air my way. "Ah, not a boyfriend exactly," he said. "Her and a guy came here a lot. They didn't come together, mind you. They met up here, though. All the time."

"All the time?" I repeated. "Like, how often?"

"Two or three times a week at least. Sometimes more than that."

"Did they . . ." Bruce blushed. "I mean, were they here for, um, romantic purposes?"

Oscar wheezed out a laugh, covering his mouth again. He shook his head and rocked forward. "Shouldn't'a said 'boyfriend,' I guess." He wheezed. "No. Not a chance. He was forty, maybe forty-five. She was, well, old."

"Sixty-five isn't old," I said.

Oscar grinned. He bobbed his head again. "I agree. I hope to get to that age myself someday."

The front door opened and Scott called out, "I'm back. Could use a little help."

Bruce boosted himself to his feet and took off. "Keep talking, I'll take care of it."

Oscar turned toward the sound of Scott's voice. We were in the back warehouse part of the first floor. Scott had come in through the front. Oscar leaned forward as though ready to bolt. The wary yet eager look on our vagrant guest's face led me to believe he worried that Scott had returned, not with food, but with the police in tow.

"It's okay," I said. "I'm sure whatever Scott brought will be delicious."

Oscar's gaze flicked over me. He didn't relax until Scott and Bruce returned, smelling of savory heat and laden with brown bags. Scott carried two by their handles. Bruce held one in his arms. Grease spots dotted one side.

"I didn't know what to get, so I got everything that looked good," Scott said. He set the bags on the table and glanced around, assessing the area. "Whatever I could get fast, that is."

"There's a bigger table in one of the office areas up front, isn't there?" I asked. "In what used to be one of those waiting rooms."

Scott snapped his fingers. "Perfect. And I made sure to get plenty of napkins, tableware, and condiments. We could probably hole up here for a week and still have food left over."

Oscar worked his lips as he eyed the bags. "Smells good," he said, his fear apparently evaporating in the aroma of hot food.

"Come on." I stuffed the promised fifty dollars back into my purse and grabbed the two bags of food. "Let's set ourselves up."

As much as I wanted to press for more information about Virginia's nonromantic liaison, I couldn't push Oscar while we were eating. It broke my heart to see how eager his expression grew as we unloaded the bags and placed take-out containers atop the conference table.

"Go ahead," I said when Oscar poked at a gravy-soaked sandwich wrapped in white.

He didn't hesitate. A second later, he'd unrolled the

butcher paper and grabbed the French bread in both hands. Before I blinked, he'd shoved one end of it into his mouth.

"Hot?" I asked.

He grunted in the affirmative as a sausage chunk surrounded by juicy beef pushed out of the other end of the roll. I wished I could have gotten him to wash his hands before touching his food, but he didn't seem to care.

Scott hadn't been kidding. There was more than enough food. Plenty to choose from. Sandwiches, burgers, hot dogs, and tacos. Plus a mountain of fries and a selection of soft drinks. I picked out a lemonade and cheeseburger and settled myself across from Oscar. He'd finished the sausage and beef sandwich and was studying the feast laid out before him with undisguised glee.

Just as he reached for one of the bags of French fries, Scott interrupted. "We have a washroom around the other side of this wall." He pointed for emphasis.

"I know where it is," Oscar said. "Only cold water." He turned to me. "I don't like the cold."

"Hot water is working again," Scott said. "I know you're hungry, but if you wanted to wash up or something . . ."

Before Scott could finish his sentence, Oscar's grimy face lit up and he took off around the wall. "Be right back," he mumbled. Then, more clearly. "Don't finish all the food without me."

The facilities were far enough away that we were comfortable talking while Oscar was gone. We brought Scott up to speed on what we'd learned so far.

Scott: "And you believe him?"

"I do," I said. "I don't think he has any reason to fabricate Virginia's male friend."

"What's his name?"

"We hadn't gotten that far," I said.

"Greg or maybe Craig," Oscar said as he rounded the wall to rejoin us. "I couldn't help hearing them talk, but her voice was so soft so I couldn't make out everything she said."

I fought to tamp down my surprise, and from the looks of it, my roommates were attempting to do so as well. Our homeless guest wasn't completely clean—such a feat wouldn't be possible in such a short time with so few resources—but he'd effected a stunning transformation. He'd scrubbed his face hard enough for bright pink to bloom on his cheeks and forehead. His beard was still braided and his hair still scruffy, but his hands had morphed into flesh-colored from their ashy gray. Still a little damp, in fact. There remained plenty of black crud under his nails and in the creases of his fingers, but he had made an effort and seemed quite pleased with himself.

"Can you give me one of those napkins?" he asked as he reached for a cheeseburger. "Thanks," he said when I handed it over. "Don't want to stain my clothes," he added with a dry laugh.

"You're saying that Virginia and this guy, Greg or Craig, had conversations here," I prompted, to bring the focus back. "What did they talk about? Why did they meet here in secret?"

Oscar's cheeseburger was halfway gone by the time I got my questions out. Watching him eat with such joyful abandon was at once both gratifying and sad. I wondered about getting him some fresh clothes.

"Pretty sure it's Craig." He talked around a cheek full of cheeseburger. "Y'understand, I didn't hear a whole lot. Most times, when they'd show up, I'd beat a path out of here fast. Once in a while I didn't move quick enough and I'd hafta sit really quiet until after they left."

"I don't know about this mysterious man, but Virginia was here to check on the building," Bruce said. "That was one of her responsibilities at the bank."

Still chewing, Oscar crooked up one side of his mouth. "That what she told people?"

Dinner forgotten, I leaned forward. "Why was she here? What do you know?"

I hadn't lost sight of the fact that Oscar could be making up a load of lies but I trusted my gut. The man was cagey when it came to his personal information, but given his circumstances, that was hardly unexpected. Once he'd come to understand that all we wanted was information, he'd dropped his guard. His answers, thus far, had been delivered with an openness that surprised me.

Now he shook his head. "I don't know," he said with an emphasis on the word. "There's no way I could because whenever I was able to make out what they were saying, I couldn't figure out what they were talking about. I was hiding, and all the stuff they were working on was out in the open where I couldn't see."

"Stuff they were working on?" Scott repeated. "What do you mean?"

Oscar grabbed a bag of fries and spilled them onto the wrapping that had held his cheeseburger. He pinched a wad of them and levered it into his mouth, all while making a face that said, "Give me a minute."

He swallowed. "There's this closet," he said, pointing downward, "at the back end of the basement, kinda in the middle. I'd push myself deep in there. I could hear some of what was going on, but I couldn't see much through the small crack around the door."

I tried picturing it, but had no luck. "Near the stairs?" I asked.

He wrinkled his face as he grabbed more fries. "There's two sets of stairs. Kinda between them, closer to this one, I guess." He used the bunch of fries to gesture. "A couple of times when the two of them came in, I was in the basement and didn't hear them until they were almost all the way down. They woulda seen me if I ran."

"Makes sense," I said. "So you hid. And that's when you overheard them talking."

"Yeah. Didn't happen but a handful of times. Mostly I'd stay upstairs, where it was usually warmer. I didn't steal nothing, y'understand. Nothing ever."

"I believe you," I said. And I did. "But I would like to take you downstairs to show you where some items were that are missing now, and ask you if you remember seeing them. But first, why don't you tell us what you overheard?"

He'd stopped eating, glancing from me to Bruce to Scott, as though trying to ascertain whether we had any tricks up our sleeves.

"It's okay," I said, hoping to put his mind at ease. "I promise, whatever you tell us, it's okay."

He sat back again, looking a little more relieved.

Just then, my cell phone rang, startling us all. I fumbled in my purse and looked at the caller ID. Joe Bradley. As much as I wanted to answer, I didn't have it in me to casually mention seeing him at Myrtille today. More important, I didn't want to squander a moment of questioning Oscar.

I hit the button to silence my phone.

"Back to what you overheard," I said.

Chapter 12

OSCAR RAN A HAND ACROSS HIS MOUTH. "LIKE I said, I wasn't in a good spot to be hearing whole conversations. And I could only see a little bit. I picked up enough, though, to know that the two of them had a thing going."

"But not romantic," I said.

"Right."

"What did Craig look like?"

"I dunno. Like I said, maybe about forty or fifty years old. That's how his voice sounded. Middle-aged maybe? I don't see so good no more." He shrugged. "He's a white guy. I think he had dark hair, but I can't say if he was good looking or ugly. Never got close enough."

My shoulders slumped. That description wouldn't be much help.

Oscar sat up straight, pressed his fingers to his stomach, then let out an extended belch. "Whoa, that felt good," he said, covering his mouth again. "Haven't brought up a power burst like that in who knows how long."

Bruce and Scott exchanged a glance.

"Anyway," Oscar continued, settling back in, "whatever Virginia and Craig were doing here, it wasn't something they wanted anyone else to know about."

"What makes you say that?" I asked.

"Well, for one, even though they both had keys to the building, she always came in the front and he always came through the back."

"Is there a Craig who works at the bank?" I asked my roommates.

"Doesn't sound familiar to me," Bruce said.

Scott shook his head. "And it isn't a very big branch, either. With all the times we've been in there, I think we would have run into him by now. I don't think there's a Craig or a Greg there."

"I'll have to ask Neal Davenport about him," I said. I turned to Oscar. "Go on."

"Craig always got here first. Virginia came after. She was always nervous and he was always telling her that everything would be all right. She'd bring something to him every time. A bunch of papers."

"What kind of papers? Were you able to see them at all? After they left, I mean?" I asked.

Oscar shook his head. "Craig was always real careful about cleaning up everything when he was done."

"Done doing what?"

He shrugged. "Don't know exactly. Was out of my line of sight. But whatever it was took him hours. I got real cramped in there. Didn't like it a bit."

"Hours?" Scott asked. "How long did the two of them stay down here?"

Oscar shook his head. "Virginia came and left pretty quick. Craig is the only one that stuck around."

"Let's go downstairs for a minute," I said. "So you can show us where you hid and where Craig was when you couldn't see him."

Oscar wiped his mouth with a napkin and surveyed the table. "You all aren't going to throw away that leftover food, are you?"

"You're more than welcome to all of it," Scott said. "We brought in a refrigerator today. You can store it in there."

"You're not kicking me out, then?" Oscar turned to me. "Is he on the level?"

I gave a helpless shrug.

Scott, as though realizing what he'd implied, began to stammer. "I mean, of course you can't live here anymore. We plan to open a restaurant and we can't have anyone living on the premises."

"I could be like a security guard," Oscar said amiably. "I was a bouncer at a disco when I was young and buff."

Bruce began clearing the leftovers. "I think what Scott's suggesting is that we hold on to this food for you. Come by whenever you want it. We should be here most days."

Oscar frowned.

"I'd be happy to talk with people around town to see about getting you a job, if you'd like," I said, eager to turn the topic back to Virginia's secret meetings.

"You'd do that for me?" he asked.

Logic warned that this might be a futile endeavor, but I always trusted my instincts. Plus, I couldn't help myself. I liked Oscar.

"I'll do what I can."

He lifted a hand to cover his teeth when he smiled again. "Thank you, ma'am."

We traipsed down the steps, Oscar leading us to a closet at the basement's back end. He opened the door to reveal a small, cluttered space filled with mops, brooms, and buckets, one of which was upended. "I sat on that," he said. "I tried to make it so I almost didn't breathe. Didn't know what would happen if they caught me spying on them."

"Hang on," I said. "Give me a minute."

I shooed Bruce, Scott, and Oscar to the side and stepped into the closet and started to pull the door shut. "Show me how open it was when you were watching them," I said.

Oscar obliged, pushing until only about an inch remained open between the edge of the door and the jamb.

"Okay, now." I raised my voice a bit. "All three of you move out of the way. I want to see what my view is from here."

When they'd stepped aside, I sat on the upturned bucket and stared out. I couldn't make out much beyond the rows of equipment that took up most of the basement. Lingering odors of disinfectant did little to mask the stuffy sweat smells of the small room. Wrinkling my nose, I leaned forward, looking hard to my right and then my left, hoping to be able to stretch enough to see the dusty table that we'd noticed the day we'd found Virginia at the bottom of the stairs, but it was too far left. Even opening the door another inch, then another, didn't allow me to see that far.

"Where was Craig when you couldn't see him?" I asked when I emerged from the closet. "Too far this way or that?"

Oscar pointed. I wasn't surprised when he indicated a spot far left. "He worked there for hours," he said again. "I could hear him. And I couldn't leave until after he did."

I tapped a finger against my lip as I made my way over to the dusty table. "Could he have been working here?" I asked.

Oscar followed me. Shrugged. "Can't say for sure."

"You see these dust marks?" I asked, pointing them out.

The clear spots on the table had developed a coating of dust of their own, making it a little more difficult to spot clear lines of demarcation. "Can you tell me if anything is missing from this table? If anything was stolen?"

Oscar took a step back. "I told you I didn't steal nothing. Not even once."

"We think someone else stole the items, Oscar," I said soothingly. "I'd like to know if you remember what may have been here." I pointed again. "It looks like a few items that had been here awhile are now missing."

He scratched his chin and crouched to study the dust patterns. "Yeah." When he stood up again, he shook his head. "Can't remember. But I didn't pay a lot of mind to any of the stuff that was down here, y'understand. I just came in here for shelter mostly."

"No problem," I said. It had been a long shot anyway. "But you said you heard him working. Could you tell what he was doing?" I asked. "By the sound, I mean?"

"Nah," he said. "And I tried to figure it out. Surely I did. I had enough time in there to try to put pieces together and get an idea, but it wasn't anything like I ever heard before. A solid noise. A repeating one. Louder than typing on a keyboard, but not heavy like hammering. Not that hard. And only sporadic hits. Not rhythmic like a machine."

I tried to imagine what sort of equipment might make such a sound. "Do you mean like the devices that print receipts for bank deposits?"

"Been a long time since I made a bank deposit," Oscar said with a laugh, "but no. That makes a tick-tick-tick-tick sound." He closed his eyes as though to aid his memory. "This was more like crank-crank, whumpata-whumpata-whumpata."

"Hmm." An idea was beginning to form. I thought about

those credit card blanks that had been found beneath Virginia's body. "What else can you tell us about Craig's activities?"

He scratched the back of his head. "Craig would yell at Virginia sometimes and say that the list wasn't long enough. That there weren't enough names."

"Names?" Bruce repeated.

"That's what he said," Oscar insisted. "He kept saying she needed to bring him more names."

Now I was sure this had to do with those blank credit cards.

"One more question," I said. "How did you get in and out of the building without a key?"

He smiled widely, self-consciously covering his teeth again. "I was wondering when you'd get around to asking me that. There's a window in back behind some overgrown weeds. You'd miss it if you didn't know it was there." He gestured for us to follow. We did.

He headed back toward the stairs where we'd found Virginia and pointed to a stack of boxes near the back wall. "Behind there."

Bruce, Scott, and I peered around the towering pile. Plenty of room for a full-grown adult to maneuver. And as promised, there was an extra-large window—the kind designed to allow people to escape a basement in the event of an emergency. The sliding panes were closed, but I pushed one side open with ease. Didn't even make a noise.

"I keep it lubricated," Oscar said. "So nobody hears me come in or out."

Scott nodded. "We would have found this eventually but I'm glad to know about it now." He turned to Oscar. "Does anyone else use this building for shelter that you know of?"

Oscar shook his shaggy head. "All mine," he said. Then with a wistful look on his face, he added, "At least it was."

We all headed back upstairs. I pulled the fifty dollars out of my purse and added another twenty. "You've been an enormous help, Oscar," I said. "Thank you."

Chapter 13

THE NEXT MORNING I CALLED JOE BRADLEY from my office phone. I knew he usually didn't see patients on Wednesdays, and thus I was a little bit surprised when the connection went straight to voicemail. Debating briefly, I opted to leave a message.

"I'm sorry I missed your call yesterday." I kept my tone lively and casual. "Believe it or not, my roommates and I met the homeless person who'd been living in the Granite Building. He was in the middle of sharing information with us when your call came through. I didn't want to give him any reason to stop talking." I drew in a quick breath. "Rodriguez gave me an update about Virginia's autopsy. He said you determined that it's definitely a homicide. I'm assuming that's why you tried to get in touch. Let me know if there's more to discuss." For a half second, I considered mentioning seeing him at Myrtille but decided it would be cowardly to leave that in a message. He knew I saw him; I knew he saw me. If we were ever going to address the matter, we'd do so face-to-face, no games. "Talk to you later," I added, then hung up.

With both hands on the receiver, I blew out a breath.

"So now it's in his court, is it?" Frances asked from the doorway. She crossed the room and sat down.

"Yep." I pulled my hands back and forced myself to assume a devil-may-care attitude.

"But he knows you went to lunch with Davenport, does he?"

"Yep," I said again.

"And how does he know this? Because you ran into him at Myrtille?" Before I could come up with a witty deflection, she went on. "Let's assume you did. And let's further assume that he backed out of his own lunch plans at Myrtille when you spotted him."

"Nothing gets past you, does it? Which of your grapevine minions brought you that bit of intelligence?"

She shrugged. "Doesn't matter. What matters is what you plan to do about it." She nodded toward the phone. "That was a pretty good first step."

"I'm so glad you approve."

My sarcasm must not have registered because she gave a self-satisfied smirk before continuing, "Next thing you need to do is find out who the woman is. I understand she was a looker."

"A looker?" I repeated. "What is this, the nineteen-fifties?" Before she could retort, I waved my hand. We were finished with this subject. "Were you able to get in touch with Neal Davenport?"

"Now there's a catch if I ever saw one," she said. Frowning, she continued, "Yes, I got in touch with him. He said he'd be happy to meet you here or at the bank. Whichever is more convenient. He also suggested dinner or drinks instead."

Dinner or drinks. Or both. Exactly what Joe and I had planned on.

"I'd like to see the bank. Meet some of the people there if I can. If you wouldn't mind setting that up, Frances? I'd do it myself but I think that having you run interference sends the signal that I'm interested in Davenport only on a professional level."

She snorted. "And that's your problem. You can't be tying yourself down to one guy when you don't even know for sure that he's worth your attention. You have to play the field a little bit. Expand your horizons. Make men understand that you're not sitting home, pining. Waiting for them to call."

"No one thinks that," I said. "And it wouldn't matter if they did. What matters is how I feel about things. I'm hardly pining. And I'm not interested in Neal Davenport."

"Yet," she said.

I rolled my eyes.

"Oh, and Flynn called. Said he's returning your call to Rodriguez. They had some kind of incident that kept them busy until late last night. Rodriguez thought it was too late to call back, so they're both stopping by later."

I glanced at the clock that sat on the mantel above the fireplace. Among the perks of occupying an office that had formerly housed a bedroom suite were the rooms' sweeping views and the cozy fireplaces. "Still early," I said, "and the day has already taken off at lightning speed."

I stared out the wall of mullioned windows to my left. "If Joe calls, put him through. Even if Rodriguez and Flynn are here." I considered a bit longer. "And even if Bennett stops by."

Frances smirked again. "Why? So that you have an excuse to keep the conversation short?"

"Hardly," I said. "Joe and I have a lot to discuss. The sooner we get started, the better." Annoyed that she'd lulled me back into that topic, I countered with, "Where is Bennett today?"

She frowned. "Talking with his lawyers, but he didn't say what it was about."

"Probably Liza."

"That's what I thought, too."

"I'm not planning to come in to work the day she gets out," I said. "My goal is to pick her up from prison, get her settled in the new apartment, and tell her what her monthly stipend will be—which is extremely generous on Bennett's part, if you ask me. I intend to make it clear both to her and to our aunt that my responsibility to them ends there."

"Admirable," Frances said.

I waited for the snark, but Frances remained silent.

"Out with it," I said. "You don't think it's going to be that simple, do you?"

"When are things ever simple with your sister?"

Frances's outer door opened, but before either of us could get up to see who had arrived, Rodriguez's voice boomed through. "We come bearing gifts, ladies."

Frances arched a brow. "A muzzle for Flynn would be nice," she said under her breath.

That made me laugh.

"What's so funny?" Flynn asked as they came into my office.

Frances stifled a chuckle. I held up my hands. "Always happy to see the two of you," I said. "When you add the mention of gifts, it makes your visit even more appealing." I made a show of looking them up and down. "And as you're both empty-handed, I assume your gift falls under the category of information."

"Right you are," Rodriguez said. "And from the message you left, I presume you have some to trade."

"That I do," I said.

Once we were all settled into our regular spots, I held out a hand to Rodriguez. "You first."

He nodded. "I thought you'd appreciate an update. But before I begin, a quick question about the squatter you met. You're sure he's the same one who's been living in the Granite Building?"

"Absolutely," I said and gave him a quick summary of meeting Oscar last night. I decided to hold back telling him what Oscar had shared about Virginia's clandestine meetings until I heard what the detectives had to tell me.

"Interesting." Rodriguez frowned as he jotted notes. When he glanced up again, he said, "One more question: Why is the place called the Granite Building when it housed a glass factory?"

"That doesn't have anything to do with the investigation," Frances said in a snit.

Rodriguez gave a mild shrug. "Can't a guy be curious?"

"From what I understand," I said, "the building originally housed a granite company. Years later, when they expanded and moved out, the glass company moved in, but the building's name stuck."

Flynn snorted. "Good luck getting people to call it by the wine shop name, then. Losing proposition, if you ask me."

"Good thing we didn't," I said sweetly. Turning to Rodriguez, I asked, "Don't keep me in suspense, Detective. What news do you have to share?"

"First things first," Rodriguez said as he sat back, making the seat creak. I recognized the movement for what it was: He was settling in to tell me a story. "How much do you know about Virginia Frisbie's daughter?"

"I think she lives in Oklahoma and that she has a child," I said. "Otherwise, nothing."

Rodriguez and Flynn exchanged a glance that told me they'd expected that answer.

"Is she a suspect?" I asked.

"Don't jump the gun," Flynn said. "We're only following evidence where it leads us and the money trail seems to be pointing to her."

Frances scooched forward on the sofa. "How so?"

"What's her name, by the way?" I asked. "The daughter."

Rodriguez lifted a finger, letting Flynn know that he'd take it from here. "Kayla Frisbie. Kept her name. Married, one child, another on the way."

The image of a pregnant woman pushing her own mother down the stairs was too horrible to contemplate. I must have grimaced because Rodriguez spoke quickly. "If the daughter is involved, and that's a very big if"—he sent a scathing look at his partner—"she could not have done it herself. She hasn't been away from home at all recently. Hasn't missed a day of work. Rock-solid alibi."

"That doesn't mean she didn't hire someone," Flynn said.

"Thank you, amigo," Rodriguez said without pulling his gaze from mine. "What my partner is particularly excited about is the fact that Virginia had been sending money—lots of money—to her daughter on a regular basis."

"Kayla's husband's a real loser," Flynn said. "Hasn't been able to hold a solid job for more than a couple months at a time. Keeps getting fired for flagrant insubordination." He wagged his eyebrows. "The guy's got anger management issues."

"Takes one to know one," Frances said from the sidelines.

Before Flynn could react, Rodriguez continued talking. "Kayla's got a big house, a mountain of debt, and she's the family's sole support."

"Plus, she's pregnant," Flynn said.

Rodriguez arched one eyebrow. "Yes, that's been established."

I thought about it for a second. "How much was Virginia sending her daughter?"

"Roughly speaking, a little less than ten thousand a month." Rodriguez leaned forward, his dark eyes sparking with interest. "More than she made on her bank salary."

I whistled. Poorly. "How was she able to do that?"

The older detective sat back, lacing his fingers across his almost-slim middle. "That's the question of the hour, isn't it? We got a warrant to look at her investment portfolio, and that information should be coming in soon."

"Seems to me that if her mother was sending money regularly, Kayla's the last person who'd want Virginia dead," I said.

Flynn practically hopped out of his seat. "That's because you don't know about the insurance policy."

Out of the corner of my eye, I saw Frances perk up. "How much?" she asked.

"Ten million. Not kidding." Flynn looked incredibly pleased with himself. "She took it out about four years ago. Daughter is the primary beneficiary."

"Ten million is a staggering sum," I said. "And you're saying Virginia opened it four years ago? At her age, premium payments had to be crazy expensive. How could she afford them?"

"How indeed?" Rodriguez said.

"Ten million smackeroos," Flynn said. "And every penny

goes to the daughter." He grinned. "That kind of money makes ten grand a month look like chump change."

My head spun with questions. "You're telling me that the daughter knew about this insurance policy?"

"Unclear," Rodriguez said. "That's another thing we're looking into."

"And how Virginia afforded all this," I said. After our talk with Oscar, I had an intriguing theory rolling around in my brain. One I was eager to share. "A pricey policy, monthly stipends to her daughter, not to mention the cost of living here herself."

"We're hoping her investment portfolio sheds some light," Rodriguez said. "Who knows? Could be Virginia inherited a fortune when her husband died. Could be she only worked at the bank for something to do. All this may make perfect sense once we have all the facts."

I wrinkled my nose. Though Rodriguez was right and every bit of this could be easily explainable, it didn't jibe with what Bruce and Scott had told me about the woman. But like they said, Virginia's salary at the bank may not have been her sole source of income.

"Does the name 'Craig' mean anything to either of you?" I asked.

The detectives shook their heads. "Why? Should it?" Flynn asked.

Rodriguez leaned forward. "This have anything to do with your conversation with the squatter?"

"Oscar," I said. "It does. Remember those credit cards that were found under Virginia's body?"

"Two of them," Rodriguez said, holding up fingers. "Blanks."

"Right. What if I told you that I suspect Virginia and a

mystery man named Craig were producing credit cards in the basement of the Granite Building?"

Flynn jumped to his feet. "You are out of your mind, you know that?"

I didn't react.

Rodriguez studied me, blinking slowly. "What makes you think that?"

"According to Oscar, Virginia and this Craig person met at the building a couple of times a week."

"So, this is actually the squatter's theory," Flynn said as he paced. "Did you ever think that maybe he's making stuff up to keep you from looking more closely at him?"

I ignored his overreaction, returning my attention to Rodriguez. I'd already bounced the idea off Frances. From the sofa, she gave me a nod of support.

Lowering my voice, I began again. "This isn't Oscar's theory; it's mine. He talked about Craig demanding names from Virginia. Yelling at her because there weren't enough names on her lists. Oscar also told us about the times he was stuck hiding until Craig left. Though he couldn't see what the man was doing, he heard sounds." I mimicked the noises Oscar had made for me.

Flynn was red in the face. "That's hardly proof," he said.

"I'm aware of that," I snapped back. To Rodriguez, I said, "According to Oscar, Craig worked for hours after Virginia left, making these random noises. If you add the two credit card blanks we found to the fact that Virginia spent a lot more money than her salary should have allowed, plus the fact that she was providing lists of some sort to Craig, I couldn't help but wonder if she and Craig were working together, producing bogus credit cards."

Rodriguez lifted his gaze to Flynn, who'd stopped pacing.

"No," the younger detective said, waving a finger. "Don't even go there."

A ghost of a smile played on Rodriguez's lips. "Why do you refuse a gift when it lands in your lap?" he asked.

Flynn flung an arm out, pointing at me. "Dumb luck, that's all it is. That's what it always is with her."

"This may be just the break we've been looking for," Rodriguez said before turning to me.

I sat up straighter, blinking my surprise.

"As you know," he continued, "my partner and I were unable to take your call last night. What you're unaware of is why. My friend here and I were taking a statement from a resident whose credit card account had been accessed fraudulently."

I said the first thing that popped into my head. "I thought you two were homicide detectives."

The older man's face split into a wide grin. "You keep us plenty busy with that, Miz Wheaton, but every once in a while Flynn and I get called in to help some of our brother officers when they're stretched thin."

Flynn threw up his hands in frustration and began pacing again.

"There's been a rash of credit card fraud reports and last night we stepped in to help ease the load."

"I hadn't heard about this," I said.

"No reason you should." Rodriguez shrugged. "Card numbers get stolen every day. As soon as fraud is detected, the credit company cancels the account and issues new cards. Because of that, victims figure that their job is done. Most of them don't call the police. But lately, that's changed. We've been getting more and more reports every day. The more information we get, the better chance we have of getting to the bottom of things."

"A friend of mine had her card number stolen a couple of weeks ago," Frances said. "I told her to call the Emberstowne Police and she did. You can thank me for making your jobs easier."

Flynn rolled his eyes.

"Interesting," I said.

Rodriguez leaned forward to rest a meaty forearm on my desk. "Interesting is right," he said. "With what you've come up with, I think we need to start looking for Craig, whoever he is."

One thing bothered me. "Emberstowne is a good-sized municipality," I said. "But I can't imagine our population being large enough to support this level of criminal activity for very long without being detected."

"Me neither," Rodriguez said as he got to his feet. "But just because we don't know of any other fraud cases around the country doesn't mean they don't exist." He gestured for Flynn to stop pacing and follow him. "My partner and I have some digging to do."

"Okay," I said. "Will you let me know what you learn?"

Flynn jerked a thumb to indicate Frances. "As long as you and Mouthy Mabel here keep it quiet."

Frances harrumphed.

"Oh," I said, suddenly remembering. "I asked Tooney to take a look at Virginia's daughter, too."

Flynn made a motion as though shooing a fly. "Tell him he can back off. We've got this one. I don't want him bumbling into our investigation and ruining everything."

"He's just eager to help." Turning to Frances, I said, "We'll have to come up with some other lead for him to track down. There are so many questions this time; I don't have a clue where to start."

"You got that right. No clue." Flynn rolled his eyes again. "Good one."

Rodriguez reached into his pocket. "How about you have him interview this woman?" He handed me a business card.

I recognized Cynthia Quinn's name. "The building inspector?" I wiggled the card, realizing belatedly that it was a refrigerator magnet. "I thought you already interviewed her."

Flynn blew raspberries.

Rodriguez sighed. "We met with her," he began.

"She's a flake." Flynn spread his arms wide. "No other way to describe her. A loose wing nut. A lunatic."

Rodriguez waved him down. "She's not so bad as all that." Turning his dark gaze to me, he added, "She is a little difficult to pin down. Perhaps Mr. Tooney will have better luck." He shrugged. "Maybe you could join him when he talks with her?"

I wondered what made this Cynthia Quinn such a challenge. "Sure," I said.

"I'll call Tooney when we're done here," Frances said.

"Thanks, Frances," I said.

The detectives were almost out the door when Flynn turned around.

"I can't believe you and your roommates plan to keep food on hand for this Oscar character," he said. "You don't want people like that hanging around. And not just because they stink. Living on the street changes people. They don't think like you or me. Shift your attention from this guy for a minute and he'll stab you in the back."

Frances clucked her approval. "First time I find myself agreeing with you," she said, arms folded across her chest. To me: "You trust people too easily."

"Thank you both for your concern and criticism, but the boys and I are happy to provide Oscar with a little help."

At that moment, the phone rang and Frances trundled to

her desk to get it. "Joe Bradley," she said, her brows arching skyward as she picked it up and said hello.

Rodriguez brightened. "Oh?"

With a tight smile, I patted him on the shoulder. "Thanks for stopping by, Detectives. I'm sure we'll be in touch."

Chapter 14

THE MINUTE THE DOOR SHUT BEHIND THEM,
I pivoted and pointed toward my office. "I'll take it in there."

Frances had put Joe's call on hold. "There's probably no
chance of you letting me listen in, is there?"

Despite the absurdity of the request, I laughed. "Not this
time." As I crossed the threshold into my office, I turned
back. "And I'm closing the door."

She frowned. "Make sure you tell him you plan to visit
Neal Davenport."

"Sure," I said. "I'll just pop that into the middle of our
conversation. Great suggestion."

I heard her answer, "Suit yourself," as I shut the door.

I drew a breath, bounced my head from side to side, and
worked up a smile as I clicked into the call. "Good morning,
Joe. How are you? I take it you got my voicemail."

"I did," he said.

The line was quiet between us for a long three seconds.
He cleared his throat. "You're right. I was calling to give

you an update on Virginia Frisbie's autopsy. But it seems that Rodriguez beat me to it."

"He and Flynn have a new lead to follow," I said. "They just left here, in fact. Not two minutes ago."

"That sounds promising."

I made a noncommittal noise. "It's something."

We endured another couple of seconds of silence.

"I was wondering," he said, then coughed, "if you'd still be interested in meeting to discuss the case."

"I'm very interested in discussing the case," I said. "Do you want to meet here at Marshfield? How does your schedule look for later today?"

Just then my office door opened and Frances marched across the room. She slammed a screaming yellow sticky note on top of my desk, the message turned toward me for easier reading. It said: *Meeting at 5:30 with Neal Davenport at bank tonight. Dinner afterward.* Beneath that, underlined, she'd added. *Tell the doctor you're taken!*

She shot me a pointed look, turned on her heel, and marched back out, shutting the door crisply behind her.

"I could come out there," Joe said. "Or we could meet somewhere local if you prefer. Maybe for dinner."

I peeled up the sticky note and frowned at it. Frances had set up a meeting with Neal, exactly as I'd asked. Well, almost exactly.

I fanned the note. "Is that a good idea?" I asked. "I mean, I wouldn't want to take you away from anything more important." *Like your girlfriend?*

"I could say the same," he said. "As much as I'd like the two of us to get together, I wouldn't want to presume anything."

I shook my head and stuck the little note back down on my desk top. "I think you and I need to talk in person."

It sounded as though he blew out a breath. "I do, too."

"Then dinner may be our best opportunity." We agreed to meet at six thirty. "Where?" I asked.

He named a new restaurant I hadn't yet had the chance to try. "See you there?"

"Yes, absolutely." We said our good-byes and hung up. My turn to blow out a breath. Yes, we were handling this like adults. If that "looker," as Frances had termed her, was indeed Joe's girlfriend, so be it. I preferred knowing the truth, whatever it might be.

But even more, I looked forward to telling Frances to call Davenport back to let him know that I had other plans for dinner tonight.

"YES, DETECTIVES RODRIGUEZ AND FLYNN came out to talk to me this afternoon," Neal Davenport said as he ushered me into his office.

I didn't know what I'd been expecting, but I thought that a bank president would warrant something a little grander than this fifteen-by-fifteen space that looked as though it hadn't seen a decorator since the mid-1970s.

He gallantly waved me into one of the wood-framed chairs at his desk. The orange and mustard patterned seat showed very little wear. But, I reasoned, that's to be expected with Naugahyde. I supposed the bank ought to be congratulated on its fiscal responsibility. Why bother replacing a perfectly sturdy, if less-than-fashionable, piece of furniture as long as it still served its purpose?

"I know you're eager to meet those who worked closely with Virginia," he said smoothly as he sat across from me. "I've asked a couple of them to stop in and say hello while you're here. But I thought it would be good for you and I to chat a bit first. I understand you have more questions for me."

So far, it seemed as though Frances had done her job to set exactly the right tone.

"I do, thanks. I know Virginia handled the sale of the Granite Building to my partners, but what other areas of the bank did she oversee?"

His eyes widened in a "too much to describe" way as he sat back. "It's probably easier to tell you the areas she didn't oversee. She'd been here for so long, she pretty much had a hand in everything. Actually, now that I think about it, there isn't a single department Virginia didn't work with at one point or another."

Here came the sticky part. "What about credit cards? Would she have had access to applications and approvals?"

"We don't issue credit cards locally. Applications are sent directly to our corporate headquarters for processing. We do offer debit cards to all our banking customers, though."

"Did Virginia handle the corporate credit card applications at all?"

"Unlikely, unless she was handing an application to a customer. Most customers take the blank forms home and fill them out at their leisure and mail them in from there. We'd love to get people to turn them in on the spot, but that only happens from time to time."

I frowned.

"What about a person named Craig?" I asked.

Davenport began shaking his head almost immediately. "The detectives asked me about him, too. I had our HR department go back through their files to see if that name popped up." He held his hands open. "No luck."

Reacting to the look on my face, perhaps, he added, "Sorry."

"Not your fault, of course," I said. "It's just that every-thing seems to hinge on finding this mysterious Craig. I'd hoped he was a coworker, but I suppose that would have been too easy."

Davenport sat up straight as a man stepped into the small office. "Here's Louis," he said, waving the fellow in. "He used to work with Virginia. I'll step away while you talk with him."

I spent about fifteen minutes meeting and talking with several of Virginia's former colleagues. They all expressed great regret at her untimely demise but none of them was able to shed any light on who Craig might be or what sort of lists Virginia may have possessed.

Davenport returned as the last one departed. He'd clearly been busy with paperwork while he'd been away because he dropped a stack of legal-sized pages onto his desk blotter before he sat down.

"There's one other woman you may want to talk with. She's been with the bank almost as long as Virginia had been. Patsy heads up our personal account customer service department." He pushed his papers aside, turning them slightly, as he scribbled a note for himself. "She should be back in the office tomorrow. I'll talk with her and ask her to give you a call."

"Thanks," I said, scanning the legal-sized pages strewn across his desk. They'd been filled out with names and per-sonal information, but that wasn't what interested me. A flash of realization hit. "What is this?" I asked, pointing to the top document.

"I'm sorry," he said as he gathered the sheets back up. "My bad. I shouldn't leave customer information out where it can be seen."

"No, that's not what I'm asking," I said as he shoved them out of sight. "Do you have a blank form like that one?"

"Sure." Clearly puzzled, he nonetheless opened a nearby drawer and sorted through the forms in it until he found what he wanted. A second later, he placed it in front of me. "But I can't imagine your need for an auto loan, given your financial circumstances."

"That's not why I want to see it." I scanned the form, quickly finding the exact section I knew must be there. "Here, look." I twisted the page to make it easier for us both to study it.

He leaned forward, tilting his head sideways. "This is a standard loan application."

"Right." I tapped the page for emphasis. "One that requires applicants to provide their credit information. Did Virginia have access to these? Completed forms, I mean."

"Of course she did." He shook his head. "Every loan application requires two officers to sign off on them. There are four of us here in total, but Virginia always offered to do the lion's share of approvals."

Thinking quickly, I asked, "About how many approvals would you estimate she performed every week?"

He leaned back in his chair, staring upward and away as though replaying scenes in his head. "Not that many," he said, squinting. "Ten? A dozen?"

Considering the huge amounts of money that Virginia had spent, I didn't think that ten to twelve accounts per week would fund her lavish expenses.

Davenport blinked repeatedly, his teeth set tight as he continued to study the ceiling. I hated to pile on the bad news, but I suspected we'd only touched the tip of this particular iceberg.

"What about corporate files?" I asked. "Did Virginia have access to your patrons' credit histories at other branches? In other states?"

Davenport's expression fell as all color drained from his face. "Oh my God," he said.

I took that as an affirmative.

He reached for his desk phone. "I'm sorry, Grace. I need to make a call."

"I'll see myself out," I said.

He nodded. "Thank you," he said, then winced. "I think."

Chapter 15

BEFORE HEADING HOME TO CHANGE FOR MY meeting with Joe tonight, I talked with Tooney, then called Rodriguez to tell the detectives about my discussion with Davenport. "No proof yet, of course, but judging from Davenport's reaction, I think it's very likely that Virginia had access to thousands of credit reports."

"Thanks, Grace," Rodriguez said. "Flynn and I will follow up. You heading home now?"

I shook my head although I knew he couldn't see me. "Meeting a friend," I said.

"Oh?" he asked in a suspiciously hopeful tone. "Anyone I know?"

"Good night, Detective."

He chuckled. "Try to enjoy yourself for a change."

The restaurant Joe had picked was an upscale, casual spot that had opened off Main Street about six weeks ago. Even better, it was a quick ten-minute walk from my house. The place had gotten rave reviews for its food, but had been dinged slightly for subpar service. The reviewer had made an effort to note that the waitstaff at most new establishments took a while to find their footing and suggested that the superior menu and meal warranted further consideration.

Joe was waiting out front when I arrived. Wearing jeans, a tan blazer, and a striped button-down shirt with the collar open, he exuded a perfect gave-my-appearance-some-effort-but-didn't-get-too-dressy vibe. He had his cane with him today. Even the way he leaned on it made him look jaunty.

"You came," he said, instantly looking apologetic for the surprise in his tone.

"Of course." I pointed to the manila folder he held at his side. "I take it that's the autopsy report."

"It is." His gaze was tight and questioning. "That's why you agreed to meet, isn't it? I'm sure it wasn't solely for my company."

Subtle, but there was no doubt in his meaning. He wanted to know who I'd met for lunch at Myrtille. Awkward, because that's exactly the same information I wanted from him.

"Let's sit down," I said. "I think we have a lot to discuss."

Disappointment clouded his features for a scant second. A moment later, he smiled and—cane and all—held the door open for me.

Inside, a young woman stood before an ochre wall with Rosabi, the restaurant's name, formed out of multicolored glass bits. "Good evening," she said. "Do you have reservations?"

We did and the young woman smiled coyly as she confirmed Joe's request for a quiet, private table near the back. She gave him a quick once-over. "All of our dining tables are up or down a set of stairs. Is that all right with you, or would you prefer to sit at the bar?"

Joe's cheeks colored. "I'm fine on stairs, thanks."

I didn't know how a busy place like this could offer a private table until she led us around the welcoming wall and I saw that the restaurant took up three levels. There was a gleaming bar along the left end, shaped like an undulating river of gold. A three-member singing group was in the process of setting up across from it, and a small dance floor separated the two.

The hostess led us past cheerful revelers to the open stairway and up to the balcony level, where patrons sitting along the rail could enjoy the music and watch the goings-on. The place was stunningly beautiful. A real gem and—assuming the food quality lived up to the hype—a real boon for Emberstowne.

On the way up the stairs, I slowed to take another look around. With my hand on the railing, I paused to once again appreciate the sleek bar with its shiny bottles and upbeat atmosphere.

And then I saw him.

He saw me, too. Then quickly turned away.

It was the man who'd been eating alone at the restaurant where I'd met Neal Davenport for lunch. The man who'd been reading his newspaper.

There was nothing odd about running into the same stranger more than once in a week. But the baseball cap he held by his knee shocked me with recognition. This man was the same age, shape, and size of the guy who'd caught taking photos of the Granite Building the day we'd found Virginia dead on the floor.

Worse, I got the distinct impression this man had been watching me.

"Grace?" Joe and the hostess waited for me at the top of the stairs.

"Sorry, I thought I saw someone I knew," I said as I

joined them. Funny, I'd uttered almost the exact same words to Neal Davenport the other day when Joe and his date had walked in.

"I hope this spot works for you," the hostess said.

"Thanks very much, this is great," Joe answered her.

The table was great. A booth, actually. High backs, cushy seats, and secluded in a deep corner. But that wasn't what concerned me right now.

"Joe," I said the moment the hostess left us. "Did you notice the middle-aged man sitting at the end of the bar?"

"No, why?"

"I don't know. Maybe I'm being silly," I said. "I think he's following me."

"Hang on." He scooted out from his side of the booth, but held up an extra second. "Middle-aged, you say? Anything else?"

"He was drinking coffee and holding a baseball cap on the top of his leg. It's navy blue. Plain."

Joe nodded, grabbed his cane, then made his way to a space between tables at the balcony's edge, taking his time to examine the area below. When he returned, he said, "I didn't see anyone who fits that description."

At that moment, our waiter appeared and introduced himself as Ethan. He handed me a menu printed on parchment.

I accepted it from him with my thanks, then held up a finger. "I'll be right back."

Scooting over to the balcony, I ignored the quizzical looks customers at the nearby tables were throwing me as I searched for my quarry. The middle-aged guy was gone, his stool empty. I traced a path to the door with my gaze, but there was no sign of him.

"Sorry," I said to the waiter when I returned.

"Is everything all right?" he asked.

"Yes, thanks." Across from me, Joe narrowed his eyes.
The waiter evidently decided to ignore our odd behavior
and, learning that this was our first visit to Rosabi, launched
into a welcome speech to explain the establishment's
farm-to-table approach. As much as I appreciated the information and the idea behind it, I couldn't wait for the earnest
young server to leave us alone.

"Can I get you started with anything to drink?" he asked.

"I'm going to need a couple of minutes, thanks."

"Got it," he said with a lilt of his pen. "I'll check back in
a few."

"Was he there?" Joe asked when the kid was gone.

I shook my head, but I was already pulling out my phone.
"I need to talk to Rodriguez."

"Do we need to leave?" Joe asked.

"No, hang on." Geez, it seems as though I was saying that
a lot tonight. When Rodriguez answered, I told him about
the man at the bar and how I believed it was the same guy
I'd seen snapping photographs outside Virginia's crime
scene. He asked me for a more detailed description, which I
provided. "There's one more thing, though," I said. "I've seen
him one other time. I didn't put it together until just now."

"When was that?"

"Remember I mentioned having lunch the other day at
Myrtille with Neal Davenport—the banker—to ask him
about Virginia?" When Joe heard the qualifier "the banker"
that I'd thrown in for his benefit, an expression of surprise,
or possibly relief, crossed his features.

"I remember. He was there, too?" Rodriguez asked.

"He was. Sitting by himself. I didn't pay him any attention because I didn't realize he was the same man with the
camera phone until now. I'm sure that was the same guy. I
think he's following me."

"We'll get right on this, but in the meantime, you be careful, Miz Wheaton."

"I will," I said, glancing up at Joe again.

"You're out to dinner with the doctor, right?"

"Nothing gets past you, does it?"

"Make sure he walks you to your door."

I gave a resigned sigh. "Let me know what you find out about this guy, okay?"

"You got it."

I hung up and tucked my phone back into my purse. "Sorry about that." I was apologizing a lot tonight, too. "There's so much going on these days, I don't know what's key to the investigation and what isn't. If there's one thing I've learned, however, it's to not take chances."

"Always a wise decision." He looked as though he was about to say more when Ethan returned to our table with an eager-to-please expression on his face.

Taking pity on the kid, and not wanting to send him away without at least a drink order again, I opted for a raspberry lemon martini, one of my favorite concoctions, especially on nights I wasn't driving. Joe ordered a bourbon and cranberry juice.

When we were alone again, Joe leaned forward. "I couldn't help overhearing. You had lunch with one of Virginia's coworkers?"

"Her boss, actually," I said smoothly. So, he wasn't wasting any time tackling the awkward topic. "I met with him again this afternoon but this time at the bank so that I could chat with a few of Virginia's colleagues."

"Did you learn anything of interest?" he asked.

"Some," I said, explaining Virginia's access to sensitive customer data and my theory about how she may have misused it.

"That's more than Rodriguez and Flynn have shared with me," he said.

"Most of this came about today. I'm sure they have every intention of bringing you up to speed next time you talk with them."

He tapped the manila folder he'd placed on the tabletop. "And they've already shared my findings with you."

"I'd like to go over those findings in more depth," I said. "If you don't mind."

"Of course, that's why I brought this." He glanced away for a moment, looking as though he wished he were somewhere else.

Time for me to push past my awkwardness. "What about you?" I asked.

He gave me a puzzled smile. "About me?"

"Myrtille turned out to be a popular lunch spot the other day, didn't it?" I asked with a cheerful lilt. "It's unfortunate you and your companion changed your minds about eating there. The food was delicious."

"Yeah," he said, glancing away again. "Yeah, about that." I waited.

"It's not—that is, please don't think—" He rolled his head back and stared at the ceiling for a long moment. A tiny growl escaped from his throat before he faced me again. "I'm doing a terrible job at this."

"Here you go." Ethan set our drinks down in front of us. "Would you like to hear tonight's specials?"

I smiled up at him. "I think we'd like to enjoy our drinks for a few minutes first. We'll let you know when we're ready."

"No problem," he said. And mercifully took off.

I raised my martini and waited for Joe to raise his bourbon. When he did, I reached across the table to clink the edge of his glass with mine. I had a sense that whatever he was about to tell me wouldn't be easy to hear.

"No pressure," I said.

"No pressure," he repeated wryly. "Sure. Let's start there."

Chapter 16

JOE PLACED HIS DRINK BACK ON THE TABLE.
"Alima is my lawyer." The tight expression on his face gave
me the impression that he was wincing inwardly. "Remember when you asked if anyone had been injured in the car
accident that left me with this?" He rested his hand atop the
curve of his cane.

"You were T-boned by a drunk driver," I said.

He nodded. "There's more to it. A great deal more."

I waited.

He picked up his drink, swirled it a bit, then took a swig.
"I'm not trying to be purposely vague, but this is tough for
me to talk about."

I could only imagine. He must have lost a loved one in
the accident. His wife, probably. "Then don't," I said. "Let's
find something easier to discuss first."

He tapped the manila folder again. "Like Virginia's
murder?"

Despite the morbid humor, I chuckled. "That's not much better, is it?"

He shifted his weight in the seat and leaned forward, hands on either side of his on-the-rocks glass. "Grace," he said, "this is the first—well—date I've been on." He glanced at his bare ring finger. "In a very long time."

I kept quiet, sensing he had more to say.

"I have a story to tell you. It's a long one and it doesn't have a happy ending." He made a face. "I'd like to be brave and tell you the whole tale, but I have to admit, I'm fearful."

"Fearful of what?"

"Dumping too much on you all at once."

Ethan returned. "Just checking in to see if there's anything you need."

Right about now I wished we would have chosen to have dinner at McDonald's.

Joe appeared so uncomfortable I decided to give him a little breathing room. "Why don't you tell us your specials?"

After Ethan completed his spiel, I sent him away with an appetizer order. The minute he was gone, I said, "I hope you like shrimp. Otherwise, this appetizer may turn out to be my entire meal."

"Thanks," he said. "I appreciate your patience with me, and yes, I love shrimp."

I took a sip of my martini.

A couple of uncomfortable seconds later, he said, "I'd like to beg your indulgence tonight. I had every intention of being upfront with you but I'm finding it difficult to put everything into words at the moment."

"That's fine." I wanted to hear every word of the story right here, right now. But he looked so incredibly broken I couldn't help but want to take his pain away. And besides,

I understood. If Joe and I were to ever get to know each other better, I had my own story to tell. About Liza. I suppressed a shudder.

"My lawyer is helping me get through all of it," he said. "That's what we planned to discuss at lunch the other day when you spotted us. She and I couldn't have had a frank conversation with you right there. Not until I had a chance to explain what's going on." He frowned at his drink. "I panicked."

When I opened my mouth to dismiss the implied apology, he tapped his hand against the tabletop. "I should have at least come over to say hello. It was a mistake not to. And then I didn't want to because I thought"—he blushed lightly—"that I'd be interrupting your lunch date."

"I thought you were there with a date, too," I said.

"Well then, at least we're both clear on that matter now," he said.

We managed to stick with noncontroversial topics while we enjoyed the spicy shrimp appetizer. And when Ethan cleared the empty ramekin from our table, we put in our dinner orders as well.

"Let's get to work then, shall we?" Joe asked as he opened the autopsy file. He and I had gone over one other report like this about a month ago. That victim had been male, and my assistant, Frances, had been accused of his murder. This time, even though the victim was female and no one I knew was suspected of having committed the crime, I was just as interested in Joe's results.

Even better, the live band on the main floor began warming up. The music would help keep our conversation private.

I leaned forward to look. Two line drawings representing Virginia's body took up the center of the first page of the report with notes and arrows handwritten in the margins.

"A lot of updated coroners and medical examiners have computerized these reports. We're still in the twentieth century here in Emberstowne. But to be honest, I prefer it this way. I find I'm better able to be specific when I physically write things down."

"I can appreciate that."

"I don't know if any of this information may help you," he said, tilting the page toward me, "but here are a few key things I found."

Although Joe didn't have more information to share than Rodriguez had, he went into more detail describing his findings and Virginia's defensive wounds. "Preliminary tests uncovered a different blood type under her nails."

"And DNA?"

He shook his head. "Too soon for results. And even when we get them, they're only going to help us find our killer if his or her DNA is on file with the local, state, or national DNA databases."

"Right now, all we have is one suspect's first name. Craig."

"And his blood type," Joe said. "But type O, unfortunately, is the most common. Not much help."

"What about Virginia's blood type?"

He pointed. "B-positive."

"That's the same as mine."

"I doubt that you had anything to do with Virginia's death."

I smiled, thinking about how my blood type, my mother's, and Bennett's were all the same. "Your confidence is well placed. But that means, at least, that it couldn't have been her daughter, right? Because a B-positive mother couldn't have a type O daughter?"

He shook his head. "It's entirely possible that a type B

individual could parent an O child. There are alleles and antigens at work behind the scenes."

I twisted my mouth, concentrating. "This is starting to sound like my high school biology class."

He laughed, then sobered. "Sorry to say that this doesn't clear Virginia's daughter."

"That's all right," I said. "I don't really consider her a viable suspect. Not sure if Rodriguez or Flynn do, either. She had too much to gain by her mother staying alive."

Ethan must have taken the earlier hint because we didn't see him again until he arrived to deliver our dinner order. Joe quickly slapped the manila folder shut.

As the music from the main floor surrounded us, warming me with memories that stretched back to high school dances, we dug into our meals and moved away from topics of car accidents and murders. Gradually, I realized that our initial awkwardness was long gone and that conversation had became effortless.

Joe maintained eye contact whenever I was speaking. He smiled easily and often, and if he had one noticeable habit, it was scratching his chin with the side of his hand whenever it was his turn to talk as he paused to consider his words.

He was telling me a story about his first year in med school when my phone rang.

I frowned at my purse.

"Go ahead and get that if you want," he said. "It may be Rodriguez calling you with an update on the guy who's been following you."

"Thanks." I reached for the little device and glanced at the caller ID. I frowned again. "It's the Marshfield Inn calling, which is very unusual for them. I assume it's work-related," I said, but feared otherwise.

Joe started to boost himself from his side of the table. "Do you want some privacy?"

I waved him back down. "No, please stay. This shouldn't take long." I hoped it wouldn't take long.

I was disappointed, though not entirely surprised, to hear my Aunt Belinda's voice on the other end. "What's all that music in the background? Where are you, Grace?"

"I'm out with a friend," I said, shrugging at Joe. I didn't like being put on the spot and feeling defensive. "Why, is something wrong?"

"You're darned right it is. You're carousing out on the town when you brought me here to help your sister. I didn't expect to handle everything by my lonesome."

I bit back a retort. "What's going on? What is it you need?"

"I need you. Here. Right now."

Most of the time I could easily dismiss my aunt's flair for the dramatic, but because she was staying on Marshfield property and interacting with employees I valued, I pressed her for details.

"What exactly do you need me to do?" I asked, slowing my words in an effort to express a measure of calm.

"Welcome your sister back into society, for one."

Her words took an extra second to register. "What do you mean? Liza isn't scheduled to get out until Tuesday."

"She's here now," Aunt Belinda said. "And she needs a place to stay. This suite of yours only has the one bed. She needs a room, too. And they won't give her a room without charging her unless you okay it. Poor Liza doesn't have your deep pockets. She can't afford a room in this place."

Speechless from surprise, I glanced up to see Joe's intent gaze and furrowed brow. I waved weakly, as though to diminish his concern. A hundred thoughts zipped through my brain at once, but I focused on the key issue and moved the phone away from my ear long enough to check the time. "It's eight o'clock at night and you're telling me that Liza was just released. I find that hard to believe."

"Of course, she didn't just get released. It's taken us this long to get back to the hotel."

My head spun. "From where?" Aunt Belinda didn't drive. The plan had been for me to pick Liza up at the prison. I'd intended to use the drive back to make it clear to my sister that my assistance, as well as Bennett's, came with strings attached. No more thievery, no more lying. Liza would have to make an effort to get a job and learn to support herself. "How did she get there?"

"I hired a car to pick her up."

That must have cost a small fortune. And my aunt was not a wealthy woman. Before I could comment, she added, "Liza got in this afternoon."

"And you're just letting me know now?"

"We've been a little busy." Her cagey tone infuriated me. A second later, she asked, "Do you want to talk with your sister?"

"No." I rubbed my forehead then glanced over at Joe. He offered a wan smile. Helpless and frustrated, I could only shrug.

Ethan stopped by to check on our progress. I turned away, allowing Joe to handle whatever disposal of our leftovers he decided on.

"I will talk with the team at the hotel," I said, "to see if they have any availability. I'll call you back shortly and let you know what we come up with."

"Your sister is tired. It's been a long day. She needs a

room right now, not sometime later tonight. Can't you understand that?"

I fought to keep my tone under control. "I hope you understand that you've caught me at an inopportune time with an unreasonable request."

She huffed. "What's so unreasonable? Doesn't your sister deserve something as basic as her own room? How can you be so selfish, Grace? Your mother didn't raise you to be so cruel."

If I hadn't lived with this constant one-sided perspective, I may have taken offense. But right now all I cared about was tamping out this particular fire as quickly and with as little collateral damage as I could.

"I'll call you back shortly," I said again. "Don't go anywhere."

"Where would I go?" she asked.

I hung up.

Taking a deep breath, I turned to Joe. "Sorry about that," I said. Our table had been cleared.

He wore a puzzled, wary expression. "Is there anything I can do to help?"

I almost laughed. "Don't I wish."

Ethan showed up at the table again, this time bearing two take-home containers. He asked if we wanted dessert and I demurred. Joe asked for the check.

As soon as Ethan was gone, Joe pointed to the containers. "I live on leftovers, but I didn't know how you felt about them," he said. "I got yours boxed up, just in case."

"Leftovers are great," I said. "Dinner was delicious and I hate to waste."

He smiled then, as though pleased that he'd made a good choice.

I waited a couple of beats, then said, "About the phone call . . ."

"No pressure, remember?" he said. "I'm happy to listen to whatever you care to tell me. It sounds as though you're dealing with a lot."

I nodded.

"Believe me, I get it. It's tough to share personal stuff."

Ethan returned with the check, and both Joe and I reached for it at once.

"Please," he said. "Let me get this."

Something in his eyes told me that my best decision was to remove my hand. "Thank you," I said. "I really appreciate it. And I had a wonderful time. Up until, well, up until now." I pulled my phone out again. "I do have to make another call. Do you mind?"

He slid his credit card into the leather folder and pointed in the direction of the restrooms. "I'll give you a little privacy."

Fortunately, the Marshfield Inn had open rooms and I was able to arrange accommodations for Liza in short order. I called my aunt back and told her that the hotel staff couldn't relocate Liza into a new room until I arrived to authorize the move. In truth, I wanted the chance to impress upon Liza the importance of behaving herself now that she'd returned to Emberstowne.

"Don't be too late," Aunt Belinda said. "We're both exhausted from our very busy day."

Again the sly tone. The emphasis on "busy."

"I'll be there when I can," I said and hung up.

Joe returned, leaned forward, and said, "I really had a nice time."

"So have I," I said. "I'm only sorry to end it with aggravation."

I should have made a move to leave, but I didn't want to.

I didn't want to rush off the moment my aunt beckoned and show up at Marshfield Inn ready to render assistance the way dependable, reliable, soft-touch Grace always had before.

For once, they could wait.

Ethan returned, but before he could pick up the leather folder, Joe placed his hand on top of it and shot me a look that held a silent question. I hesitated only a moment, then nodded.

"On second thought," he said to the waiter, "we'd like another round."

"Thank you," I said. "I'm not ready to face reality just yet."

"So tell me," he said when our fresh drinks arrived, "who's Liza?"

Chapter 17

I FINISHED A SECOND MARTINI BEFORE WE called it a night. Truth is, I'd been sorely tempted to order a third, but good sense prevailed. I still had much to do this evening.

I thanked Joe for both the lovely dinner and for his non-judgmental expressions of support. "Talk about dumping too much on a person all at once," I said as we made our way out of the restaurant. "I had no intention of telling you all about my sister tonight."

"I'm glad you did," he said. "It's a good reminder that we all have stressors. Some that aren't obvious." He offered a shy smile. "Which makes it that much easier to share my situation with you. But not today," he amended quickly. "You need to get your sister settled and I need to be up early tomorrow."

"Next time?" I asked.

"Next time for sure," he said. "I just hope you won't be sorry you asked." Brightening, he gestured toward his car.

"You mentioned that you walked here. Do you need a ride?" he asked.

I opened my mouth to decline, then thought better of it. "A ride home would be great."

I don't know what I expected: another mention of a future date; a peck on the cheek; a move toward something more? But when Joe dropped me off at my front door, he merely said good night, smiled, and was off again.

I waved until he was out of sight, then let myself in.

My little tuxedo cat Bootsie bounded over to greet me, but from the silence surrounding us, I deduced that Bruce and Scott were already upstairs and settled in for the night.

One of the perks of being a joint owner of Marshfield Manor was having a driver on call whenever I needed. Up until now, I hadn't availed myself of this particular benefit, but two martinis meant no time behind the wheel for me tonight.

"TOOK YOU LONG ENOUGH," AUNT BELINDA said when she opened her hotel room door. Stepping back to allow me to enter, she gestured toward my sister, who sat slumped in one of the room's guest chairs, staring at a reality show rerun on TV.

Liza shot me a derisive glance when I walked in. "About time."

I held back my reaction. Gone was Liza's chestnut mane. Her pixie-short hair was darker than usual. Her face pale and gaunt. She wore a plaid shirt over a tank and blue jeans that looked new. Her eyes were rimmed red and her feet were bare.

"Nice to see you, too, Liza." I held up a cardboard packet that held keys for the new room. "And look. I was able to get you on the same floor. Right down the hall, in fact."

She bounded up to strip the packet from my hands. I yanked it out of reach.

"What is wrong with you?" she asked. "I'm tired and I'm cranky and all I want is to go to bed."

"You're always cranky," I said without any bitterness. It was the truth.

Aunt Belinda picked up the remote and shut off the television. "We're both very tired, Grace. I'm surprised at your selfishness, coming so late."

"I'm surprised you're here," I said to Liza. "What happened?"

"What happened is you weren't there for me like you said you would be. Again." She crossed her arms and lifted her chin toward our aunt. "If it wasn't for Belinda, I'd probably still be there, waiting for you and your empty promises to pick me up."

Aunt Belinda, I silently corrected. "You weren't supposed to get out until Tuesday," I reminded her.

"There was a plumbing issue at the prison," Aunt Belinda said as she stepped between us. "They had to relocate Liza's entire block and the other sections were already overcrowded. Anyone with a release date in the immediate future got a reprieve."

"Lucky you," I said.

Liza held out a hand. "Can I have my key now?"

"First, a couple of things."

She rolled her eyes. "Let me guess: rules. That's all you ever care about. You didn't even ask what it was like in jail. You don't care about me. You only care that I follow your orders."

I held back saying that if she'd followed my advice the last time she was here, she never would have been arrested in the first place. "I'm sorry you feel that way. But as long as I'm covering your expenses—and from the looks of it, that promises to be a long time—we need to set some guidelines."

Before she could interrupt with another complaint, I started in.

"Your apartment will be ready Monday, and until then, you and Aunt Belinda are here as my guests. Don't abuse that privilege. While the staff will do their best to keep you happy, they're not to be mistreated. Don't talk down to them."

"We're staying here until you find me a better apartment," Liza said. "I saw the pictures you sent Belinda. The place is a hole."

"It's brand-new construction in a vibrant part of town. Hardly a hole," I said. "Close enough to walk to work. Once you get a job, that is."

"Whatever." She gave a head waggle. "But it's so small. Did you see the size of the rooms?"

"Stop," I said, holding my hand up. "It's a lovely place; it has two bedrooms and two baths. And best of all, it will be affordable once you get a job. Oh wait, did I mention getting a job?"

Liza made a move toward me, but Aunt Belinda restrained her with a light touch on her forearm.

"You're sitting pretty on millions of dollars and you're talking to me about getting a job? Where's your loyalty?" Liza asked.

"I don't expect you to understand," I said. "It's called tough love. And really, with the apartment you're moving into, life isn't going to be all that tough. It's about time you take responsibility for yourself."

Liza faced our aunt. "She always does this. Makes it sound like she's the angel and I'm the devil. I do everything wrong. She does everything right, and if I don't follow exactly what she tells me to do, she makes me pay for it later."

"For now, honey," Aunt Belinda said as she gave me the side-eye. "Maybe we ought to do what Grace suggests. Just for now. Our time will come."

My aunt's not-so-subtle reminder of their intent to badger Bennett into sharing his fortune with Liza did not escape my notice.

"Bennett is a busy man," I said. "Any and all communication with him goes through me." *And I will head off every attempt to exploit him.*

"Of course," Liza said. "That's the exact same line you handed me last time I was here. You want to keep everything for yourself. What a shame. Like our aunt said, Mom and Dad didn't raise you to be so selfish. What happened?"

"I think we're done here," I said, dropping the packet of keys onto the dresser next to me. "I'll be in touch."

"You were never there for me, even when we were growing up," Liza said to my back as I navigated my way around their belongings.

I ignored her.

"Like that time I got suspended in fifth grade." Her voice rose. "You didn't stand up for me."

I spun. "Don't try to rewrite history, Liza. You were a bully. Little Josefina was afraid to come to school because of you. You were horrid to her."

"She was prissy. She deserved to be knocked down."

I locked eyes with Aunt Belinda as if to ask, "You see how she is?"

My aunt bit her bottom lip and looked away.

"I'm leaving," I said unnecessarily.

"What about the time I got hit by a car?" Liza lurched across the room and grabbed my arm. "I was five years old and I wanted my big sister. You didn't come visit me in the hospital. Not one time."

"I wanted to," I said quietly. "You know I did."

"I remember that." Aunt Belinda stepped closer to Liza and began petting her shoulder. "We were all so frightened because you lost so much blood. But you were strong. And now you're even stronger."

"Even Aunt Belinda came to visit me," Liza's voice rose again. "She came all the way from Florida to Chicago. But was my sister there? No."

"What? You think I faked having chicken pox to avoid coming to see you?" I asked, angry to hear the strain in my own voice. "They wouldn't even let me sit in the hospital waiting room. I had to go stay with the neighbors." Regaining control, I blew out a breath. "Don't change the facts to fit your version of the story. You know I wanted to come see you. I was just a kid. I had no power. I wrote you letters. I made you cards."

"Not the same thing," Liza said.

Anger and frustration threatened to get the better of me.

"This is ridiculous." Why did I allow my sister to get under my skin? "This time I really am leaving," I said. I pulled open the door and stepped out.

"I'm not moving to that dinky apartment," Liza shouted after me. "You and Bennett need to do a whole lot better than that."

Chapter 18

"I'M NOT WORRIED, GRACIE," BENNETT SAID the next morning. He, Frances, and I were gathered in my office. Outside my window the day sparkled with bright promise but my mood was dark and volatile as a storm cloud.

"I wish I shared your optimism," I said, "but there was a manic gleam in my sister's eyes that I haven't seen in a long time. Prison didn't serve to rehabilitate her, it heightened her rage."

Frances shifted in her seat. She'd remained silent while I'd brought the two of them up to date on last night's events, but her pointed look and exaggerated scowl assured me that she sided with me this time rather than with Bennett.

"We can make this go away." Bennett tapped the top of my desk to reclaim my attention. "As I've told you, I've had to face far more troublesome adversaries."

"Troublesome?" I couldn't help myself, I scoffed at his choice of descriptive terms. "She's out for blood."

"Literally," Frances chimed in.

"When does their attorney want to meet with us?" Bennett asked.

"They haven't specified. They haven't even provided their attorney's name so we can't get a jump on fact-finding."

Pushing himself to his feet, Bennett smiled down at me. "Whenever they want to meet, let's book it. The sooner we put this behind us, the happier we all will be."

"I don't want to negotiate with them. It isn't right."

"What's right? Or what's best? They're not always the same thing," he said. He tapped my desk again. "On another topic, what's the status on Virginia's murder? In the paper this morning, I read that the detectives have gone back to question the homeless man, Oscar, to try to get more information about what he may have seen while he was taking shelter at the Granite Building." Bennett looked hopeful. "Apparently they're bringing in a police sketch artist."

"The newspaper got that part wrong." I sighed. "Rodriguez and Flynn would have loved to bring in a sketch artist, but Oscar's eyesight is so bad he couldn't come up with anything more descriptive than a guesstimate on Craig's height and weight and age." I told him the rest of what I knew so far, which wasn't much. "Tooney and I are meeting Cynthia Quinn today to interview her."

Bennett gave me a puzzled look. "That name isn't familiar. Remind me who she is?"

"The inspector that gave Bruce and Scott a thumbs-up on the structural integrity of the Granite Building."

"What do you hope to learn from her?"

Frances snorted. She'd asked the very same question earlier this morning.

I didn't have a good answer for Bennett. "The inspector may have seen something she doesn't even realize is important."

Frances pivoted to face Bennett. "The inspector missed the fact that a squatter was living on the property. How observant can she be?"

"Fair enough," I said. "But I don't know what I'm looking for. I need to keep digging until something pops."

Bennett nodded, looking amused. "You've proven yourself time and again and I don't blame you for digging under these rocks, however remote the chance you'll turn up a clue." He sobered. "But please, for my sake, Gracie, be careful. Let's try to avoid a life-threatening encounter this time."

"I'll do my best," I said.

Frances snorted again.

Bennett wagged a finger at her. "That goes for you, too."

WHAT PASSED FOR CYNTHIA QUINN'S OFFICE sat in the sketchy part of town not far from where the Promise Clock used to hang. I turned toward what was left of it—gaping ragged edges stretching from buildings on opposite sides of the street. The ornate clock mechanism that had sat at its center had been blown to smithereens not all that long ago. I shuddered as I recalled the part I'd played when the clock met its untimely and violent end.

Tooney noticed. "Brings back bad memories, doesn't it?"

"Scary memories, that's for sure." I shoulder-chucked him. "But everything turned out all right. Thanks to you."

His homely face colored and he cleared his throat. "How come you wanted to be part of interviewing the inspector?" he asked with an exaggerated glance at our surroundings. "This isn't exactly an optimal setting."

Scrappy weeds poked through uneven sidewalk cracks. Many of the businesses on this stretch—long boarded shut—were so layered with graffiti that taggers' messages were lost in a faded rainbow of paint. Plenty of apartment buildings were still occupied, however, evidenced by ratty curtains dancing out from open windows.

Beside Cynthia's office, the establishments that remained in business—and I spotted only two—were a liquor store with windows latticed in iron bars, and a similarly armored tiny outlet that offered cash for car titles.

"True enough," I said. "But Rodriguez thought I might have luck with her. I don't know why. He was a little vague on that score."

Tooney shrugged, his cheeks still pink. "Not that I mind the company, of course."

Cynthia's place of business consisted of a narrow storefront wedged between two three-story apartment houses. Uneven adhesive letters—new, from the looks of them—identified this as the home of AA+ BUILDING INSPECTION. The front door and wide picture window, while clean, had dingy corners as though the glass had been wiped in a hurry.

Tooney pulled open the door, making the three-bell chime above ring out our arrival. Two people, one man, one woman, glanced up. Facing us from behind brown metal desks, they wore identical expressions of eager anticipation. Other than the two desks, a set of guest chairs for each, and a single four-drawer filing cabinet in the back corner, the place was empty. I speculated the company had either just moved in or was on its way out.

The woman got to her feet first. "Good morning," she said, giving us an obvious once-over. "I take it you're looking for home inspection services? Are you buying or selling?"

Tooney cleared his throat before reminding her—almost apologetically—that he'd made an appointment to speak with her today.

Except for her voice, so high and squeaky she sounded

like an animated rodent, Cynthia registered average on just about every measurement I could think of: height, weight, looks, build. About forty years old and a little shorter than me, she had what my mom used to call mousy brown hair pulled back into a messy bun.

"Oh, that's right," she said, her tone straining for new heights.

I did my best not to cringe.

"I almost forgot," she said with a smile that shocked lines into her face so fast I couldn't believe the transformation. I revised my estimate. This woman had fifty in the rearview mirror.

"Come sit down," she said.

The man sitting at the other desk grumbled lightly, picked up a leather portfolio, and pulled keys from his pocket. "I'm going out," he said. "If I'm not back when you leave, lock up."

Cynthia gave him a dismissive wave. He circled his key ring around an index finger, palmed the set, and pushed his way out the front doors, sending the bells into another spasm of jingles.

"What can I do for you?" Cynthia asked when Tooney and I were settled in the hard plastic seats across from her.

Frustration crossed Tooney's features for the briefest moment. "As I mentioned on the phone, we're here to talk with you about your inspection of the Granite Building," he said, pulling out a notebook. "I know the police interviewed you about what you may have seen or not seen while you were there, but I'd like to go over the facts with you one more time."

She nodded, then turned to me. "Are you his wife?"

Tooney blushed again. "No," he said very quickly. "This is Grace. I work for her. As I mentioned in my phone call, she's partnering with the Granite Building's new owners."

"Oh, that's right," she said, tapping her forehead. "Silly me. Grace. From Marshfield. Right."

I'd introduced myself when we'd first walked in. This woman either had a lot on her mind or the attention span of a flea.

"You know that a woman was killed at the Granite Building, right?" I asked. "The police told you?"

"I have an alibi," she said. "I told them that."

"Of course you do," I said, beginning to understand why Rodriguez hadn't gotten much out of her. "We're here to ask you about things you may have seen or experienced while you were inspecting the building." A thought occurred to me. "You did perform the inspection yourself, correct? You didn't ask someone else to do it for you?" I gestured vaguely toward the empty desk where the man had sat moments ago.

"I do all my inspections myself," she said with no small degree of pride. "And as I told those two officers, I didn't notice anything of interest while I was there. The lady hadn't been killed yet, remember." She sat up straighter, her voice growing defensively shrill. "How on earth could I notice something before it happened?"

Tooney leaned forward. "What sort of things do you evaluate during an inspection?" He smiled gently and kept his tone even.

The calming technique worked. Her shoulders relaxed as she enumerated the many key areas that required attention in order to perform a satisfactory inspection.

When she finished, I asked, "How long does all this take? Generally, I mean."

"Several hours," she said. "And in this instance, I went back a couple of times. The assignment was simply too big to complete in one visit."

One of the many things she claimed to examine was

evidence of vandalism. "Did the police mention the fact that someone was living on the premises?"

"The squatter?" she asked. "I saw nothing that made me suspect anyone had broken in." A second later, she added, "Of course, there was so much stuff lying around that I could hardly be held responsible for knowing what belonged in the building and what a bum may have dragged in. I'm not there to take inventory, you understand. I'm there to ensure that the structure is sound."

"What about Virginia?" I asked. "She hired you, didn't she?"

Cynthia shook her head, her mouth a prim line. "Oh, no. The bank couldn't hire us. That would be a conflict of interest. They want to sell the building. They want a clean inspection. Your partners hired me."

I could have sworn Bruce and Scott told me that Virginia had set up the inspection for them. "So you never worked with Virginia?" I asked.

She squirmed. "No, you misunderstand. Virginia and the other bank officers know what a wonderful job this company does and they recommend us to their customers."

"Aha," I said. Now it made sense. Of course my roommates would have depended on Virginia's recommendation. "How often does that happen?" I asked. "That your company is called to do inspections—due to a bank officer's suggestion?"

She squirmed in her seat again. "Now and then."

"Now and then?" I repeated.

"All right, pretty often. The bank is one of our best sources for new leads. But it's all on the up and up."

"You mentioned visiting the building more than once," Tooney said. "Did you have keys of your own?"

"Oh, no," she said. "I always had to pick them up from Virginia first. And then return them immediately afterward."

"What time of day did you go there?" he asked. "Usually?"

"Mornings or early afternoon. When the light is best. Even though the electricity was on, there's nothing like natural daylight when you need to get a close look." She smiled, looking old again. "Of course, I always carry a bright flashlight. Don't want to miss those dark corners."

I thought about the windows out front here and their dirty corners. "Do you own AA+ Building Inspection?"

She laughed. "Heavens, no. I only work here."

"How long?" Tooney asked.

She squinted. "Three years, give or take."

Oscar, the homeless man, had told us that Craig and Virginia used to meet at the building after banking hours. And Virginia controlled the keys. Which meant that Cynthia probably had never run into them there. But then again, Oscar had also mentioned that Craig sometimes worked in the building on his own.

"Does the name 'Craig' mean anything to you?" I asked.

"Greg?"

"No. Craig," I said enunciating more clearly.

She started to shake her head, then stopped. "Wait, do you mean Craig who used to work here?"

Tooney and I exchanged a look. "I don't know," I said. "What's his last name?"

"It's . . ." She held up a finger. "Give me a minute."

Could it be this easy? I imagined that, in seconds, we'd find out that Craig had recently left AA+ Building Inspection and that he'd had access to the Granite Building via Virginia. Once we had his full name, Rodriguez and Flynn could start checking him out.

I held my breath.

"Oh, darn," Cynthia said. "I can't remember."

I pointed around the office. "Is there some file here with former employees' names? Maybe you could look him up?"

"Are you kidding?" She laughed as though I'd asked the most ridiculous favor. "We have nothing here. Literally." She half turned to look at the filing cabinet in the far corner. "You see that? Our open assignments are in there, and maybe three months' worth of records. Enough to keep us afloat until we move into our permanent space." She wiggled her fingers in the air. "This is temporary. Our lease was up and our new spot wasn't complete yet. This is the only location the boss could find." She shrugged. "I would prefer to work from home."

"How long ago did Craig leave the company?" I asked.

Cynthia scrunched her nose. "Has to be a couple of years, at least. We only worked together a few months. Not even a full year, I don't think."

My hopes fell. This long-gone Craig was probably not the man we were looking for after all.

"What about your boss?" Tooney asked. "Is that the man who left? Would he know Craig's last name, or where Craig went to work next?"

"The guy who left started here after I did. He wouldn't have a clue. The boss is out of the country on vacation until our new space is ready."

"He may remember Craig's last name," I said, though I knew we were grasping at straws.

"I'm sure it's possible," she said. "Even though the turn-over here is crazy." She thought about it and twisted her mouth to one side. "The thing is, all our old records are in storage. I don't have time to get out there and sort through boxes. Not when I have a full boat of inspections to finish."

As though to punctuate her statement, she looked at her jewel-encrusted, giant-faced watch. "I'm due to meet a potential client in an hour."

"Tell me about this Craig," I said, unwilling to give up even a scrap of a lead. "What does he look like? What kind of personality does he have?"

She twisted her mouth again as though to convey that she found my questions odd. "He's a heck of a nice guy," she said. "He kept in touch for a year or so."

And she couldn't remember his last name?

"How did he keep in touch?" I prompted. "Via e-mail?"

"No, he used to call." She pointed to the desk phone. "Just to chat and ask about how business was going and what I was up to. I haven't heard from him in a while, though." She frowned. "Now that I think about it, he always called me. I didn't ever get his phone number. Not that I would have used it. I wasn't interested in him that way." She shrugged. "Sorry."

"What does he look like?" Tooney reminded her of my question.

"I don't know. Average, I suppose. Maybe forty or forty-five years old. Nice head of hair."

"Color?" I asked.

"Brownish, I guess," she said.

"Ethnicity?" I asked.

"I don't know. White?"

"Tall, short, heavy, thin?"

She shook her head and held up her hands. "Like I said: average. Not bad looking, I suppose. But no George Clooney."

"Any distinguishing characteristics?" Tooney asked.

She couldn't think of any. "Sorry," she said again.

We asked her a few more questions but she made it clear she wanted us to leave in order to make her next appointment. As Tooney and I reached the door, I thought of one more thing.

"Cynthia." I waited until she looked up. "You mentioned that you work with the bank a lot."

She nodded.

"How long has AA+ worked with them?" I asked. "I mean, did your company have a relationship with the bank back when Craig worked here?"

"Oh, sure," she said. "He handed the bank business off to me when he left."

"So, he knew Virginia."

"Definitely."

"Great, thanks," I said. "And don't forget: If you're able to get Craig's last name, I'd really appreciate it."

"I'll try to remember to ask the boss when he gets back," she said, tapping the side of her head.

The minute the door closed behind us, Tooney said, "Don't hold your breath."

Chapter 19

ON OUR DRIVE BACK TO MARSHFIELD, I TOLD Tooney about the fellow I'd noticed taking photos at the crime scene and how I'd spotted him at the bar when I went to dinner with Joe.

"Would you mind keeping an eye out for him?" I asked, providing the best description I could. "I know it isn't much to go on, but I can't help but believe he's involved in this situation somehow."

"You think he's this elusive Craig person?" Tooney asked.

"Could be, but the truth is, I don't know. No one has been able to give me a detailed enough description of Craig to discount this guy, though. They're both very ordinary."

We drove for a few moments in silence.

"So, you like this guy, then?" Tooney asked.

It took me a second to realize he was referring to Joe. I half smiled and shrugged. "I think so. There's a lot I don't know about him yet."

Tooney kept his eyes on the road. "Want me to check him out for you? I'd be happy to."

I reached over to pat his arm. "Thanks," I said, "but I think this is a route I need to follow on my own."

He nodded without looking at me.

BACK AT MARSHFIELD, I CALLED NEAL DAVEN-port.

"Grace," he said with a smile in his voice. "How nice to hear from you."

Before I could say a word, he interrupted.

"Regarding the matter we discussed the other day," he said as he lowered his voice, "about Virginia and the loan applications, there's nothing I'm at liberty to share with you right now. I hope you understand."

"Yes, of course," I said. "I'm sure this situation is causing a great deal of angst."

"You don't know the half of it," he said. "But what can I do for you today?"

"I may have a lead on this Craig fellow the police are looking for," I said. "I'm hoping you can help me."

"Whatever I can do, although you remember that we looked through all our personnel files and didn't come up with anyone with that name."

"Right," I said. "But I believe he interacted with your staff. It turns out that the inspection firm your bank recommends had an employee named Craig several years ago."

"Okay," he said slowly.

I pounced on his pause. "Is there anyone there, other than Virginia, of course, who may have worked with an inspection service firm? Specifically, AA+ Building Inspection?

Perhaps someone there will remember him and be able to provide a last name."

"Offhand, I wouldn't know," he said. "But I'll be happy to check with Patsy and ask her what she knows."

"Patsy?" I repeated. "That's the woman who was out of the office when I was there, isn't it? The one who used to work with Virginia?"

"That's right," he said. "I'll see what she knows and call you back."

"Would it be all right if I spoke with her directly?"

He drew in a quick breath but then said, "Sure," and provided her extension.

"Thanks very much," I said.

"Give me a call if you need anything else," he said. "Or if you just want to get out of the office sometime to talk."

"Thank you, Neal. I appreciate it."

When I hung up, Frances poked her head in. "How's Mr. Dreamboat?"

"Let him sail on without me," I said as I picked up the phone again and started to dial.

"Come on." Uninvited, she sat across from me. "It wouldn't hurt to give him a chance."

I was spared commenting when Patsy picked on the first ring. After identifying myself and assuring her that her boss had approved my contacting her, I launched into the reason for my call.

"It's my understanding that you worked closely with Virginia Frisbie," I began.

She answered with a snort. One Frances would be proud of.

"I'm sorry," I said into the phone, sending my assistant a look that told her I was confused, "do I take that to mean that you didn't work with Virginia?"

"I worked with her all right," Patsy said. "But 'closely'? If that's the word Mr. Davenport actually used, he's even more clueless than I realized."

I tilted the phone slightly away from my ear and Frances leaned forward to listen in.

"I'm sorry if I misspoke," I said, shrugging to let Frances know that I wasn't quite sure why Neal thought it would be a good idea for me to talk with this woman. "What I'm really interested in today is knowing if you ever worked with AA+ Building Inspections."

She made a noise of dismissal. "'Course I did."

"Great." I injected cheer into my tone to try to turn this conversation into something more positive. "I take it you know Cynthia Quinn, then?"

"Sure I do. The bank uses that company a lot."

"Did you know one of the men who worked there a few years ago?" I asked. "First name 'Craig'?"

"Yeah," she said but with less vigor. "That sounds familiar. Kind of a charmer? Not too bad looking?"

"I think that's him." Her description, at least, didn't contradict what I'd gotten from Oscar and Cynthia. "You wouldn't happen to remember his last name, would you?"

"You'd think I would. After all, I had dealings with him for a couple of years before Virginia shooed me into a different department and stopped me from having anything to do with loans."

"When was this?" I asked.

"Geez, maybe five years ago, give or take." She made a thoughtful noise. "Everybody here thinks that Virginia was the best thing to happen to this bank."

Frances and I exchanged a look. "You disagree?"

She snorted again. "She wasn't a bad person. That's not what I'm saying. I don't want to speak ill of the dead or anything, but she was one of those super-sweet old ladies who had a core of steel underneath."

I'd never met Patsy, but by her voice, I judged her to be in her fifties. "That's interesting," I said to keep her talking.

"People like Mr. Davenport, they love the Virginias of the world. Those women do everything they're asked to do plus a whole lot more. They try and make themselves indispensible. Nobody's indispensible," she said. "The bank hasn't closed since she died, has it?"

"No, it hasn't," I agreed.

"Yeah, well, there you go. But until Virginia didn't show up for work Monday morning, Davenport would've been terrified to run this place without her. The rest of us are just as competent. But did we ever get the promotions and the perks Virginia did? Not a chance. She hogged all the plum assignments. Didn't know the meaning of the word *delegate*."

This was the first negative assessment of Virginia that we'd come up against. "I appreciate your candor," I said. "How are things going now? Is there a lot of work to divvy up?"

She made another impertinent noise. "It's a mess. Virginia kept everything locked up tight and password protected. We haven't been able to get into most of her files. It's chaos here."

"Neal Davenport has been putting up a good front then," I said. "He seems the picture of calm."

"Because he doesn't know how deep this goes," she said. "I predict that there will be more aggravation before there's less."

"Are you saying that Virginia may have participated in something illegal?" I asked.

"I never said that," Patsy said. "I don't think she was embezzling from the bank, if that's what you're suggesting.

We've got too many controls in place for anyone to get away with that. But do I think she was a control freak? Oh, yeah."

"Thanks," I said.

"Not that I want to speak ill of the dead," she said again.

"I understand," I said. "And about that Craig from AA+, have you been able to think of his last name?"

"Not for the life of me." A half beat later, she added, "But you know what? I can probably dig through some of my files from back then. Maybe it's recorded somewhere around here."

"Thanks, I'd be grateful." I gave her my office and cell phone numbers as well as my e-mail. "It's a bit of a long shot, but whatever information you have on this Craig will be appreciated."

"You think this guy killed Virginia?"

Frances shot me a look that said, "What did you expect her to think?"

"That's for the police to determine," I said. "But I suspect they'll want to talk with him."

"I'll take a look today."

Frances frowned when I hung up the phone. "While you had her talking, you should have asked her for the scoop on Neal Davenport."

MY PHONE RANG LATER THAT AFTERNOON but Frances picked it up in her office before I could even read the caller ID display.

Less than a minute later, she hurried into my office, pointing. "Your sister's lawyer. Wants to talk with you about setting up an appointment with Bennett."

I nodded, working to quell the sudden gyrations in my stomach. "Here we go," I said, then picked up. "Grace Wheaton."

"Good afternoon, Ms. Wheaton, this is Everett Young calling on behalf of my client Liza Soames."

So my sister was keeping Eric's last name. Well, that would make things easier. Wheaton versus Wheaton could get messy.

"What can I do for you, Mr. Young?" I asked.

He chuckled as though my question came as a surprise. "I'm sure I don't need to tell you that your sister has engaged me to explore her options as they apply to making a claim on Bennett Marshfield's property. Unfortunately, when I've attempted to open a discussion with Mr. Marshfield, his assistant informed me that all communication must be routed through you."

"I'm surprised Liza didn't advise you of that requirement before you went through all the effort," I said. "I made that point quite clear to her."

He chuckled again. "We do not need to be adversaries, Ms. Wheaton. We're both on the same side."

"Really?" I made no attempt to disguise my indignation. "Liza is attempting to wring money from our uncle. How can you possibly contort facts to presume that puts her on my side?"

"What I mean," he said smoothly, "is that your sister has had a spate of bad luck."

"More like she's created her own bad luck and is sorry to have to pay the price."

He continued as though I hadn't spoken. "She's destitute and dependent on family for her sole support. I know that as her sister, and as a compassionate human being, you don't want to see her on the streets. You don't want to commit her to a life of poverty. You know as well as I do that when individuals have nothing, they have nothing to lose. That's where crime begins."

I bit back a retort. This man was Liza's advocate. There was no way I'd sway his stance. It would be futile to try. "You mentioned wanting to speak with Bennett," I said to bring us back on track. "I can tell you that he's open to a meeting."

"I'm glad he's seeing reason."

I bit my cheeks again. The time to negotiate—or to kick them out on their backsides—was not now. I needed to bide my time. I needed to wait until we knew exactly what we were up against. And as Bennett had suggested, the sooner the better. "How does tomorrow afternoon look for you? Say about three o'clock?"

"Wonderful," he said and began to give me his office address.

"Let's meet here," I said.

"Even better."

I hung up and let out a long breath before calling Bennett to let him know that the game was on.

Chapter 20

BRUCE AND SCOTT HAD DINNER READY WHEN
I walked in that night. "Hope you don't mind Southwestern
chicken with quinoa," Bruce said. "It'll be on the table in
five."

"One of my favorites," I said.

"Bootsie has already been fed, by the way," Scott said
when I picked up my little cat to say hello. "She's been pretty
chatty this afternoon. It's almost as if she senses that we've
got a big project ahead of us and wants to help."

I nuzzled her neck and scratched behind her ears for as
long as she tolerated the attention, then put my soft, squirming bundle down on the floor.

"Let me run upstairs real quick to change." As much as
I liked wearing skirts and flats at work, I much preferred
getting comfortable in pajama pants, a T-shirt, and socks
when I was home.

Dinner was on the table when I got back. We all dug in
immediately.

"How's Oscar doing?" I asked between mouthfuls. "This is delicious, as always, by the way."

"Thanks," Scott said. "I particularly love these one-dish meals. Super easy, yet healthy."

"And full of flavor," I said, spearing an artichoke heart. "What a great combination."

"Oscar is"—Bruce made a so-so motion with his fork—"a challenge."

"That doesn't sound good," I said.

"We waited for him tonight—he was supposed to stop by before we left for the evening—but he never showed up," Scott said. "Poor guy may not eat tonight."

"I feel bad for him," I said. "He probably isn't used to a regular schedule."

Scott shook his head. "I was sure he'd be there before we left. He said he was looking forward to another hot meal."

"It's not his fault," Bruce said. "He probably lost track of time. He simply isn't used to interacting with people so closely and so regularly. We're working on getting him to do things like wash his hands after using the bathroom. And change his clothes more often than he's used to doing."

"Does he have a change of clothes?"

"We picked some things up for him at the secondhand store," Bruce said.

Scott nodded. "And we've been giving him cash to get his clothes cleaned at the Laundromat. We hope he actually uses the money for that, but we can't watch over him every minute."

"That reminds me," Bruce said. "When we talked with him this morning, Oscar remembered something else about this Craig fellow that he wanted us to tell you."

"Oh?" I stopped with the fork halfway to my mouth. "Anything good?"

"He said that the reason Virginia and Craig were arguing had something to do with chips."

"Chips?" I repeated.

"Oscar didn't know whether they were talking about computers or potato chips. He said that they got into a heated discussion about it, though. And that Craig kept saying that, without chips, they were finished. He wanted Virginia to get him these chips."

"Credit cards have chips nowadays," I said, thinking back. "But I'm pretty sure the ones Joe found under Virginia didn't."

"I'll bet that's it," Scott said. "Oscar said Craig talked about how, without chips, everything could be ruined."

"Thank you, guys," I said. "I'm convinced now that we're on the right track."

As we finished dinner, we talked a bit more about plans for the new Amethyst Cellars and I found out that they'd arranged to interview three contractors over the next few days. Anton had recommended two of them and they'd come up with a third choice on their own.

"Good luck with that," I said as we finished up dinner. "Keep me updated."

"We will," Scott said. "Speaking of updates, is everything set for Liza? She arrives Tuesday, right?"

I groaned.

"Uh-oh," Bruce said. "What don't we know?"

I told them about Liza's unexpected arrival last night and Aunt Belinda's demands that I drop what I was doing to meet her at the Marshfield Inn.

"You went out with Joe Bradley last night?" Scott feigned hurt. "Keeping secrets now?"

"Not at all." I laughed. "There's simply too much going on these days. Everything is blending together and I can't keep my days straight. Half the time I can't remember who I talked with or what I said."

As we cleared our plates and began to wash the dishes, Bruce said, "I get that. I feel as though it's been a month since we took possession of the Granite Building. In reality it's been less than a week."

"How did it go?" Scott asked. "The date, I mean. Not your visit with your sister. That, I can imagine."

"It went well," I said.

They both stopped what they were doing to look at me. "That's all you've got?" Bruce asked.

"There isn't that much to tell," I said. "We talked. We laughed. We had fun. We went over autopsy results." I shrugged. "Not exactly high-time romance."

"Oh, Grace," Bruce said. His tone was one of disappointment, but he smiled. "You plan to see him again?"

"I hope so." I'd learned the hard way not to get my hopes up too soon. "But I get the feeling this one will move slowly. He's got baggage he isn't ready to share yet."

"Everybody has baggage," Scott said.

"True enough." My mind immediately whipped back to all the accusations Liza had hurled at me. She resented me, no question about it. I suppose I could have been a better sister to her, growing up. But for the life of me, I couldn't imagine how. At the time, I thought I was doing my best.

Bruce dunked his hands into the sink's soapy water. He glanced up when I placed the baking dish next to him. "Why the scowl?" he asked.

"Me?" I shook my head. "Letting my mind wander, I guess. Something Liza said earlier is bugging me."

"Don't let her get to you," Scott said. "She's toxic."

"She is," I agreed. "But it's not that. She reminded me of a time when she was in the hospital and I wasn't allowed to visit her." They both stopped to listen. "I had the chicken pox and the doctors wouldn't let me near her. I made Liza cards and drew pictures, but they didn't want to risk her catching the disease, so I had to stay home. Liza remembers it differently."

"And she's making you feel guilty?"

"Attempting to," I said. "I know what I know. She'd been hit by a car and was in pretty bad shape for the first day. I was out of my mind with worry."

"Wow, hit by a car?" Bruce said. "Poor thing."

"Liza lost a lot of blood and had to have transfusions. I remember my parents being terrified about that." I frowned again. "I know I was young at the time, but I remember there was a problem."

"What kind of problem?" Scott asked.

"That's the thing. I don't remember. Our parents weren't the type to discuss worries with eight-year-olds. I just recall a lot of whispering and plenty of phone calls."

Bruce started rinsing the dishes again. "They were probably calling friends and family."

"Probably," I said. "I just seem to think that there was something more going on."

"I doubt Liza will tell you, even if she knows," Bruce said.

"True enough." My phone pinged an incoming e-mail. A quick glance told me it was from Patsy at the bank. With an attachment.

I pointed upstairs. "Do you guys mind if I grab my laptop for a second? I'll come back in a bit to help."

"Don't worry about it," Scott said. "A one-dish meal makes for easy cleaning."

Bootsie bounded up the stairs with me, crossing my path and staring as though trying to start a conversation. "Sorry,

Boots," I said as I hurried into my bedroom to fire up my laptop. "I want to see if Patsy came through for me."

She had.

Patsy's e-mail was brief. In it, she stated that she'd found some of the old invoices Craig had signed off on, but that his penmanship was so bad that she couldn't make out the proper spelling of his last name. She offered her guess and also attached several copies of invoices so that I could try to decipher his scrawl myself.

I downloaded immediately and enlarged the documents as much as I could. This Craig was a scribbler, no question about that. He started his first name with a giant *C*, but the rest looked like little more than a bumpy flat line with a loopy *g* at the end. His surname clearly began with a *W*. I studied the first document and thought that Patsy's guess of "Wedestia" wasn't bad.

I compared three documents on my screen. The loopy center consonant that Patsy had identified as a *d* could actually be an *l*, I thought. The extra stroke before it could be an *x*. A bit more scrutiny and I decided that Craig had a specific twist to the *r* in his first name. Which put that consonant at the end of his last name.

I tried that combination. Wexlstir. Probably not.

Except. That final vowel could easily be an *e*.

"Wexlser." As soon as I said it aloud, I could see the potential. Maybe Wexler. "Oh, yeah," I said to Bootsie. "Time to call Rodriguez."

"Grace," the detective said when he picked up. The odd note in his voice took me aback. I didn't have time to react, though. "How did you hear?"

"Hear what?" I asked.

"Why did you call me?"

"I may have a lead on Craig's last name."

"Hold on." In the background, I heard him tell someone else that he'd be right back. He lowered his voice. "Give it to me."

I did and could tell he was writing it down.

"Why did you think I called?" I asked.

I heard his sharp intake of breath. Before he could refuse to answer, I said. "Please tell me."

"I'm at the hospital. Your friend the squatter was just brought in. Somebody did a number on the poor guy."

"Oscar?"

"Yeah. Beaten up pretty bad. But he'll live," he assured me. "Lucky that a Good Samaritan stopped it from being worse."

"Who attacked him?"

"Unknown," Rodriguez said. "The witness couldn't provide much of a description beyond 'male' and 'average.' We plan to question Oscar as soon as the docs give us the all clear."

"The papers this morning said—"

"We know. Could be this Craig trying to tie up a loose end. Could be as simple as another homeless person wanting a share of Oscar's good fortune. Don't worry, Grace. We'll find out who did this."

Chapter 21

MY ROOMMATES WERE HORRIFIED BY THE news.

"I knew something was wrong when he didn't show up," Scott said later when we were all gathered in the parlor. "I should have done something."

"What could you have done?" I asked.

He threw his hands in the air. "I don't know."

"I feel responsible," Bruce said from the sofa. "Poor guy."

"The police agree that it may have been Craig who attacked him," I said, "but there's no way to know for sure. Not yet."

"If only the newspaper hadn't mentioned the eyewitness," Scott said.

"I know." I'd pulled out some of my mother's old photo albums and now drew one of them onto my lap. "I really wish they would have specified that Oscar provided the police zero description."

Scott came to peer over my shoulder. "What are you

doing?" he asked, pointing at a photo of me and Liza in our plastic backyard pool. "Is that you? Look at how blond you were."

"I know. I was a real towhead back when I was seven."

He sat down in the chair across from me. "What's with the trip down memory lane, Grace? I can't imagine you're trying to conjure up warm feelings for your sister."

"No," I said with a sad laugh. "I'm doing the exact opposite. I'm trying to figure out what's bothering me about her stay in the hospital." I ran my finger along the bottom of the sunny backyard photo. I was standing up to my ankles in the water, mugging for the camera. Behind me, Liza held a bucket of water poised to dump over my head. "I remember that Mom stopped her from dousing me. Liza kept insisting that I'd dumped water on her first." I glanced up. "I hadn't."

"Some things never change," Scott said. "Some people, either."

I slid the photo out of the album and turned it around to check the date my mother had recorded there. "This was about a year before Liza got hit by the car," I said. "My mom was a fanatic about dating pictures."

"Do you have any from when your sister was injured?" Scott asked. "Maybe something in them will trigger a memory of what's bugging you."

"Good idea," I said, flipping forward. I got to the last page of the collection but the album ended with New Year's Eve. "Let me grab the next one."

I'd pulled out five of my mom's albums. There were plenty more where these had come from. All carefully categorized.

"Here we go," I said as I turned to the center of the book and paged forward a little until I got to the summer pictures.

Bruce got up from the couch and looked over my shoulder the way Scott had.

"There I am with my chicken pox," I said, pulling the photo out and glancing at the date on the back. I passed it up to Bruce.

He took it without comment then handed it to Scott, who said, "Pictures are great for dredging up forgotten memories."

Bruce started to take a seat. "Hang on," he said. "Anyone want a little wine?"

I smiled up at him. "That sounds delightful."

The three of us repositioned ourselves, sitting cross-legged on the floor in front of the quiet fireplace. Bruce had opened up a smooth rioja that eased down my throat like warm silk. Even though my roommates couldn't possibly help me in my quest to snag that elusive memory, they each took an album and perused pages slowly—commenting often—as they turned.

"Who is this?" Scott asked, tilting the book at me. "She's beautiful."

"That's Aunt Belinda, believe it or not," I said. "Oh wait, you haven't ever met her, have you? She was gorgeous."

Scott studied the photo then checked the dates. "These are from before you were born," he said.

"I didn't mean to grab one from that early," I said. "But now the picture makes sense. From what I understand, Aunt Belinda lived near us until she got married and moved to Florida. After that we hardly saw her." I wrinkled my nose and thought about that, too. "Except once, I think. She came to stay with us for a little while. To help my mom take care of me when Liza was born."

"How old were you then?" Scott asked.

"Almost three."

"How can you not remember these?" he said, then pointed at another picture of my aunt from before I was born. "Check out those plaid hip huggers."

Bruce leaned over to look. "She sure rocked them, though."

I turned the next page of the album on my lap to see the WELCOME HOME sign my parents had made for Liza when she got out of the hospital. I'd still been contagious at that point, so I had to wait to return home to see my sister.

"Finding anything?" Bruce asked.

"Nothing that triggers any important memory," I said. "Liza spent most of the next few days on the couch, as I recall. When I finally was able to return home, most of the living room was covered in toys." I laughed. "My mom didn't even complain about the mess. That was a first."

"How long did Liza recuperate?"

"I don't remember," I said. "At that point, I was only eight. I do remember that the doctors said she was still too weak to do the stairs so my dad had to carry her up to bed every night." I had a quick mental image of my dad lifting Liza up. How the belt of her bathrobe trailed down between his arms. How Mom hurried over to tuck it up so that he wouldn't trip. "She'd lost so much blood. They said that it could take some time before she felt strong again."

"That had to be one heck of a trauma," Bruce said. "Blood transfusions are a very big deal."

"They are," I agreed absentmindedly. I placed both hands facedown on the open album in front of me. "That's what I forgot," I said. "That's what the problem was."

"What?" they asked in unison.

"My parents wanted to do a directed-donor option because they didn't trust the blood supply," I said. "This was shortly after that young boy in Indiana was banned from his school. He'd developed AIDS from a transfusion he needed because of his hemophilia."

"I remember that," Bruce said. "Even though I was just a kid, too."

"I'm glad we've come such a long way to understand the disease and how to prevent it," I said.

"Though we still have a long way to go," Scott added.

"True enough," I said. "The thing is, because everyone was terrified about contracting AIDS, my parents thought that they'd donate blood for Liza directly so that it would be safe."

"Two pints probably wasn't enough," Bruce said.

"That wasn't the problem," I said. "They weren't the same blood type as Liza."

"What blood type is she?" Scott asked.

"I don't remember," I said. "But I know my parents were both B-positive because that's what I am."

"How can Liza be different if your parents are both the same?" Bruce asked.

I thought about my discussion with Joe where he'd started to explain how Virginia's daughter could have a different blood type than her mother. "I'll have to ask my favorite doctor," I said. "That'll give me an excuse to call him."

At that moment, my phone rang. I glanced at the display and smiled as I held it up for the boys to see. "Speak of the devil."

"I hope I'm not calling too late," Joe said when I answered.

I clambered to my feet and arched an eyebrow at my roommates signaling that I'd take this call upstairs. Bruce made a kissy face and Scott shooed me out.

"Not at all," I said. "In fact, you saved me the trouble. I have a question for you."

"What can I help you with?"

"You first," I said. "You made the call."

He made a noise that sounded like hesitation to me. "No, go ahead. What's your question?"

I decided not to argue the point. "Remember when we were talking about blood types and you mentioned how Virginia's blood type could be different from her daughter's?"

"Sure," he said. "A child's blood type comes from a combination of both parents."

"What if both parents have the same blood type?" I asked. "Shouldn't their children have all the same blood type, too?"

"Not necessarily. Why? Do you know Virginia's husband's blood type?"

I chuckled, embarrassed. "I'm asking for myself this time. My blood type is the same as my parents' but my sister's is different."

"That's not impossible," he said. "If both parents are A or both parents are B, they can have a child with type O. That's not unusual."

"Hmph."

"You sound disappointed."

"No, just curious." I gave a sad laugh. "Let's move to better subjects," I said, shaking off my melancholy. "Like the reason for your call."

He coughed. "About that."

A stab of awareness pinched me in the gut. *Uh-oh*.

"Let me guess," I said slowly, "this is not a happy subject."

He cleared his throat again. "I really like you, Grace."

Here it comes. The let's-just-be-friends conversation.

Disappointment twisted deep. I liked Joe a lot more than I'd allowed myself to admit. And until this minute I hadn't been honest with myself enough to realize just how much I wanted to pursue a relationship with him.

I swallowed. "I'm glad," I said, keeping it light. I waited a beat, but when he hesitated again, I said, "Go ahead."

"What do you mean?"

"You said, 'I really like you, Grace.' There's a silent 'but' hanging between us right now. I'd like you to feel free to share what's on your mind." I forced a smile into my voice. "Go ahead. I'm a big girl. I can handle it."

To my surprise, he chuckled softly. "That's exactly the sort of thing I'd expect you to say," he said, "but I'm mucking it all up. You have the talent of being direct without being unkind. You're strong, compassionate, and honest. I can't help thinking that anyone you choose to share your life with is a very lucky person indeed."

I tried to ignore the bittersweet sting of his words. Although he couldn't break up with me—not technically, at least—because we'd never been a couple, he sure delivered a very touching, sincere-sounding "It's not me, it's you" speech.

Better now than later, when it would hurt even more. "But that person isn't you," I said. I blew out a breath. "No worries. I understand."

"Jeez," he said. "No. You don't. I told you I was mucking this up." He made a noise that sounded like "Aaah," then gave a frustrated growl. "I really like you, Grace. Period. You're fun, fascinating, and I enjoy being with you. I want that to continue."

I didn't know what to say. There was still that nagging "but." I kept silent.

"I would love to give us a chance, to see where this relationship goes," he said. "If you're willing, that is. But there's a lot I haven't told you about myself."

"The story that you don't want to dump on me all at once," I prompted.

"Exactly," he said. "But I realize I need to trust that you'll understand."

Even though he couldn't see me, I leaned forward, intrigued. "Go ahead," I said again.

"Not now." Another soft chuckle. "I don't mean to be mysterious but this is a tale I need to tell in person. My goal tonight was to commit to you to doing so. And to make a date."

"Okay." I was both disappointed and vaguely relieved. "Whenever you're ready."

"Tomorrow?" he asked.

"Tomorrow sounds perfect," I said.

When we hung up, I meandered back downstairs wondering what it was that Joe intended to tell me.

"Well?" Bruce asked.

I reclaimed my seat on the floor. "Dinner tomorrow night at Hugo's." When my two roommates gave a whoop of glee, I raised both hands. "Not so fast. It seems that the handsome doctor intends to use our date to share all."

Bruce and Scott exchanged a glance. "That's pretty brave of him," Scott said.

"You don't know what he plans to tell me."

"True, but the fact that he's being straight up about it and not playing games—well, that's unusual," he said.

Bruce nodded. "Admirable."

Leaning sideways to sort through the photo albums, I said, "Let's see how we feel about him after he spills his story." But I couldn't imagine anything bad enough to make me change my mind about the man. "Back to the project at hand."

It took a minute to find the album I was seeking and hoist it onto my lap. Liza's baby book.

"What are you looking for now?" Scott asked.

I shot him a sheepish grin. "I can't help thinking that I've missed something but—I know it sounds weird—I have an idea about what it is."

"What is it?" Bruce asked.

"Hang on," I said.

A few minutes of paging brought me to the section I was looking for. I placed the open book back onto the floor and pulled up another album—my baby book. "Here," I said, pointing. "Look at all the photos of my mom when she was pregnant with me."

Bruce and Scott peered over my shoulder. My dad had taken pictures of my mother throughout her pregnancy, and as I paged through them, we watched her progress from barely showing, to glowingly ready to give birth, to smiling as she held me at the hospital.

"Pretty normal," Scott said.

"Right." I reached to lift up the album I'd set aside. "But look at these. This book starts with Liza already born." The photo I indicated showed my mom holding her new infant daughter, while I sat on my dad's lap and smiled for the camera.

"No pregnancy pictures, you mean?" Bruce asked.

"Exactly. Why not?"

Scott made a thoughtful noise. "That's not unusual with second or third kids. At least from what I've been told. Parents are so busy herding their little ones, they don't have a chance to pick up the camera."

"I guess," I said as I continued to page forward. "Except my mom was crazy about her photos. And she managed to get lots of shots of us after Liza arrived. From the looks of it, she took at least one of us every week to chart our progress."

"What are you saying?" Bruce asked. "That you think your sister was adopted?"

"Outrageous, I know. But we don't look alike. We don't act alike. We're more different than we are similar."

The boys were skeptical. "Your dad had dark hair like Liza's."

"That's true. Probably just wishful thinking on my part."

Chapter 22

I KNEW BENNETT'S BLOOD TYPE AND I KNEW mine. What I didn't know was Liza's. But I was determined to find out.

The next morning before heading into the office, I stopped at the Marshfield Inn. When my sister didn't respond to my knock, I tried Aunt Belinda's room. No answer there, either. Drawing on my deductive skills, I made a beeline for the dining room, where I found them enjoying the hotel's lavish breakfast buffet.

Liza speared a ripe strawberry with her fork. Aunt Belinda lifted a delicate china cup to her lips.

I blew out a breath. I could do this.

I stepped up to their table and placed my hands on the back of one of the empty chairs. They both froze, mid-motion, wearing twin looks of horrified surprise.

"Good morning," I said. "I'm glad I found you here. Big meeting this afternoon, right?" When neither of them spoke, I pulled out the chair and sat down. "The two of you, plus your attorney, plus Bennett, plus our attorney," I reminded them. "And me, of course."

Aunt Belinda returned her cup to its saucer with a gentle clink. "I'm looking forward to meeting the illustrious Bennett Marshfield," she said with a tight frown. "Liza tells me he can be quite charming." She shot a knowing look at my sister before returning her gaze to me. "When he manages to break free from your clutches, that is."

I raised up my hands and wiggled my fingers. "These clutches?" I asked, immediately sorry to have so easily snapped up my aunt's bait. I forced a light laugh and shook my head. Time to marshal restraint. "Bennett is his own man, I assure you," I said. "But you'll find that out for yourself later. I'm not here to argue with either of you." I raised my hands again, this time in supplication. "I just wanted to catch up with both of you before the big meeting this afternoon."

Liza tossed her head, the speared strawberry on her plate long forgotten. "Right," she said. "All of a sudden you want to play nice because you know I have the same claim to Bennett's fortune that you do."

I wrinkled my nose. "Let's not get into that, shall we? Let's leave our differences to the attorneys." I worked to keep my expression neutral. "We left things on a bad note last time we talked and I wanted to smooth things over."

"Smooth things over?" Liza repeated. "Exactly how do think you can do that?"

"Fair enough," I said. "I was thinking about what you said about that time you were in the hospital and I couldn't come up because I had chicken pox."

Liza rolled her eyes. I ignored that.

"Mom and Dad were especially worried for you because of something to do with your blood. You needed a transfusion. Do you remember that?"

"Not really."

Aunt Belinda leaned forward. "What does this have to do with smoothing things over?"

I shrugged. "My parents were worried about HIV," I said. "That was back when we knew very little about the virus and before the blood supply went through as rigorous testing as it does now. They didn't tell you any of this?" I asked.

"I can't recall." Aunt Belinda shook her head. "That was a long time ago."

Liza pushed her plate forward and folded her arms on the table. "Where is this going?" she asked.

"Mom and Dad wanted to donate blood to you directly," I said. "I wanted to, too, but I was too young."

Liza lifted her hands as though to say, "So what?"

"Family is often asked to donate blood when a loved one is in the hospital," Aunt Belinda said. "That's nothing new."

At that moment a waitress stopped by the table and touched the edge of Liza's plate. "Are you finished here?" she asked.

"Yes," Liza said with emphasis. "I've lost my appetite."

As soon as the waitress was gone, I continued. "But Mom and Dad couldn't direct their donation because you have a different blood type than they do."

"Wait, I remember now," Aunt Belinda said. "Your mother called me. You're right, she was very worried. But it wasn't anything about blood. It was about something else. I think maybe an infection."

"I'm pretty sure it had to do with Liza's blood type being different," I said as I turned to my sister. "Out of curiosity, what is your blood type?"

"How should I know?" she asked.

"I thought everyone knew their blood type," I said. "We had to test it in high school biology."

Liza barked a laugh. "Of course you remember back to high school biology, Little Miss A-plus. I don't."

"Well," I said, "I suppose it doesn't matter. I was just curious. And you'll find out your blood type soon enough."

"I will? How?"

"If you're going to try to lay claim to Bennett's estate, you're going to have to prove you're related, just the way I did."

Aunt Belinda waved a finger. "She shouldn't have to do that. She's your sister. Everybody knows that."

I shrugged. "The lawyers insist on it." I'd made that part up on the spot. I had no idea what the lawyers might require, but it sounded reasonable enough.

"No big deal," Liza said. "I've given blood before. Plasma, too. Sometimes it was the only way to raise cash."

Aunt Belinda looked stricken. "You see what your poor sister has had to deal with? What a tough life she's endured? While you're living in the lap of luxury? How can you be so cruel to her?"

Time for me to leave before this escalated again. "I'll talk with you both later."

I left the hotel's restaurant and said hello to a few employees as I made my way across the lobby. I was nearly out the hotel's front door when I heard Aunt Belinda call my name.

I turned. She hurried across the marble expanse, her arms pumping like kinked pendulums providing momentum. By the time she reached me, nearly breathless, her face was red. She grabbed my arm, but I didn't know if it was for emphasis or her own stability. "Don't do this."

"Do what?" I asked.

"Make her take a blood test."

"Why? What don't I know? Why aren't there any photos

of my mother when she was pregnant with her? Was Liza adopted?"

"Don't push this, Grace. Leave well enough alone."

Sharp curiosity kept me frozen to the spot.

Aunt Belinda glanced back the way she'd come. "I told your sister I had to use the bathroom so I'll make this quick. Your mother . . ." Her voice cracked. She took a quick breath and started again. "Your mother, well, I don't know how to break this to you . . ."

I waited.

"Your mother, she . . ."

"You're not saying anything," I said. "Tell me."

"Have it your way." Aunt Belinda straightened. Her mouth twisted ever so slightly before she said, "Your mother had an affair. That's why you and your sister look so different."

The lobby walls pulsated around me. Shock pounded my head. "I don't believe you."

"Just like our mother with old man Marshfield, your mother had a child with a man who wasn't her husband."

Although the pieces fit, this felt wrong. "No. My parents had an amazing marriage. Neither of them would ever have cheated on the other."

"Yes, well. Your father forgave her."

"No," I said again. "That doesn't explain why there aren't any pregnant photos in Liza's baby book. There were plenty when she was expecting me."

She winced, then glanced back toward the dining room again before answering me. "Your father didn't want any pictures to remind him of your mother's infidelity."

I was reeling from the impact of this revelation, but unwilling to give up. She was not describing the parents I knew. "You're telling me that he refused to allow photos, but he accepted a child—a living, breathing reminder of infidelity—to raise as his own? That doesn't make any sense."

"Stranger things have happened, young lady. It's about time you realized that."

I rubbed my forehead, trying to sort out all the questions in my mind. "Who is Liza's father?"

A sad look washed over Aunt Belinda's face. "My husband."

I couldn't help myself. I gasped.

"You thought your mother was a saint, didn't you? All this time." With a burst of anger she added, "It doesn't matter anymore. He's dead." She gave another terrified glance back. "I've been away from the table too long. She's going to suspect something. You can't let Liza know that she wasn't your father's child. It'll break her heart."

Chapter 23

I MADE IT TO THE OFFICE, REELING FROM AUNT Belinda's disclosure. Could it be true?

"You're running late today," Frances said as I strode past her.

"Yes." I wasn't in the mood for conversation.

I sat at my desk for several minutes, weighing options and staring across the room seeing nothing at all.

The moment I picked up the phone to call Bennett, Frances poked her head in. "What happened?"

I ignored her. When Bennett answered, I got right to the point. "I'm going to reschedule our appointment with Liza's attorney," I said.

"The meeting this afternoon?" he asked.

"Yes."

He waited a few beats, no doubt expecting me to provide a reason for the sudden change in plans. When I didn't, he said, "If you think that's best, Gracie, I trust your judgment."

"Thank you," I said. "I'll explain later."

"I know you will."

By the time I hung up, Frances had crossed the office. She sat across from me. "You want me to call their lawyer to cancel?" she asked.

"If you don't mind." I frowned out the window. "See if we can push it off for a week or so." I needed to regroup.

"Won't your sister have moved into the new apartment by then?"

"She's made it clear that she had no intention of moving into such lowly accommodations."

"What's wrong with that girl? It's a perfectly fine place." I appreciated Frances's outrage on my behalf.

"Tell her that." I drew in a breath and faced my assistant again. "Tell the lawyer to let Liza and my aunt know that today's plan has changed. When I saw them this morning, I hadn't yet made up my mind."

"This morning, you say?" Pressing her hands to her knees, she got to her feet. "That explains your sour mood."

"Just when I think things are going well, they swing a bat into my face."

She flinched but didn't ask what I meant by that. "I hope you know what you're doing."

"I don't, but this gives me time to figure it out." I grabbed my purse. "Speaking of which, I'm going home."

BRUCE'S CAR WAS IN THE DRIVEWAY WHEN I got there. He wasn't on the main level, but the basement door was ajar and the light was on so I poked my head in and shouted that I was home. He called back a muffled reply.

After changing clothes, I dug out two more giant boxes of albums and brought them into the parlor, where I set them out according to year. I then poured myself a cup of coffee and sat on the floor ready to dig in again. "I need more clues, Mom," I whispered into the empty room. "There's a story here you never told us, isn't there?"

A few minutes later, Bruce bounded up the steps and trotted into the parlor, Bootsie in his wake.

"What are you doing home?" we said in unison.

"The termite control company was able to fit us into their schedule sooner than expected. That's good because we were afraid we'd have to wait a month. The problem is that when they're fumigating a location, no one can be on the premises. So anything we hoped to get done today over there is a no-go."

"How soon before you can get back in?"

He shrugged. "Tomorrow, thank goodness. Scott should be home soon. He's visiting Oscar in the hospital. I hope to get there later myself. Oh, wait." Bruce blinked as though he'd just remembered something. "We're interviewing another contractor today, but because of the fumigation, we invited him here. If that's inconvenient for you, we can meet somewhere else." He gave the mess on the floor a pointed look.

"Feel free to hold the meeting here," I said. "This house is as much yours as it is mine. And I'm playing hooky. There's no way you could have expected that. As long as you don't mind me hanging around."

"Not at all," he said. "Why are you home?"

I feared that speaking Aunt Belinda's allegation aloud would make it worse—make it seem more real—but being able to share my anger and distress was the relief I needed. Bruce listened carefully as I recounted the conversation.

"I don't buy it," he said. "I realize I only knew your mother for a short time but such a thing seems completely out of character for her."

"I agree."

"Another thing that seems odd," he said. "Why is your aunt so concerned about Liza's reaction?"

"I don't know." Recollecting a conversation I'd had with my sister shortly before she'd been arrested, I mused, "Liza suggested the very same thing when she was here last."

"That she was the result of an affair?"

I nodded.

"What did you tell her?"

"Of course, I thought the idea was preposterous. But because she believed that was the reason our mom was so tied to this house, I let it slide. At the time, I was so relieved that she hadn't heard about our relationship to Bennett that I didn't argue the point."

"But now she knows the truth—that Bennett's father was your grandfather."

"Which doesn't mean that my Aunt Belinda is wrong. I suppose it is possible that my mother had an affair. But it doesn't feel right." I pressed a hand to my middle. "Gut-level wrongness. I know better. But how to prove it?"

"What about your DNA test with Bennett?"

"Our DNA traveled through our mom, who is Bennett's relative. It wouldn't preclude an affair."

"Then what is your aunt afraid of? Why doesn't she want Liza tested?"

I wrinkled my nose. "Good question. She says that she doesn't want to break Liza's heart."

"Don't tell me you're buying that. Your sister is as hard as they come."

"I know. But there's a piece missing. I can't let it go. Not until I understand what's really going on."

"So you're searching through your mom's things again?"

I shrugged. "I've told myself a hundred times that I

needed to dig through all this stuff, but never actually got around to it. Considering the bombshell I discovered in my mom's things the first time, I should have made this a priority."

"You've had a lot on your plate since then."

"True, and I was focused on my mom's history, not my sister's. I don't even know what I'm hoping to find, but I believe I'll know it when I see it."

"With any luck, you'll find out you're not sisters after all."

"Fat chance of that. I've got thirty years of memories that say otherwise."

"Half sisters, then."

I shook my head. "I'd rather be able to prove that Aunt Belinda is wrong and that my mother didn't have an affair. Even if that means Liza remains a thorn in my side for the rest of my life."

"Well, if anyone was aware of the affair, it was probably your aunt, right?" he asked as he headed toward the door. "Were your mom and aunt close? Before this alleged affair, that is?"

After he left, I thought about that. My mom and Aunt Belinda weren't particularly close. My mom had claimed to dislike her sister's husband and Aunt Belinda didn't even come to see my mom when she was dying. Didn't come in for her funeral. Both husbands had been long dead by then. Why didn't Aunt Belinda come?

Could they have been close thirty years ago? If my mother had had an affair with my uncle—which I still couldn't reconcile with the childhood I knew—why would she have done such a despicable thing to her own sister?

It sure would explain a lot about their fractured relationship and my aunt's obsession with my sister, however. She and my uncle had never had kids of their own. Maybe Liza was as close as she would get.

But no. I couldn't believe it. I refused to believe it.

I sat back against the sofa, trying to remember the sisters' relationship back when I was a kid. All I remember was that our parents took care of us. Other adults sliding in and out of our lives were of middling interest. I could remember my mother's best friend, Arlene, being a much bigger part of our lives than my aunt. It seemed as though Aunt Belinda was always unable to come see us. Always making a phone call and an excuse for not visiting, whether it be for holidays, my parents' anniversaries, or a family friend's death. If what Aunt Belinda had said was true, though, her absence in our lives made sense.

I sat up. I exchanged Christmas cards with Arlene. And as far as I knew, she was happy and healthy and still living out in Seattle, where they'd moved when I was in college. Would Arlene know if my mother had had an affair with my uncle? More important: If she did, would she tell me?

I dug out her number and picked up the phone.

Arlene didn't answer so I left a message. "Hello, this is Grace Wheaton. How are you? Hope everything is great. If you have a minute, could you give me a call? I have a question I'd like to ask you about my mom." I left both my home and cell numbers.

Cryptic? Possibly. But if Arlene knew the truth, she'd probably suspect why I was calling. If there was a secret, would she share it with me because I asked, or would she keep it hidden away out of solidarity with my mother?

I willed the phone to ring.

In the meantime, I returned to my digging. I had some time before Bruce and Scott's potential contractor would arrive. Plus, I had dinner with Joe tonight. My stomach did a somersault thinking about what the evening might hold.

MY MOTHER KEPT SHOEBOXES OF LETTERS. A half-dozen dusty shoeboxes of letters. As well as folders full of files. I had no way of knowing if she'd kept every single bit of correspondence she'd ever received, but it certainly seemed as though she had. Hours later, I'd gotten through about half of the boxes, skimming most of them, fully reading some, but not one of them provided any insight into Aunt Belinda's allegation of an affair.

Bruce had taken off to meet Scott and run a few errands before their meeting, so Bootsie was the only one keeping me company in the big house this afternoon.

I stopped to grab a quick ham and pickle sandwich then washed it down with lemonade before returning to my dusty task. Bootsie folded herself into a cat-loaf atop one of the photo albums I'd been poring over the other day—Liza's baby book. When I resumed my seat on the floor, Bootsie gave a wide-mouthed cry, then stood up and rubbed against my forearm.

"Oh, all right," I said to my little tuxedo cat. "I'll take another look."

I dragged the album onto my lap, leaned back to bolster myself against the front of the wing chair, and began paging through once again. I took it slowly, examining the backgrounds of each candid, looking for clues.

Of what? My mother's infidelity? How could a photo prove or disprove Aunt Belinda's accusation?

Whatever "it" was, I told myself again that I'd know it when I saw it.

I'd gotten through about half of Liza's baby book realizing that although my mom's photos in this album under-standingly focused on my little sister's progress from birth to age one, I appeared in plenty of the shots. It made sense. While there were pictures of Liza alone taking her first steps, there were many with us together, such as infant Liza and three-year-old me posing with our dad and a Halloween pumpkin. The two of us on Santa's lap—Liza howling, her little round face red and sweaty. They'd taken pictures of us together wearing silly hats on New Year's Eve. Normal sibling shots. Nothing unusual.

Bootsie nuzzled my arm again.

"What are you trying to tell me, sweetie?" I asked.

I turned back to page one. Our first family photo with Liza. My mother didn't look particularly tired. Not like she had in her hospital pictures immediately after I'd been born. But then again, second births were rumored to be easier.

And then it hit me.

I'd been focusing on Liza's pictures. Maybe I should be focusing on mine.

"Good idea, Bootsie girl," I said, even though she hadn't made a noise.

I stood, tiptoeing around the piles of albums, shoeboxes, and files that I'd strewn all over our parlor floor. Ignoring my baby book this time, I sorted through until I came up with one of our family albums.

My mom had kept first-year books for the two of us, but after that, she'd maintained family albums. I paged quickly through one, then another.

"Here we go," I said when I opened the one that started in the summer before I turned three. I knew what I wanted to see, or rather, what I didn't want to see, so I took my time.

As always, my mother had dated each and every photo. I pulled out one—dated mid-June—of me at a leafy green resort where we'd vacationed that year. They'd put me in a bright red swing and my dad had posed behind me, smiling. No photos of my mother, though.

Anxious now, I gave up the idea of taking in the photos slowly and zipped through them, looking for any shots of my mom. Nothing. Nothing. Nothing.

Until.

My third birthday party.

There she was, standing by with a knife and serving spatula, waiting for me to blow out the candles on my birthday cake, out on our backyard patio.

My mother was wearing a summer dress. But the frock wasn't form-fitting enough to define her shape.

I counted on my fingers. Liza would be born in twelve weeks.

My mom would have had to be six months pregnant in this shot.

Maybe my birthday had been celebrated earlier that year?

I peeled out the photo and checked the back for the date.

My birthday. Exactly.

I squinted at the puffed-out cheeks of little-me trying to blow the candles out. I hadn't ever been around children enough to easily determine their ages. Could this be my second birthday and not my third? Could my mother have dated the photo incorrectly?

That's when I noticed the number three candle in the center of the cake.

The only other option was that my mom had hosted this party a few weeks earlier that year and simply recorded my actual birth date on the back.

I squinted at the photo. I'd heard the myriad stories of women who didn't gain much weight, who had no outward signs, who never knew they were pregnant until the day they gave birth. Could that be what had happened here?

The room spun and my head hurt. I leaned back against the chair and stared at the ceiling. "What does all this mean?"

Chapter 24

WITH PAINSTAKING CARE I WENT OVER THE albums of my life leading up to, and including, Liza's birth, jotting notes and dates and including commentary about my mother's figure. There was not one picture in any of those my mother had kept where I could say with certainty that she'd appeared pregnant.

Aunt Belinda's voice nagged in the back of my brain reminding me that, in order to appease my father, my mother would have taken great care to make sure there were no photos in any albums with her pregnant with Liza.

"Grace?"

Startled out of my reverie, I raised my voice to answer Scott. "In here," I called.

He and Bruce came in from the kitchen. "How's it going?" Bruce asked.

"Wait until you see what I found," I said as I got to my feet and brushed dust off my jeans. I bent to reach for the family album with photos from my third birthday.

At that moment, the alarm on my cell phone rang.

"I didn't realize the time," I said as I silenced it. "I'm meeting Joe in an hour. And look at me."

"What did you find?" Bruce asked.

"It'll have to wait," I said as I tried to rearrange the albums, boxes, and notes into some semblance of order. "What time is your contractor supposed to be here?"

"Any minute now," Scott said.

As if on cue, the doorbell rang.

I pointed. "Good luck. I'm running upstairs to change and then I'm heading out."

As I got dressed, my cell phone rang. Thinking it was Joe, I snatched it up, only to be disappointed to see a Marshfield Inn number on my device's display. The chances of this being Aunt Belinda or Liza calling to complain that I'd canceled today's appointment were sky-high. I declined the call. A few moments later came the signal indicating a voicemail.

I listened to the first few seconds of Aunt Belinda berating me for my inconsiderate behavior. Apparently their attorney had waited until just now to deliver the news that our negotiation meeting had been rescheduled.

"You're welcome," I said as I clicked out of her angry diatribe and tossed the phone onto the bed.

Thirty minutes later, I took the stairs down to the main level at a more leisurely pace than I'd hurtled them going up. With the weather changing for the better every day, I'd changed into a summery cotton dress, silver flats, and sweater for when the night turned cool.

My roommates and their contractor were discussing plans in our dining room, which, unfortunately, provided a wide-open view of our cluttered parlor.

I could have easily slipped out without interrupting. But

I had plenty of time to walk to Hugo's and still be early. I didn't want the boys to think I wasn't interested in the preparations and plans for the reimagined Amethyst Cellars. While I may be their silent partner, I didn't have to remain invisible.

"Hi," I said as I stepped into the room. "I hope I'm not interrupting."

Bruce and Scott sat on one side of the table with their backs to me. The man opposite them leapt to his feet the moment I walked in.

"Not at all," Bruce said. "Grace, let me introduce Jeremy King of JK Contractors. Jeremy, this is Grace."

He came around the table to shake my hand as Bruce made introductions. "Very pleased to meet you," he said.

About the same height and build as my roommates, Jeremy had bright, dark eyes and an engaging smile. Frances wouldn't put him in the same category as dreamboat Neal Davenport, but he was an attractive man.

"Nice to meet you, too," I said. Because it seemed polite to continue the conversation slightly before taking off, I asked, "I can't say that your company name is familiar. Is your firm local?"

"Almost local," he said with a smile. "We're located just outside of Piedmont Springs."

I knew where that was. "This isn't too far for you?"

He shook his head and smiled again. "For a job this size, not at all. This is a fabulous opportunity to partner on a stellar project, and I'm lucky we connected." He gestured toward Bruce and Scott. "I was just telling them that I could see this one winning awards. I will always make time for a chance like this."

"That sounds great."

"But I don't want to get ahead of myself," he said. "The

guys have a big decision on their hands and it may make more sense to use someone closer. For cost containment. Totally understandable."

"I agree," Bruce said. "As much as we want to make the new Amethyst Cellars a showplace, we will want to keep our out-of-pocket expenses reasonable." From behind Jeremy, he winked at me. Apparently they hadn't told him of our financial arrangement.

"And," Scott said, "Jeremy hasn't had a chance to actually tour the space yet. Until he gets a look at the bones of the location, we can't make any real projections. Those fumigators." He waved a hand in front of his face. "At least we can get back in there tomorrow."

"Unfortunately, I have a commitment tomorrow." Jeremy nodded thoughtfully. "I'm looking forward to seeing the building, though. From the few pictures you've shown me, it looks perfect for your purposes."

"Speaking of pictures," I said to my roommates. "Do not let me forget to show you what I found this afternoon. But for right now, I need to run. I don't want to be late."

Jeremy reached into his pocket and drew out a business card. "Here." He handed it to me. "In case you have any questions. Or anything."

I MADE IT TO HUGO'S ABOUT TEN MINUTES early and Joe hadn't arrived yet, so I put my name in for a table. I debated waiting outside, but the air had begun to turn cool. I decided to sit at the bar to wait for him instead.

What with all the digging I'd been doing into Liza's life, sorting through letters and photos and such, I hadn't had much time to think about what Joe had promised to divulge tonight. Whatever it was, it was related to the car accident

that had necessitated his using a cane and it made him uncomfortable to talk about. I was convinced that someone
had died. Based on his ring finger tan line, it was probably
his wife.

I imagined that he still carried guilt for her death and
that he'd relocated to Emberstowne after the tragedy in order to make a fresh start.

"What can I get you?" the bartender asked.

I ordered a glass of Amethyst Cellars's cabernet even
though there were cases of that exact wine sitting in our
basement this minute. The more orders Hugo's took for my
roommates' wares, the better for future business.

My wine appeared a short while later. "Thank you," I
said. "I'll close out now, though, rather than run a tab."

The bartender tilted his head to the far end of the bar.
"Compliments of the lady down there," he said.

Surprised, I turned to look where he indicated. A woman,
several years older than me, lifted a beer bottle in greeting.

"I don't understand," I said to the bartender, but he'd
already moved on to take care of someone else.

By the time I turned back to the woman, she'd vacated
her chair and was making her way over. She was shorter
than I was, maybe five foot three, with freckled olive skin,
short blond hair, and a hard body. Black jeans and a matching turtleneck snugged slim curves. She didn't smile.

"Don't worry," she said as she slid into the empty seat to
my left, "I'm not trying to pick you up. I like guys."

"I wasn't worried," I said.

"Tell your face that." She took a swig from her beer bottle. "Meeting your doctor boyfriend here tonight, are you?"

My stomach made a fist. "He's not my boyfriend."

"Oh no?" Her mouth turned up at one corner and she

gave me a sideways stare. "That's not the way it looks from where I sit."

"Who are you?"

"My name is Yolanda," she said. "I'm a private investigator. We've been shadowing the good doctor these past few weeks. Gotta say, we find his activity—particularly as it relates to you—very interesting."

"What are you investigating, may I ask?" I'd had enough experience with imposters in the past that I wasn't about to swallow her line without substantiation. "Has he done something wrong?"

"You tell me," she said easily. "Exactly how close are the two of you?"

I pushed my wine away. "This conversation is over," I said as I gathered my purse.

"Not so fast." She gripped my forearm. When I glared, she loosened her hold but didn't let go. She brought her face close to my ear. "He's got a wife. Did you know that?"

Startled, I jerked away.

"No, I guess you didn't," she said. "Because of him, she's unable to walk, can't do anything for herself. And what does he do? As soon as she could no longer take care of him the way she used to, he up and left."

The car accident. I'd asked him if anyone else had been injured. That was the moment he'd gone silent.

The woman continued, "She's heartbroken. She's been begging him to come back. But he's a cruel man, your doctor. Left her with nothing. The only hope she has now is to catch him trying to worm his way into some other unsuspecting woman's heart." Yolanda shrugged. "Maybe it gives her grounds for a settlement in their divorce. Something that allows her to pay her food and hospital bills. Maybe it just makes her feel good to save someone else from getting her heart broken."

"I don't believe it," I said. True, I didn't know Joe well, but this description didn't jibe with what I knew of the man.

Yolanda was ready for me. She whipped out a photo, placed it on the bar top, and pushed it toward me. Joe was utterly recognizable in his wedding picture—with a radiant wife. She wore vivid pink lipstick, a perfect complement to her pale hair and porcelain skin. Her wild, ecstatic expression seemed to shout, "We just got married!" The two of them seemed so young, so happy. My inexpert guess dated the photo from about five years ago.

"Now this one." She offered another picture, this one of Joe's wife in a hospital bed, hooked up to a myriad of machinery. She was unconscious.

"That was taken shortly after the accident for insurance purposes," she said.

I didn't touch the photo but I couldn't look away.

"This one was taken last week."

The final shot was again of Joe's wife. This time she was seated in a wheelchair in what looked like a home's living room. Her once beautiful face had grown gaunt, her hair stringy. With an afghan draped over her legs, she stared into the camera from sad, troubled eyes.

Yolanda collected her pictures and slid off her chair. "I'll leave you to your date now," she said. "Have fun."

For a long few minutes I stared at my wine debating my next move. Part of me wanted to get up and leave before Joe got here, but that was a coward's way out. I reminded myself that every story has two sides, but images of those photos swarmed, clouding my brain. Did I really have such bad luck with men? Was this always to be my lot in life?

Again, the urge to leave overwhelmed me. But—I'd learned—the easy choice was rarely the right one.

My cell phone rang. Aunt Belinda again.

I silenced the device, pulled my wine closer, and waited for Joe to show up.

Chapter 25

JOE'S FIRST WORDS TO ME WERE, "SORRY I'M late. I was on the phone with a patient." His next were, "Something's wrong. What happened, Grace?"

This conversation didn't belong at Hugo's bar. I didn't want to have it at a table, either. The very idea of dinner revolted me right now.

"Can we leave?" I asked.

Momentarily perplexed, he opened his mouth as though to ask why, then changed his mind and said, "Sure, where would you like to go instead?"

"Outside." Hugo's had become suddenly claustrophobic. I needed fresh air and I needed it now. I got off my chair and headed for the door.

"Your tab?"

"Paid for," I said over my shoulder. Part of me didn't want him to follow. But I needed him to. As I passed the hostess, I thanked her for holding our table and told her she could release it.

A second later I was out in the cool spring night, facing west into the orange and purple sky. This was not how things were supposed to turn out. I started walking without a destination in mind.

"Grace," Joe called from behind me.

I stopped long enough to let him catch up.

"What's going on?" he asked.

Despite the evening's chill, there were still plenty of people out on the street. "Not here," I said. I walked to the corner and made a right down the first side street.

He fell into step next to me and I tried to ignore the worried glances he repeatedly threw my way. I waited until we'd walked a full block away from the busy area before I stopped.

When he faced me—concern and fear darkening his eyes—I faltered. How even to begin this conversation? There would be no easing into it like drifting into cool water at the beach. I had to dive straight into the deep and suffer its icy impact.

"You're married," I said.

The worry in his expression flashed instantly to shock, then sorrow, then fear. He turned his face away and covered his eyes with his hands. He pulled in a deep breath and held it before blowing it out and turning back to me.

"Are you?" I asked.

"I am," he said.

I reacted audibly. Whether I'd realized it or not, I'd been holding out hope that it wasn't true.

"I'm sorry," he said.

"You're sorry."

"This is what I wanted to talk to you about tonight." He reached his hands out as though to keep me from bolting but stopped before actually making contact. I wouldn't run;

I intended to hear him out completely. That way there could be no question later. No rationalizing—"if he'd only been allowed to explain"—when weeks from now, doubt wormed into my brain in the middle of the night.

I would force myself to listen completely. Only then would I leave. No regrets. For either of us.

"Your wife can't walk? She's paralyzed?" I asked.

"No. Not at all." He winced. "There's more to it than that."

"Oh?" I hated the accusatory lilt in my tone but couldn't stop myself from applying it. "More to it, as in you've left her high and dry without means of support and she's destitute?"

"She isn't destitute." For the first time, anger sparked in his eyes. He bit down hard on his lower lip. His hands shook. Again, he drew in a deep breath and blew it back out in a rush. "May I ask who told you all this?"

I gestured back the way we'd come. "A woman at the bar. Yolanda. She claimed to have been hired by your wife to follow you. Somehow she knew that you and I were meeting here tonight. She decided to forewarn me."

He nodded as though this answered a question that had been nagging at him. "Was she about forty years old? This high?" He held out a hand. "Blond?"

"You've met her?"

"No, but our receptionist has." He shook his head in disbelief. "While I was with a patient earlier today, this Yolanda came into the office and asked to see me. She said she didn't have time to wait right now, but told our receptionist that she was an old friend and that our families went back years together." He turned to the side again and made an incoherent, angry noise. "Of course our receptionist bought it. My wife has an arsenal of knowledge that this woman must have relied on to provide a convincing performance."

Arsenal. Interesting choice of words. I remained silent.

"The receptionist—thinking she was being helpful—mentioned my plans for tonight." He shook his head again. "She's young. It wasn't her fault. And when she realized that I had no idea who this woman was, she was apologetic. I didn't think much of the situation. Not until now. Now it makes perfect sense."

"Seems quite a lot of effort to simply ruin your evening."

He glanced at me sharply. "If you only knew," he said. A moment later, he softened. "I swear I had every intention of telling you the whole sordid story tonight. You should have heard this from me."

"You're right. But now I know," I said. "Thank you, at least, for not lying to me. Have a good night." I started toward home.

"Grace, wait." He grabbed my arm lightly.

I glared. He let go.

"Please," he said. "There's more to the story."

"Of course there is." I tempered my anger and reminded myself to hear him out.

"Can we"—he glanced at our surroundings—"go somewhere quiet to talk?"

I hesitated for the briefest second. Turning my back now would not help me decide which version of Joe was the real one—the man I'd begun to get to know or the one Yolanda had described to me tonight. Truth, I'd learned, usually fell somewhere in between. The fact that he was still married was no longer the issue. There could be no relationship between us now. There would be no equivocation on that score. What I wanted to know was why he'd made an effort to connect with me when he was not free to do so.

"This way," I said.

He didn't say a word as I led him to a children's

playground on the next block. In the dusk the bright-colored equipment formed shadowy battlements with tall, jail-like bars.

Talking quietly at the far end, in an area meant for toddlers, three teenagers sat cross-legged in the grass at the foot of a plastic slide. Otherwise the area was empty.

One of the youngsters glanced up as we arrived. He didn't seem particularly disturbed by our presence, but I decided to give them a wide berth and took a seat in one of the four vacant swings in the nearer, older kid section.

Joe took the swing next to me.

"It's quiet here," I said. "And relatively private."

"I appreciate your understanding."

"Let's not get ahead of ourselves," I said. "You're married, your wife is severely injured, and you've broken her heart by leaving her. But she isn't destitute, so that makes it all right. Have I summed it up properly?" I came across as flippant, but I couldn't let him hurt me more than he already had.

Tall river birch trees lined the perimeter of the park. As Joe stared up over the tops of them, he worked his jaw. "Nothing about this situation is all right," he said.

My swing began to sway gently. I jammed a toe into the gravelly ground to stop the movement. "I agree."

"I can't apologize enough." He rocked back in his swing, planting both feet on the ground, leaning his elbows on his knees and clasping his hands together. "Will you let me tell you everything?" he asked. "I mean, will you let me get it all out before you ask any questions? This is hard—very hard—for me to talk about."

He glanced at me sideways.

I drew a breath. What choice did I have? "Go ahead."

"Thank you." He stared down at the ground and worked his jaw again. "I've been in therapy since before the accident," he said. "And even there I find it difficult to discuss everything that happened." He shook his head and glanced toward me again.

I nodded.

"Believe me, Grace, I'm sorry." He gave a sad smile. "And I promise to tell you the absolute truth."

I swallowed and glanced over at the carefree teenagers. Two boys and a girl. I couldn't make out what they were saying but their voices rose and dropped in animated conversation, punctuated with bursts of laughter. How long had it been since I'd spent twilight sitting with good friends under a darkening sky, believing that my future was limitless? Though the world was open to me now—in a far different way than I could have ever imagined back then—I couldn't help but wonder: Would I ever be so relaxed again?

"Dorie and I were set up. A blind date," Joe said. "Her cousin was engaged to one of my best friends and they decided to bring us together. I'm not blaming either of them. They thought we would made a good couple, I guess." He frowned at some middle distance, making me wonder what he was seeing.

"Dorie was beautiful," Joe said. "And her family is well known and respected." He squinted up at the sky. "This next part is going to come across as cruel and angry. Vindictive, even." He shrugged. "And maybe it is. Maybe I am. Maybe I'm not as compassionate as I'd hoped to be at this point in my life.

"Dorie made me believe she was someone she wasn't. She turned herself into a different person. Whether she was doing it to fool me or to fool herself, I don't know." He glanced at me again as though to gauge my reaction. "It's harsh to say. But that's the truth. I saw the warning signs and dismissed them. My friend—the one who set us up— tried much later to make me see that Dorie wasn't who she pretended to be. I wouldn't listen to him."

He spoke, staring away as though seeing images play out before him.

"I'm not innocent here, I promise you," he said with another sideways glance. "There's more than enough fault to go around. I was young, and although that's no excuse, it's the truth. Dorie made me believe that the only thing she wanted in the world was to be married to me. To have our children. To grow old together in retirement. She loved the idea of my being a doctor. Her parents loved the idea, as well."

I was having a tough time not asking questions. Nothing he'd told me thus far seemed very much different from what you'd find in a B-level tear-jerker. But at the end of those sagas, the couple always reconciled and went on to live happily ever after. Once the churlish husband realized the error of his ways, of course.

"I ignored my gut," he said. "I pretended that every time she changed plans or begged out of an event at the last minute, she was being spontaneous. Or because her migraine headaches were back." He sucked in his cheeks. "She played me on that score," he said. "She must have memorized every possible migraine symptom because she convinced me. I'm a doctor." He pointed both hands to his chest. "I should have known better. I should have recognized the lies."

After a long moment, he went on, "I felt sorry for her.

That she was never feeling completely well. But when she was in a good mood"—he shook his head ruefully—"she was wonderful. Everyone's best friend. Alert, happy, confident. Too happy, as it turned out. Too confident."

I waited.

"Drugs." He turned to face me. "And not the prescription kind. The kind that can get you locked up." Staring back at the ground, he went on, "We didn't live together before we were married—her parents were dead set against that—so I missed the blatantly obvious signs. Plus, I was building my practice and not paying close enough attention. Looking back, I realize that all of her last-minute cancellations were because she was high or sick with tremors, and her parents didn't want me to find out. They thought they could get her clean. And apparently she had gone long stretches without using. That's when she spent the most time with me." He raised an eyebrow and shook his head.

I couldn't help myself. "Your friend didn't tell you about the drugs?"

"He didn't know. Dorie's cousin didn't even know. Let me rephrase that: The cousin knew Dorie had had drug problems as a teenager, but believed she'd beaten her addiction. She wanted Dorie to have a good life—one not spoiled by her past offenses—so she kept the secret from her fiancé." He gave another wry laugh. "They wound up breaking up before their wedding, believe it or not." Gazing up at the sky again, he said, "Smart man."

"I'm sorry," I said.

"That isn't all of it." He didn't seem particularly upset that I'd interrupted even though I'd promised not to. "Once we were married—once I understood the problem—I tried to get her into rehab. Of course, her parents offered whatever financial help I needed. I think they were so utterly relieved to have someone else assume responsibility for her that they would agree to do anything to support me."

A cool breeze washed over us, bringing with it the teenagers' distant laughter.

"We were married for five years," he said. "An eternity with someone as volatile as Dorie. After more attempts and failures to stop her from using than I can count, I had nothing left anymore. We signed up for counseling as a couple and as individuals." He gave another wry smile. "I went. She refused. I felt my life slipping away." He turned to me. "I watched her life slipping away. And I'm a doctor," he repeated. "I'm supposed to save people, not usher them along a path to destruction.

"My therapist encouraged me to ask for a divorce. She told me that Dorie needed tough love. Something that she'd never gotten from her parents. What I couldn't bring myself to admit to my therapist was that"—he blew out a long breath—"I couldn't give Dorie tough love because I didn't have any love to give. Whatever had lived between us was dead and had been for at least two years. The divorce, however? Yeah, I wanted that."

There was truth in his words. I could feel it.

"And then, the accident."

The crux of the story. Where he would tell me how guilty he felt for his wife's injuries. How he may no longer love her, but he couldn't, in good conscience, leave her.

"I asked for a divorce," he said. "I'd already talked with my attorney. We were ready to file. I simply felt that I owed her the decency of telling her in person before putting paperwork into place. I packed up some of my things and told her that I'd be staying at a nearby hotel until we could work out an agreement.

"She freaked out." He turned to me again, his eyes narrowed with pain. "Freaked. Out. I'm not exaggerating. She'd been drinking again—that was yet another issue—and she came at me with her fists at first, then started throwing things at me. I ran out and got into my car, hoping that she'd calm down once I left.

"I called her parents as I drove to the hotel to let them know that I was leaving their daughter. Permanently. They weren't surprised, of course. They tried to talk me back home, but I'd hit my breaking point.

"I called them from my actual cell phone while I was driving—not via a hands-free connection. That was my first mistake. My second mistake was underestimating Dorie's rage. And telling her where I planned to stay."

I realized I was holding my breath.

"When I told you I was T-boned by a drunk driver, what I didn't tell you was that the driver was my wife."

I gasped.

"I spent a week in the hospital and six months in physical therapy. Dorie walked away from the wreck. She was too drunk, or too high, or too infuriated with me to realize she'd been hurt. When the paramedics arrived, they tried to calm her down, tried to get her into the ambulance. I was barely conscious at this point, mind you, so I'm recounting what I've been told. She fought them off and started running. But she was delirious and didn't get far. She ran into oncoming traffic and got hit by a delivery truck." He frowned down at the gravel. "Thank goodness for gapers' blocks, I suppose. Speeds had dropped as drivers slowed to view our T-boned vehicles. Dorie could have been killed. Instead, she escaped with just a broken leg and minor injuries. She walks perfectly; she simply prefers to pretend otherwise when it serves her purpose."

"I'm so sorry," I said again.

He faced me directly. "What does it say about me that my own wife tried to kill me? How can I even consider trying to engage in a new relationship? What if it wasn't just the drugs that pushed her over the edge? How can I know that it wasn't me? That she wasn't trying to kill herself, too?"

I didn't know how to answer that. Didn't know if I should even try.

"I left my practice just outside Rosette and decided to start over and relocate where no one knew me. Divorce papers have been filed, but Dorie is contesting everything and her lawyer has arranged for a ridiculous amount of continuances. Dorie wants to present herself as a helpless woman who deeply loves her misguided husband and who needs him for her very survival. But the truth is she has considerable personal wealth, including a tremendous trust fund. Not to mention parents who think every problem can be solved by throwing money at it. What Dorie wants—and can no longer have—is to control me. And that infuriates her."

The teenagers were gone. I hadn't even seen them leave. We were alone in the chilly park on our uneven swings listening to the late-night chorus of bugs and birds around us.

"When I came to Emberstowne, I met so many great people. My colleagues, Rodriguez, you," he said with a sad laugh. "I could say that my faith in humanity was restored, but that's not all it was. I began to believe in myself again. I hadn't in a very long time."

This was too much to take in at once. I sat silently, aware that my swing was drifting back and forth ever so slightly. Even though it was dark, the park lights and the glow from the moon were enough to see that Joe was studying me, waiting for my reaction.

I didn't know what to say. What to do. Where I fit in all this.

"I realize you've heard two conflicting stories tonight. Dorie's version and mine," he said quietly. "And there's no way you can know which is the truth. Or if the truth lies somewhere between the two." He echoed my very thoughts from when we first sat down. "I'm not going to try to convince you to believe me. You either do or you don't. And I'm not going to pressure you to make that decision right now." He half laughed. "I'm not going to pressure you to make that decision at all. What I am going to say is that I admire you, Grace. You're kind and warm. You're genuine. You're direct. And I'd like the chance to see where this can go. All I ask is that you think about it."

That much I could agree to. I nodded.

"Are there any questions I can answer for you? Anything?"

I had a hundred questions though none I wanted to broach right now. Maybe not ever. I needed time. And I needed to think. "I'd like to go home."

He got to his feet.

I stayed where I was, wishing I could sit here and stare at the sky all night. Wishing I could be a blithe teenager again.

"I'll walk you home," he said. "It's late."

The world felt so heavy all of a sudden. "I'd rather walk myself, if you don't mind."

"But is it safe for you—"

"I'll be fine. Thanks."

He gave a quick nod. "Take care, Grace, and thank you for hearing me out."

I got to my feet. "Good night."

He tried to smile. "You know where to find me." He shoved his hands into his pockets and turned away.

I waited until his form disappeared into the night, then walked home, alone.

Chapter 26

WITH THE MORNING NEWSPAPER IN ONE hand, a mug of coffee in the other, and the sound of footfalls on the stairs, I braced myself.

"Good morning." Bruce sniffed the air as he made his way across the kitchen. "You're up early. And coffee's ready. What's the occasion?"

Scott stretched in the doorway. "We got in really late last night," he said to me. "Anton may be twice our age but he's got the gusto of a twenty-year-old." As he padded across to join Bruce at the coffee machine, he asked, "What time did you get in from your date last night? How did it go?"

Seated at the table, I had my back to them. "I've had better evenings."

Two beats of silence followed; clearly that wasn't what they'd expected to hear.

My roommates sat down to join me. They both leaned forward, concerned expressions on their faces.

"What happened?" Scott asked.

Bruce's mouth set in a grim line. "Is the baggage that bad?"

These two men were my best friends in the world. If I needed to pour my heart out to anyone, I couldn't ask for a better audience.

I placed the newspaper on the table and set my coffee mug next to it. "I got to Hugo's a little early," I said, and then told them everything.

By the time I'd finished, both men were sitting back in their seats. All our coffees had grown cold, so I got up and started a fresh pot.

"He's left it in your court, then," Scott said. "What will you do?"

I had my back to them again. I shrugged. "I don't know yet."

When I returned to my seat, Bruce tapped the table top. "You're torn because you don't know the truth."

"Exactly," I said. "On one hand, Joe is the victim. On the other, he's a soulless cad."

"Remember that one scene in *Lord of the Rings*?" Scott asked. "I think it was the second movie when they're worried about Frodo and Sam. That interchange between Aragorn and Gandalf?"

Bruce sat up straighter. "I know what scene you're talking about. But that was the third movie."

"You sure?" Scott squinted up at the ceiling, then said, "Yes, you're right. Definitely, the third movie."

We'd watched the trilogy together enough times that I knew exactly the scene they referred to.

I couldn't help but smile. "You're asking what my heart is telling me, is that it?"

They nodded.

"I believe Joe. Everything he said felt true." I blinked down at my coffee mug. "But what if it's simply because I want his version to be true?"

"You have good instincts," Bruce said.

I thought back on some of the men I'd dated in the past. "Not always."

"Maybe you need to find proof, then," Scott said.

"Where exactly?"

Neither of them had an answer to that.

The two men exchanged a look that I didn't understand. "What?" I asked.

Scott shrugged. "Believe me, we're hoping things work out with Joe and he isn't the 'soulless cad' that investigator made him out to be."

"But?"

They exchanged another glance.

"That contractor, Jeremy, who came here last night?" Bruce asked. When I nodded, he went on, "When you left, he made an offhand remark about your date being a lucky guy."

I smiled at their attempt to cheer me up. "He was being polite."

"He gave you his business card, didn't he?" Bruce asked as he got up to empty and refill our coffee mugs. "And he wanted to know if you were seeing anyone seriously."

"What did you tell him?"

"That we don't share details about our friend without her permission," Scott said.

"Thank you."

Bruce placed a steaming mug in front of me and pushed the cream container into reach. "And before you tell us that the only reason he's interested in you is because of your relationship to Bennett, I'll spare you the effort."

I poured cream in my coffee and rolled my eyes.

"He didn't even know who you were," Bruce finished as he sat down.

"How did that come up?" I asked.

"It didn't," Scott said. "Which is weird. I think it's because he's from out of the area. Every other contractor so far has managed to bring up your name in conversation even though we never share with them that you're our silent partner. I guess it's common knowledge around town."

I took a sip and savored the hot brew as it slipped down my throat. "Maybe Jeremy is more polite than most."

"Actually, he didn't know about you at all," Bruce said. "He didn't realize we had a roommate until we introduced you. I think your presence confused him."

I thought about Jeremy. He had a nice smile. But moving toward a new romantic interest without closure on this one was not the least bit appealing.

"What did you think of this guy otherwise?" I asked.

"Too early to tell," Bruce said.

Scott agreed. "I think part of our hesitation with Jeremy is that we weren't able to walk through the building with him. Until he's able to see the place for himself, he won't be able to provide the sort of creative solutions we've heard from the other contenders."

"I assume you're planning to do a walk-through with him soon?" I said.

"That's another issue," Bruce said. "Because he's headquartered so much farther away than the other firms, getting him all the way out here is a little tricky."

"He said he'll do his best to get back out here as soon as possible, though," Scott said. "I hope so. I'd like to make a decision."

"Anton said that he plans to talk to a few more people in the business. It's important that we connect with a contractor who understands our vision," Bruce said.

Scott nodded. "That will take time."

"And legwork," Bruce agreed. "We can't just hire a contractor who sounds good. We need proof that they're talented and conscientious."

"Proof," I said, recalling the remark Scott had made earlier. "That reminds me. Let me show you what I found in the photo albums."

Bruce and Scott were taken aback by the evidence I'd uncovered. But even as I pointed out my mother's slim figure in the photos leading up to the date of Liza's birth, even though I was convinced I'd uncovered something profoundly important, my thoughts strayed back to Joe.

If everything he'd told me turned out to be true, then he was being made to suffer for someone else's contemptible behavior. That made me complicit because I wasn't giving him the benefit of the doubt.

But what if he hadn't told me the whole truth?

"You okay, Grace?" Bruce asked.

Belatedly, I realized Scott had asked me a question.

"I'm sorry. My mind wandered. Yes, I plan to ask my aunt about all this. I can't imagine how she'll explain these shots," I said as I pointed. "I'm hopeful that my mom's friend Arlene returns my call first, though. It would be better for me to have the whole story before I confront Liza."

"What if Arlene doesn't call?" Scott asked. "Or won't tell you because it's some dark secret your mother made her promise never to divulge?"

"Then I'll figure it out another way," I said. "I always do."

THAT AFTERNOON, AS I WAS FINALLY PUTTING away all the albums, boxes, and files that I'd pulled out in order to investigate Aunt Belinda's allegations about my mom, the house phone rang.

I trotted into the kitchen and scanned the caller ID display.

Marshfield Inn. That meant it was either Liza or Aunt Belinda again. I ignored the call but waited for the answering machine to kick in. The moment it did, the caller hung up.

Less than thirty seconds later back in the parlor, my cell phone rang, offering the same phone number on its display.

I dropped it back onto the wing chair's seat, letting it ring until it silenced itself.

No voicemail here, either.

"Sorry to disappoint you," I said aloud, then shrugged. "No, not really."

Bootsie leaped up onto the chair and settled herself atop the quiet phone as though to protect me from my aunt's spite. I leaned down and scratched my little cat behind her ears. She purred.

"What do you think?" I asked her. "Will Arlene call? Will I ever find out the truth about Liza's father?"

When the back door banged open, Bootsie jumped over the chair's arm to greet Bruce and Scott.

"You home, Grace?" Bruce asked.

"In here," I called back.

They'd returned from their errands in a jubilant mood.

"Hey, Grace, guess what?" Bruce said as Scott followed him in. "Oscar is out of the hospital."

"That's wonderful news," I said.

"We stopped in to visit him this morning and found out that he was being released," Scott said. He glanced at his partner. "There was no way we were going to let him go back to living on the streets."

"Not after what happened to him there," Bruce added.

"Exactly," Scott continued, "so we offered him a job and a home."

Taken aback, I blinked. "At Amethyst Cellars?"

"Why not?" Bruce asked rhetorically. "There's plenty of

room. He'll be safe there and we can sure use help getting the place together."

Scott nodded. "He seemed blown away by the idea. He couldn't agree fast enough."

"I know we're making a leap of faith here," Bruce said, "but we feel strongly about giving Oscar his best shot."

"That's wonderful," I said and meant it. I, too, felt as though Oscar was a lost soul who needed a helping hand. "What will you do for accommodations, though?"

"For now, we've only set up a camp bed and brought in some supplies," Scott said, spelling out a list of items they'd picked up for him. "As we move forward with renovations, we'll look into creating a more personal space."

"We'll have to make sure we're not breaking any zoning laws or building codes before we make this permanent," Bruce said, "but I think we're okay for now."

"Has he been able to provide the police with a better description of his assailant?" I asked.

Scott shook his head. "He can't remember much of the attack."

"How is he feeling?"

"He's got one arm in a sling and a few cuts and bruises on his face," Scott said, "but he's in good spirits and is thrilled with the new arrangements."

"I'm glad," I said. "You guys are good people."

"Don't worry, once he's fully recovered, we plan to put him to work. He seems to be looking forward to that most of all."

"Speaking of being useful," I said, "check this out. I'm finally tidying up the place. Won't you both be glad to come in here and not see piles of Wheaton family history on every horizontal surface?"

Scott waved the air. "No biggie."

"Instead of spending the day cleaning," Bruce said, "why don't you come with us? We're meeting Anton out in West-ville. A friend of his called and suggested we come out to take a tour of his restaurant. His place has the ambience we're hoping to cultivate."

"Strictly a business outing," Scott said with a grin.

"With Anton? Are you kidding me? That guy is a fish. My guess is that after your excursion, he'll spirit you off to one of his favorite bars for the rest of the night. No thanks."

"He's a good man," Scott said.

"I know he is. And I know he has great business instincts. But I'm not in the mood for a raucous night out. Not after yesterday. Not with the situation between Liza and Bennett still looming." And not when I was waiting for a phone call from Arlene.

"We hoped an evening out might help take your mind off of . . . things."

"I appreciate the thought," I said. "Have a nice time. And if you've had too much and need me to pick you up, just call. No matter how late."

"You got it," Bruce said.

Later, after the boys had gone and all the piles of stuff I'd pulled out had been returned to their dark corners to be reexamined another day, my cell phone rang again.

Bootsie had disappeared and was probably sleeping up-stairs. I couldn't count on her to shield me from my aunt's fury.

I glanced at the display and was surprised to see Tooney's number listed there. "Grace," he said when I answered. "Are you busy? Do you have a few minutes to talk?"

I sank into our sofa and perched my feet on the ottoman. "I sure do. What's up?"

"Well," he said with such hesitation that I eased back up.

"What happened?" I asked.

"That's just it," he said. "Not a thing. I haven't been able to come up with a single lead on that guy who's been following you."

Come to think of it, I hadn't seen him recently, either. "You think it was merely coincidence that he happened to be at the Granite Building on the day of the murder, and at same restaurant where I had lunch with Davenport, and at the restaurant where Joe and I met the other night?"

"No, I don't think it's a coincidence," he said. "Your instincts are good. If you sensed him following you, then I'm convinced he is. I suspect that he realized you were on to him—especially since he knew you spotted him sitting at the bar last time—and he's stepped out of the picture for a while until he thinks the coast is clear."

"How do we find him, then?" I asked.

"Tough question. I've been shadowing you myself these past few days," he said.

"You have? I didn't notice."

"Then I guess I did a decent job of being discreet," he said with a chuckle.

"You definitely did." My leg bounced an impatient rhythm. "I don't know what to suggest. I was sure the guy had to be Craig and I figured he was after me because he knew I was there when Virginia's body was found, but now I don't know."

"I wanted to give you an update," Tooney said. "I'll continue to keep an eye on you—"

"No," I said, interrupting him. "Not necessary. If I see him around again I'll let you know, but for now let's consider the matter closed."

"I'm happy to keep tabs on the situation. It's not a problem."

"I understand, but I'm starting to feel as though this was a colossal waste of your time."

"Let's compromise then," he said. "Give it another week. If, by next Saturday, we haven't spotted this guy anywhere in town, I'll agree to fall back."

"Sounds fair," I said.

"Good, speaking of which: What are you plans for tonight?"

"Zero plans." I glanced down at myself. "I'm in comfy pajama pants and a ratty T-shirt and I have no intention of changing. So feel free to take the night off," I said with a laugh. "Go out and have fun."

He chuckled. "Thanks, Grace. Talk soon."

While I'd been on the phone with Tooney, the thought had occurred to me to ask him to find out what he could about Joe's situation. I'd stopped myself before the words came out, though. I didn't want to involve Tooney in my romantic troubles. Something about that felt very wrong.

I'd just put my phone back down when it rang again. It was Aunt Belinda.

There were only so many times I could put this conversation off. I forced a chest full of cheer into my voice. "Hello?"

Chapter 27

"IT'S ABOUT TIME YOU ANSWERED," SHE SAID. "Why did you cancel our meeting? That was very irresponsible of you. After I flew all the way here to help you with your sister, you could at least show a little respect for my time."

"Unfortunately, it couldn't be helped. A matter arose and—"

"Don't give me that. I know this is payback for me telling you about your mother's affair," she said. "You're angry and you don't want to face the truth."

"The truth—" I stopped myself. I didn't have facts, only a few photos that may not prove or disprove anything. All I had were suspicions that my aunt hadn't told me the whole truth after all. "The truth is important. And I'm not running away from it. But I do need time to get my head around everything you told me."

She made a noise that sounded like acceptance.

"Have you said anything to Liza?" I asked.

"I told you we can't say a word to her. She'll be crushed."

"She's a big girl. She can handle it," I said. "And just so you're aware, Liza must have sensed that something was amiss. Last time she was here, she said she suspected as much."

"What? No, she didn't," Aunt Belinda scoffed. "You're telling me that to convince me to spill the story to your sister. I won't do it. I won't hurt her more than she's already been hurt."

"And what about me, Aunt Belinda?" Stretched to the breaking point, I couldn't stop exasperation from seeping through. "When have you ever worried about how much Liza's indiscretions affected me? I've been responsible. I've taken care of my finances, my life, and even our mother while she lay dying. Where was Liza? What has she done with all the opportunities that have come her way? She squandered them."

Aunt Belinda tried to interrupt but I talked right over her.

"Don't argue. You know it's true. What galls me is the way the two of you are working together to force Bennett to subsidize Liza's cavalier lifestyle. She doesn't deserve anything from him."

"Easy to say when you're sitting on top of a fortune that you're too selfish to share with your own flesh and blood."

I nearly lost it. The temptation to reveal the clues I'd found in the family albums—as well as the burning desire to demand answers—bubbled up in my chest with a pain so searing hot I thought my heart would burst.

I drew in a deep breath through my nose. "Bennett's stipend offer to Liza is more than generous."

"Tell me another one," she said with derision. "The man is a millionaire. He can afford a whole lot more than he's letting on."

Billionaire. *But you don't need to know that.* I pulled my lips in and held tight.

"Our attorney says he's going to push to reschedule our meeting for Monday afternoon," she said when I remained silent.

"We'll do our best to accommodate your schedules," I said. "But I can't promise Bennett will be available on such short notice."

Aunt Belinda's heavy breathing whistled through the phone line. "Why do you resent your sister?" she asked. "What has she ever done to you to deserve your spite?"

I raised my fist to my lips to keep from retorting.

"Your mother was the same way with me. She never approved of me. Not ever. She was the golden child in our family. The one who could do no wrong."

Except for that alleged affair.

"You don't understand how hard it is to live up to such high standards," she said.

"What standards?" I asked. "You're eight years older than my mother."

"She was always belittling me for my mistakes."

"That doesn't sound like my mother."

"You didn't know her the way I did," she said. "She treated me like dirt."

She hung up before I could respond. Puffing up my cheeks, I blew out a long breath. So much for keeping my cool. I stared at my cell phone for a long moment before putting it back down. I then meandered into the kitchen to stare at the house phone. Could Arlene have missed my message? Perhaps she was out of town. Maybe she'd become ill or passed away.

I sighed. There was a chance I'd never know the truth about Liza's birth. And with every passing moment, time ran out. There was only so long I could delay this meeting with my sister, my aunt, Bennett, and the lawyers. If I didn't hear from Arlene before then, I'd have to trust my gut and push Aunt Belinda for details I sensed she was omitting.

An hour later when the house phone rang, I bolted to answer it. No name, but an unfamiliar number from a different area code. I couldn't remember if this was the same number I'd dialed to reach Arlene, but reasoned that this had to be her returning my call.

"Hello?" Anticipation ratcheted my voice up a few notches.

"Oh. Hi." A man's voice. Hesitant. Confused. "I'm sorry, I'm trying to reach Bruce?"

"You've got the right number," I said, trying to place him. "This is Grace."

"Grace, of course," he said with gusto. "I thought this was Bruce's cell phone and didn't expect a woman to answer."

"I suppose you wouldn't," I said.

"They gave me three phone numbers and I must have confused myself. I'm guessing this is your landline, am I right?"

"Yep, this is our house phone. We're dinosaurs for keeping one." Still unable to determine who I was talking to, I asked, "Can I help you?"

"This is Jeremy. Jeremy King?" he said. "We met last night when I was there with Bruce and Scott to discuss plans for their wine shop and restaurant."

"Of course," I said as recollection flooded. "I didn't recognize your voice."

"No reason you should," he said easily. "Turns out I'm unexpectedly free this afternoon and happy to drive out to Emberstowne. Are they there?"

"No," I said, disappointed on my roommates' behalf. "They left a little while ago and I don't expect them back until late tonight."

"Oh, that's too bad," he said. "I was hoping to get that tour of the building they promised."

"I know they're going to be sorry they missed you," I said. "They're eager to get started on the project." I thought quickly. "What about tomorrow? Will you still be around?"

"Unfortunately not. Tomorrow is my niece's birthday party back at home in Piedmont Springs. Even though she's only four and probably wouldn't miss her old uncle amidst all the hoopla, my sister would never forgive me." He chuckled. "Plus, I want to be there. She's a real cutie, that one. Makes me laugh."

"Well," I said with a smile in my voice, "for our sake, I'm sorry you're busy, but it sounds like you're making the best choice."

He made a thoughtful noise. "Let them know I'll be in touch as soon as I can. It may be a month before I can get back out this way. At the earliest."

I remembered what he'd said about being eager to make the trek for this project because an opportunity like this would be worth his time.

He must have read my mind because he added, "Any other time, I'd be back out here in a heartbeat, but I'm leaving Monday morning for a three-week stint in Guatemala."

"Vacation?"

"More or less." He chuckled again. "I'm part of a group of volunteers going out there to build houses for those in need."

"That's admirable," I said.

"Thanks, but I actually get more out of it than the poor people do." He hesitated a couple of seconds then said, "Hey, I know that your roommates may have to make a decision before I even have a chance to compete. Which bums me out. I could have been working on ideas and plans during my downtime on the trip. But that's okay. I get it. Things some-times just don't work the way we hope they will." He coughed lightly. "What about you? Is there any possibility that, when I get back next month, you'd be willing to hang out sometime?"

"Me?"

What a silly thing to say. Of course he meant me.

"Yeah." He gave a nervous laugh. "Even if they choose another partner for this project, I'd like to—you know—grab coffee or something with you. If you're interested, that is. I'm not trying to be pushy."

"You're not," I assured him. And then I faltered on how to continue. This was unexpected. Part of me was still re-covering from Joe's bombshell revelation last night but an-other part of me—a whisper, actually—asked what was the harm? Maybe this man with the engaging smile and easygo-ing manner would be nice to get to know better.

"Sure, coffee sometime would be great," I finally said. With a laugh, I added, "And clearly, you have my number."

"I do," he said. "Thanks for the update. I'll call you as soon as I get back."

"Good luck with your volunteer work. I hope you have fun."

"I always do," he said. "Thanks."

I walked out of the kitchen thinking about missed opportu-nities. Not for me, but for my roommates. Although I knew nothing about Jeremy's particular talents, I didn't like the idea that he would be automatically knocked out of the running simply because Bruce and Scott hadn't been here to take his phone call.

Bootsie curled into the room, rubbing the side of her face against the doorway corner. She stared up at me, uttered a plaintive cry, and then rubbed up against my legs. "I fed you an hour ago," I said. "You can't possibly be hungry already."

The kitchen phone rang again. Jeremy, calling back.

"Hello," I said again.

"Hey," he said, sounding as tentative has he had when we'd hung up. "Since I'm around and your roommates aren't available, is there any chance of us getting together tonight? For coffee? Or maybe even dinner?"

I glanced down at my rumpled pajama pants. I could only imagine what my hair looked like. And if I were being perfectly honest with myself, I wasn't at all in the mood to be chatty and pleasant with a man I hardly knew. Plus, I still held out hope that my mom's friend Arlene might call.

About to decline, I stopped myself and considered my roommates' predicament. They'd appreciate it if Jeremy got the chance to see the building's interior. Something otherwise impossible for a month.

"Tell you what," I said as I ran a hand through my uncombed hair and tried to catch my reflection in the window. "How about, instead, I give you that tour of the Granite Building space so you can start coming up with ideas for renovation?"

My counteroffer seemed to take him aback. "Wow," he said after a moment's pause, "that would be great. But without Bruce and Scott—"

"I have a set of keys," I said, opting not to volunteer why. "I'll need an hour or so to get ready, though."

"All right. Pick you up in an hour?"

I wasn't about to relinquish my chance to escape if he turned out to be a bore, a boor, or a buffoon. "I'll meet you there," I said and named a time.

"Looking forward to it, Grace. I'll bring my sketchpad and measuring equipment."

"Is there anything I need to bring?"

"Nope. Just yourself. See you then."

I jumped into the shower and zipped through my regular

process of getting ready. I spent far less time choosing an outfit than I normally would. Even as I pulled on a pair of blue jeans and a top, I examined my reason for this departure from the norm. I usually spent a ridiculous level of effort picking out an ensemble to send the right message. Today, however, I opted for unimpressive. That was the message I wanted to convey. Tight on the heels of that observation, I realized why.

Joe.

My heart told me that he had been truthful when he'd told me the tale of his marriage and the fury of his wife. I could be wrong about him. I knew that possibility existed. But wasn't this what taking a leap of faith was all about? The choice was clear and it had less to do with finding proof than it did with trusting my instincts.

I glanced at the clock. No time to call him right now. Not even enough time for a quick e-mail. If I thought wardrobe choices were difficult, I knew word choices were agonizingly worse.

I promised myself to make it an early evening and to call Joe the minute I got home. I wished I could simply stay home right now.

I frowned at the mirror. I was not interested in Jeremy. Not romantically, at least. But meeting him at the building was the right thing to do for my friends. I did have time to send a quick text to Bruce and Scott, letting them know about this impromptu tour. I ended with: Leaving in 5. Join us if you can.

Chapter 28

"OSCAR," I SAID. "YOU'RE LOOKING GREAT. HOW are you feeling?"

I'd gotten to the Granite Building before Jeremy and let myself in. Oscar, wearing jeans, shoes, and a rumpled polo shirt, had hurried to the front door to see who'd arrived. Dressed up, with one arm in a sling, and with his hair trimmed and beard gone, he looked more like a middle-aged dad on vacation than a homeless squatter. The transformation was astounding. His skin was pink and healthy looking. He smiled, and although his teeth weren't in great shape, he at least still had some of them.

"I'm doing pretty well, considering," he said as he lifted the casted arm. "Happy to be out of the hospital and able to come home."

Referring to the giant warehouse as home caught my heart.

"We're glad you're back." He seemed a lot healthier than I remembered. The hospital stay obviously did him a lot of good. With a little bit more effort, no one would ever realize that he'd once been homeless.

"What are you doing here?" he asked.

I explained about Jeremy coming to tour the building and my roommates' absence.

"You probably want me to stay out of the way, don't you?" Oscar asked.

"Not at all," I said. In fact, I'd been counting on his presence to keep the meeting from any potential awkwardness. "Bruce and Scott already told Jeremy about you and he's in full support of your living on-site as much as possible during the renovation."

I glanced at my phone.

"I'd better get out front," I said. "He should be here soon."

"I'll head downstairs. Got a few things to prepare down there."

Twenty minutes later, when Jeremy hadn't yet appeared, I decided to give up and return home. Truth was, I was glad. I'd done all I could to help my friends, yet through no fault of my own, it hadn't worked out. I was free to head back and call Joe.

"Not here yet?"

I jumped. Behind me, Oscar loomed, standing a little too close for comfort. "Am I in your way?" I asked, shifting position to allow him out the door.

"Nope." He gave a self-satisfied smirk. "Believe me, after all the time I spent holed up in this place, I know every creak and footstep. Came up to check on you. Been too quiet for too long."

"It looks like I've been stood up," I said. "I guess I'll head home now."

"Before you go," he said, jerking his thumb to indicate

the former lobby behind him, "you think you can give me a hand moving something?"

All of a sudden it dawned on me that, without the contractor's presence, I was completely alone here with Oscar. In any other circumstance that might not bother me, but in his cleaned-up state, his appearance—though hardly definitive—was not terribly dissimilar than that of Craig. At least as had been described to me by both Cynthia the inspector and Patsy at the bank. He looked . . . average.

And although Oscar claimed to have spied on Craig a number of times, he'd never provided us an accurate description, claiming poor vision.

"I think it's best if I take off now," I said.

"Oh." His disappointment sounded sincere. "The microwave the guys got me would be great, except it got moved by the fumigators and now it's nowhere near an outlet." He made a face. "That's okay. Cold food is better than no food, right?"

My suspicions were getting the best of me. How ridiculous to imagine that Oscar could have faked his injuries or spun the story of being attacked to shift the focus away from him.

Stranger things had happened, though. To me. To people I cared about.

I was about to decline again, politely, when I heard my name. Still in the doorway, I turned around to see Jeremy jogging across the street to meet me. I breathed a sigh of relief. He waved hello.

"Sorry." He was out of breath when he reached us. "Got tied up." He glanced at Oscar, then shot me a quizzical look.

"This is Oscar," I said. "Bruce and Scott may have mentioned him to you?" I didn't want to introduce him as "the homeless man," and hoped Jeremy remembered on his own. "Oscar, this is Jeremy King."

The contractor shifted his messenger bag to his left hand and extended his right hand to shake. Confused, Oscar squinted at the proffered hand before extending his own in return.

Oscar frowned. "I'm hungry," he said. "I'm going back downstairs now." He pivoted and left.

As soon as he was gone, Jeremy said, "That's the one who'll live on-site during construction, isn't it?" When I nodded, he said, "He looks pretty good for a homeless guy. Not too talkative, though."

"Sorry," I said. "He's been on his own so long, I don't think he's good with social niceties."

"No worries," Jeremy said with a wave of his hand. "My reason for being here today isn't to see him anyway." He offered a tentative grin.

Ooh. This could get awkward quickly. Despite my quick and altogether baseless fear that Oscar would turn out to be the murderous Craig, I was glad to have our homeless friend here after all.

"Right." I shot back a high-wattage no-idea-what-you-meant-by-that smile. "You're here to see the building. Let's get to it."

We started on the main level as I took him through the dated central reception area into the high-ceilinged warehouse in back. "I love how those high beams give this place such an airy feel," I said, pointing up. "The boys talked about replacing the old skylights and maybe adding a few more. What do you think?"

He shifted his messenger bag again, then zipped it open and pulled out a pen and paper. "Let me jot down a few notes while we walk. I'd like to see the whole space to get a sense of it before I make any suggestions."

"Fair enough." I decided to let him wander about without further commentary from me. As we made our way to the far end, he asked, "Is there another level?"

The boys had piled cases of wine along the low wall, serving to obscure the stairway where we'd found Virginia's lifeless body. "There's a basement," I said. "One set of stairs are to the left behind those boxes."

I followed Jeremy as he made his way over. When he jumped back with a gasp, I jumped and yelped, too.

"Got a problem with me coming up the stairs?" Oscar asked as he sauntered past Jeremy. "I live here, you know. This is my house."

The contractor turned to me as though to ask how to handle this.

"Oscar, this is one of the people who may be working on renovating the building. He's a friend."

"I'll decide who's a friend and who isn't."

I realized I would have to have a talk with my roommates about Oscar's future behavior.

"What kind of things are you writing down there?" Oscar asked Jeremy. "Looks like a bunch of nonsense scribbles to me."

Jeremy shook his head. "Drawings," he said. He held them up for Oscar to examine. Oscar squinted across the ten-foot expanse that separated the two men.

"I'm sorry," I said for the second time. "I'm sure Oscar doesn't mean to come across as rude. This is new territory for all of us."

Oscar folded his arms again, squinting. "I'm not sure," he said.

Jeremy shrugged. I didn't know what to do so I led him down the steps, leaving Oscar alone on the main level.

Once we'd reached the bottom, Jeremy glanced up back

the way we'd come. "You don't usually come here alone, do you? That guy seems dangerous."

"He isn't," I said. "Or at least, I never thought he was until today. He's been through a lot."

"Yeah, Bruce and Scott told me about it. I guess we ought to cut him a little slack." He perched one hand on his hip and surveyed the shadowy basement. "Where does he stay when he's here?"

I gestured vaguely. "There are a couple small rooms down that way, including a bathroom and a small kitchen."

"How did Oscar get in and out of the building without anyone noticing?" Jeremy asked.

"There's an unsecured window behind the Dumpster near the building's back door. I guess he used it as his own private entrance."

Jeremy nodded as though he was imagining the scene. "His own private door, and bedroom, and bath, and stairway." He laughed. "Probably heaven to a homeless guy."

As we made our way over to that end of the basement, I caught sight of Oscar peering at us from around a far corner. He ducked out of sight. My roommates hadn't yet cleaned away much of the storage detritus. Walls of unidentifiable equipment remained. Atop a table next to the corner where Oscar hid were three bright yellow plastic jugs. Because I hadn't seen them before, I wandered closer to see what their labels said.

"'Detest the Pest,'" I read aloud, gathering these had been left behind by the fumigators. Oscar came around the edge, doing a terrible job of being discreet with his spying. He ducked away again.

I'd had enough of Oscar's erratic behavior. "Is there anything else you need to see?" I asked Jeremy. "I'd like to wrap this up before we overstay our welcome. Again, I apologize. I had no idea Oscar would be so adversarial."

"Almost done." He wandered toward the rear of the basement. Oscar had left a door ajar. "This is where he lives?" he asked as he started in.

"Let's not disturb his privacy," I said.

"Sure, you're right," he said, leaning sideways as though to peer inside. "But I would like to get a look at the bathroom facilities. You can tell a lot about a structure by its plumbing."

I pointed up. "There's an identical set directly above these washrooms. We can check those."

He turned to face me again, tucking his notebook and pen back into his messenger bag. I started for the stairs but he didn't follow.

When I stopped and turned, he held his arms out as though to encompass the whole area. "What else can you tell me about plans for this space?" he asked.

"I'm sure Bruce and Scott will be able to give you a better description of their vision," I said. "Have you ever been inside the original Amethyst Cellars location?"

"Lots of times." I must have reacted because he said, "Why so surprised? It was a great location."

"It was," I said. "I just wouldn't imagine that someone who lives as far away as Piedmont Springs would be familiar with the place."

"Oh man, you caught me," he said with a good-natured grimace. "Truth is, I had a girlfriend who lived out here. But that's not the kind of thing I'm supposed to mention on a first date, is it?"

First date? Yow. "Good to know," I said blandly.

"Yeah, I ought to confess a little more while I'm at it," he said. "Because it wasn't that long ago that she and I broke up, and because I spent so much time out here, I actually know a little bit about you. When I heard Bruce and Scott were moving into this building, I introduced myself. I thought it was a perfect opportunity to meet you and find out if all the rumors are true."

"Don't believe everything you hear," I said.

"I don't," he said with a laugh. "But I gotta ask because I've heard it too many times: Did you really help the police catch a murderer?"

I caught myself before asking him which time. Nodding, I said, "Yes."

"Whoa," he said. "So you're like Wonder Woman or something, is that it?"

I heard Oscar shuffling behind me and a sudden sense of claustrophobia swarmed. "Not even close," I said.

"What about the lady who was killed here? I heard you're helping the police with that one, too."

"Very little," I said. "They're handling the whole investigation this time. I'm just a tiny cog in the machinery."

"That's not how your roommates explained it." He laughed. "You're in the thick of things. Interviewing people every day."

"Bruce and Scott told you about the investigation?" That wasn't like them at all. "What did they say?"

"Ah." He waved the air again. "Not much. Can't remember exactly."

"Oh, come on." I poured on the charm to get him to spill. "They exaggerate sometimes," I lied. "I'd love to hear what stories they're spinning this time."

"Just a few things." He took the bait with an affable grin. "About you trying to figure out what Virginia was doing here before she was killed. And who she was with."

"I haven't had much luck," I said.

"Yeah. Bummer."

"Did you know Virginia?" I asked. "Seeing as how you spent a lot of time in Emberstowne, maybe you met her?"

"No, can't say I did." His quick glance behind me told me that he'd noticed Oscar spying on us.

"Hey." This time, when Oscar emerged from the shadows, I didn't jump. He walked past me to point at Jeremy. "You."

Eyes narrowing, Jeremy took a step back, raising both hands.

Oscar pointed. "My microwave got moved away from the outlet and I've got this busted wing. You're pretty big. Can you maybe move it back for me?"

Jeremy gave me an amused look. "Sure," he said. To me, he added, "I guess we get to check out that back room after all."

Oscar gestured. "The light's on the left," he said.

Jeremy hesitated. "You first."

Oscar took a step farther back. "The microwave is right inside. You can't miss it."

Jeremy took a step toward him. "You aren't trying to lure me in so you can lock the door behind me, are you?" he asked. "That's not very polite."

Eyes wide and terrified, Oscar slunk farther back. Then, I understood.

I started for the stairs. "Let's go," I said to Oscar.

But he stood frozen to the spot. "You're Craig," Oscar blurted out. "You're Craig Wexler."

Chapter 29

THE MAN'S MOUTH SPLIT INTO A WIDE GRIN.
"It's Webster, actually. But close enough to cause me trouble." He didn't take his gaze from Oscar's trembling form.
The tip of Craig's tongue played at the corner of his mouth
as he chuckled. How could I ever have found him even remotely attractive? "You're sharp," he said to me. "Unfortunately for you, not as sharp as I am."

The nearer, south stairway was a good fifteen feet away.
Getting to it would involve sprinting past Craig and hoping
Oscar would follow. The other stairway lay more than fifty
feet across the basement. I eased sideways, gauging my
chances. Surreptitiously, I pulled my cell phone out of my
purse, unlocked it with my thumbprint, and positioned it
down by my side, intending to speed-dial Rodriguez.

"Oh, no you don't." Craig lunged, smacking my arm with
such force that it sent my phone skittering across the concrete floor.

"I'm sorry, Grace," Oscar said as he steadied himself

against a piece of equipment. "I didn't know for sure. Not until a few minutes ago."

"When you recognized his voice," I said.

Oscar cradled his arm and whimpered.

"Too bad for the homeless bum." Still wearing a smirk, Craig reached into his bag again and pulled out what looked like a power drill with a metal support—like a heavy-duty ruler— running from bit to handle.

When I blinked, startled, he shrugged. "Nail gun," he said. "Best I could do on short notice. Killing people isn't something I do on a regular basis." He pulled out a handful of plastic tie wraps and threw them toward me. "Why didn't you just walk away?" he asked. "Why did you have to go digging into my business?"

"Why didn't you just leave town after killing Virginia?" I countered. "You had to know the police would investigate her murder."

"You think disappearing like that"—he snapped his fingers—"is easy? Relocation takes time and planning. Anyway, I got ties here."

I'd edged closer to the south stairs. Maybe I could make it up and out the front door before he took me down.

He pointed the nail gun at me. His left hand reached up to pinch something on top of the device. "Don't even think about trying." He tilted his head toward the tie wraps. "Go on, hook yourself up to that metal pole there."

"Make me."

Craig arched a brow. "You want to play, is that it?" His left hand relaxed again and he dropped it to his side. "I got plenty of time. I was going to come visit you at your house tonight, sweetie, but your suggestion to meet here was the answer to my prayers."

I wished Oscar would try something—anything—to

distract Craig long enough for me to make a run for help. The poor man, however, was paralyzed with fear. He sank to the ground, gripping an upright beam for support.

I'd told Tooney I was in for the night. And now I regretted being in too much of a hurry to alert him to my change in plans. In truth, I hadn't thought to let him know. Although I had texted Bruce and Scott about meeting the contractor here, the chances of them arriving were slim.

"Oscar, get up," I said.

"I don't wanna die. Not now. Not when things are finally getting better."

"Shut up, you," Craig said.

"Why did you beat this poor man up anyway?" I asked. Was I stalling? For sure. My only other option was to give in and give up.

"Him?" Craig asked unnecessarily. "The paper said he was helping the cops. What other choice did I have?"

"You tried to kill me," Oscar said as he stumbled to his feet. "You would have killed me if that lady hadn't screamed."

Thank goodness he was ambulatory again. Maybe we had a chance.

"I wanted you dead, old man." Craig lifted a corner of his lip as though disgusted with himself. To me: "How was I supposed to know he couldn't identify me? I didn't. I couldn't take any chances. Like I can't take any chances today."

He took a step closer.

I took a big step back. Then another.

"Don't be stupid." He continued to move forward as I retreated and stepped closer to Oscar. Closer to the stairs and to cover behind the piles of equipment.

Craig laughed as he positioned himself between me and escape. "How long do you figure we can keep this up?" he asked. Toeing the tie wraps, he kicked them toward me. "Pick them up."

I took another step back, ducking behind the table of plastic jugs.

"Pick them up now," he said. And then he brought his left hand up a second time to grip a piece of metal atop the nail gun. Grinning, he drew it backward about an inch.

Stepping sideways, I was close enough to touch Oscar if I wanted to.

"I won't," I said.

When indecision clouded Craig's eyes, I made the choice easy for him. Stretching my leg out, I kicked the tie wraps sideways, sending them sliding along the smooth concrete to gently land at the bottom step.

The distraction worked as I'd hoped. When Craig's gaze instinctively followed the moving object, I grabbed the jug of chemicals in front of me and flipped open the cap.

I sloshed the contents of the jug at Craig. Instantly, my eyes began to tear, but I stole the extra seconds necessary to chug out more liquid, then threw the container.

Craig bellowed.

"Run," I shouted to Oscar.

I straight-armed the homeless man into motion, shoving him away from the noxious fumes. Grabbing a handful of his shirt, I half pushed, half dragged him down the long aisle of equipment, hoping to make it across the basement and back up another aisle to reach the far stairs before the spreading toxic chemicals caught up with us.

Behind us, Craig roared. With anger or pain, I didn't know, didn't care. We were overwhelmed by the smells of ammonia, sulfur, and sickly sweet lemon. I blinked repeatedly, coughing and fighting the urge to retch.

I heard pings as nails hit the floor behind us. I knew nail

guns were deadly up close, but at a distance they posed less of a threat. The quicker we made it to the stairs, the better.

We choked our way along the basement wall, Oscar stumbling as we turned the corner. The stairs were still out of sight, obscured by rows of accumulated junk.

"This way," I whispered between clenched teeth as I tugged him back up and peered around the corner of the next aisle. Even though we'd put distance between ourselves and the fumes, it still hurt to breathe. A vicious tang filled my nose and a taste of disinfectant coated my lips. My vision blurred as my body struggled to eliminate irritation from my eyes.

Craig coughed. "You've helped me more than you know," he shouted. He sounded far enough away. I fought to hush my coughing and whispered to Oscar to do the same. If we kept quiet, maybe he wouldn't be able to figure out exactly where we were.

"Accidental spill. Toxic fumes," Craig said loudly. "All I have to do is knock you two unconscious and I'm home free."

We picked our way around the collection of junk, making sure the coast was clear before racing to the next hiding spot. I ignored Craig's taunts. But that didn't mean I wasn't worried.

I could have traveled much faster on my own, but I continued to push and pull Oscar along until, finally, the stairs were no more than thirty steps away.

I still wasn't seeing clearly, but it was easier to breathe at this end of the basement. It may have been the fresher air, or the promise of freedom, that inspired Oscar to rally. Suddenly alert, and freshly stable on his feet, he bolted past me and headed for the stairs. I wasted no time hauling myself into his wake.

We emerged from the aisle and crossed the ten feet of

floor before making it to the bottom of the stairs. Our goal swam before my eyes. I sensed, rather than saw, Craig approaching fast from our left. "Go," I screamed with one hand on Oscar's back as I launched myself up the steps behind him. My other hand grazed the railing in an effort to keep myself steady.

Two pings. Three. Nails danced up the stairs, clattering as they fell next to my feet.

I'd made it almost halfway up when Craig grabbed my ankle through the stairway's metal railings. I lost my balance, tripped, and began toppling backward. My butt hit the corner of a step and I cried out in pain.

Oscar, ahead of me, turned at the commotion. He, too, lost his footing and then staggered against the rail. He dropped to his knees as I scrambled to right myself. Craig raced around the bottom of the stairs and leaped in front of me. In a smooth motion, he dropped the nail gun and caught Oscar's good arm with one hand while yanking more tie wraps from his pocket with the other.

With a grunt, Craig lurched to the side, nimbly attaching Oscar's wrist to the top of the hand rail.

With the nail gun out of reach, I full-body jumped Craig, using my fists to beat his face, groping for the soft sockets of his eyes. My own eyes were nearly closed from the fumes' irritation, and my efforts to subdue Craig proved fruitless.

He swung at me wildly. "You stupid woman."

I sensed he wasn't able to see well, either. One of his meaty hands clapped hold of my shoulder, shoving me down until a step's edge bit into my spine. Craig reached for the nail gun with his other hand. When he hoisted the weapon aloft, I screamed, rolling toward my pinned shoulder. My head banged on the stair edge above.

Craig slammed the gun into the step where my neck had

just been. The hit of the gun's metal bit against wood and the subsequent hissing thunk of a nail sinking into the stair told me exactly how close I'd come to permanent injury.

Twisting, he grabbed for me again, but my quick movement coupled with the stairs' unevenness served to knock him off balance. I kicked upward, catching Craig hard in the groin before he could try again to impale me.

I raked his face with my fingers, catching the hollows beneath his eyes and digging my nails in as deeply as I could. He howled, reaching to pull my hands from his face. The nail gun dropped to the step below, thudding hard.

With his powerful weight off my shoulder, I rolled upward, away from him. As soon as I broke free, I dropped to sit, slamming both feet against Craig's side. Groaning with effort, I shoved him down. He grabbed blindly as he tumbled, striving for a hold. I had mere seconds before he'd be back for more.

Oscar tried in vain to wiggle his hand out of the plastic restraint with no promise of breaking free. I wanted to run for help, but couldn't leave him defenseless. Craig would kill the man. I had no doubt.

My cell phone was too far away, back amid the worst of the spillage. There was no phone line installed upstairs yet.

Our only chance for survival was the nail gun lying three steps below. I lunged for it just as Craig intuited my intent. Blood leaked down his face. He wiped it away with the back of his arm and heaved himself up the bottom two stairs.

I got to the nail gun first. Gripping it with both hands and holding it up like a gun, I aimed for his face, about four feet away.

"Don't take a step closer." My words came out menacingly low. "I will shoot you."

He laughed, but backed up. "Oh yeah?" he asked as he

attempted to clear his eyes with the hem of his shirt. "Go ahead." He pulled his shirt higher and pointed to his chest. "Aim for right here. I want to see the look on your face when you try."

Something clicked. I remembered how his left hand had come up to grab the top of the gun. Nail guns are effective tools, but not terribly threatening weapons. Had I seen that on *Mythbusters*? Or had Rodriguez or Flynn dropped that tidbit when my house was being restored? Didn't matter.

The gun was getting heavy, no doubt about that. I re-aimed the device, training on Craig's center mass. Another piece of advice from Rodriguez and Flynn.

"Oh, because I need to pull this piece back?" I asked as my left hand came up and I yanked the safety backward. "Should I shoot now?"

The panic in his eyes was real. We were only about five feet apart and although I doubted that a shot nail would possess the necessary velocity to harm him in any material way, he evidently wasn't about to take chances. I didn't blame him.

"Get on the ground, facedown," I said.

"Not gonna happen."

The fumes had dissipated enough for my vision to clear. I hoped that none of us would suffer permanent damage from our exposure to the toxins. But I couldn't worry about that right now. One problem at a time.

Maintaining the high ground, I took a step closer, then another, reminding myself to stay out of his reach. Behind me I heard scraping, grunting, and scratching. I imagined Oscar was still trying to find a way to unhook himself.

"Craig," I said in a reasonable tone, "we're at a stalemate here. And we aren't getting any healthier around this poison."

"So?"

"Empty your pockets." He might be carrying a pen knife or keychain that Oscar could use to break through the tie wrap.

"Make me." He dropped to the floor, sitting solidly with his feet outstretched and palms flat on the concrete behind him. "I can do this all day," he said. Nodding toward the quivering nail gun, he asked, "The question is: Can you?"

Chapter 30

HONESTY GOT THE BEST OF ME. "NO," I SAID, taking aim. "I can't."

And pulled the trigger.

Pshew.

Craig jumped as the projectile skimmed the floor next to him.

I took a step closer. "I told you to empty your pockets."

He crab-walked backward. "You're a lunatic. This isn't fair."

"Fair?" I asked, mimicking him as I tried to fight the tremor in my arm. Nail guns, I decided, were not designed to be held aloft for long periods of time. "Talk to Virginia's family about fair."

From behind me: "Grace, I got it," Oscar said triumphantly. "I'm free."

I didn't shift my attention from my quarry. "Go get help."

"One of those nails he shot at you," Oscar said. "I used

it to cut through the plastic. And it was really hard to do with my broken arm and all."

"Go get help," I said again. "Hurry."

"Yeah, yeah, okay."

I heard him scramble up the stairs.

"Just you and me now," Craig said when he was gone.

I hoped the quiver in my arms wasn't obvious. "And the nail gun."

He started to get to his feet.

"Stay down," I said.

Shaking his head very slowly, he continued to rise. My right arm continued to shake. I would have loved to have bolstered my right arm with my left, but I didn't want to release the safety mechanism. Not even for a second.

"I'm going to leave before the police get here." He pointed to the other set of stairs. "And you aren't going to stop me."

"You don't want to do that," I said. "It isn't safe with all those chemicals in the air." It probably wasn't safe at this end, either, but there wasn't much I could do about that.

"I'll take my chances," he said.

I took a step closer and shot a nail just ahead of him, missing him by a much narrower margin than I'd expected. The nail gun's weight had affected my aim.

"Don't try it."

He raised both hands above his head. "Okay," he said. "You win."

He spun so swiftly I almost missed it. Lunging, he grabbed for the gun, trying to wrench it from my hands. Despite my throbbing arms and the sweat that poured down my face from exertion, I gritted my teeth and held tight. Howling with pain, I tightened my hold on the safety and pulled the trigger once, twice, three times.

At such close range, the nails hit their mark with soft, sick precision—like a sharp knife plunged repeatedly into meat. Craig cried out, grabbing the side of his torso. He curled into the fetal position as he tumbled once again to the concrete floor.

Blood leaked from one arm and oozed from a wound on his left side. I couldn't tell where the third nail had hit.

I sat on one of the steps to support my weakened right arm with my knee.

Below me, Craig moaned and rocked. Indecision froze me in place. How badly was he hurt? As much as I wanted to make sure I hadn't delivered a fatal blow, I feared dropping my guard.

"Please help me." Eyes clenched, features twisted in pain, he coughed and cried out. "I promise I won't hurt you. I can't." His words grew weak as he moaned facedown into the concrete. "I'll die here if you don't stop the bleeding."

Torn and helpless, I bit my lip. "Help is on its way."

He looked over to me. The right side of his face was smeared red. "You're cruel. You would let me die here." He coughed again, this time spitting blood. "You see?"

As he talked, he'd begun shifting position. Now he had one leg bent, the ball of his foot propped against the floor. One hand pressed hard on the concrete. Just like someone preparing to boost himself to his feet. The look in his eyes was murderous.

He'd deliberately opened his mouth on the bloodied floor to make me believe he was coughing up his body's vital fluid. I shook my head. "You're a wily one, Craig." I didn't alter my aim.

"I'm dying."

"No, you're not."

When he charged me again, I was ready for him. Instead of shooting nails this time, however, I leaped to my feet and swung the nail gun at his head.

He went down fast and hard, his skull bouncing along the edges of the steps until he landed at the bottom for the last time.

Shaken, I strove to steady my hammering heart. Keeping my perch above, I watched his immobile form to ensure he was still breathing.

He was. Good. No need to attempt CPR.

"Grace?" Rodriguez's voice. "Where are you?"

I turned at the sound of my name. "I'm down here. Craig's hurt. Call an ambulance."

NO DEAD BODIES THIS TIME, SO NO NEED FOR the coroner to make an appearance. Sitting outside in the fresh air, far away from the toxins, I realized how much I wished Joe would show up anyway. For moral support, if not for any official duties. But he'd made it clear that the next move was mine. And I hadn't called him yet.

As paramedics tended to Craig, and Rodriguez and Flynn took statements from Oscar, I sat on my car's bumper, stared up at the starry sky, and let my mind wander.

Craig would survive. I found myself relieved to hear it. And now that the police had his real surname, Webster, they'd be able to track his movements and investigate him thoroughly.

Flynn sauntered over. "Here's your phone," he said as he handed it to me. "Doesn't seem to be damaged at all."

I unlocked it and played with the controls for a minute. Seemed to be working just fine. "Thanks," I said. "I appreciate it."

"How are you doing?"

"Better," I said. "I like being able to breathe without feeling like my lungs are on fire."

"Yeah, about that—we're having our hazmat team come out here to assess the damage. I'll keep you posted."

"I appreciate it."

He shifted in place and looked around as though to make sure no one was listening. "You did good," he said quietly. "But I still don't like you making a habit of catching murderers."

"For what it's worth, I don't like it, either."

"I did a quick background check on your buddy," he said with a glance toward the gurney carrying Craig. "He's got a record of embezzlement and fraud. No surprise there."

"What about Virginia?"

"You already know that she first encountered Craig when he worked for the appraisal company."

I nodded.

"Craig came up with this credit card scheme and pressured Virginia to go along with it. Having an empty building to process the cards was bonus."

"Pressured her? How?" I asked.

"We're looking into allegations that he threatened the daughter's family." He shrugged. "Davenport has been keeping us updated on the bank's side of the investigation. Now that they know what they're looking for, they're finding more about Virginia than anyone expected."

"How much do you think Craig and Virginia got away with?"

"We'll probably never know for sure," he said. "Millions, though. At least."

"Wow. Poor Virginia. Too bad she didn't come to you when Craig threatened her family."

"*Allegedly* threatened," he corrected. "That's what the daughter's claiming now that we're building a case against her mother." Flynn made an impolite noise.

"You don't believe her?"

"She swears that otherwise her mother would never do anything illegal." He frowned. "Maybe Craig made threats, maybe he didn't. Maybe Virginia saw the writing on the wall: looming retirement, not enough money saved, and when Craig offered an opportunity, she jumped right in. Based on some of what I'm seeing in Craig's background, elderly women were his preferred prey."

"That's terrible."

He shrugged again. "You ask me, the daughter knew exactly what was going down. She's scared now because the feds are liable to swoop in and take all her ill-gotten goods away."

"Can they do that?"

"If they can prove the daughter was in on the scheme," he said, "you bet they can. Even if they can't make charges against the daughter stick, she's in for a rough ride. According to the the loan application information Davenport uncovered for us at the bank—thanks for that, too, by the way—Virginia was into this credit card scam pretty deep. Just like you thought."

My brows shot upward. It had to be hard for Flynn to admit that I'd helped.

He started to walk away, then turned back. "Hey, I hear Joe finally told you his troubles."

"You knew about that?" I asked.

Flynn had the decency to look sheepish. "Yeah. Rodriguez and I got the lowdown when he first moved here." He held up a hand. "Not my story to tell, you understand. It was up to him to spill."

"I appreciate that, I guess," I said.

"He's a good man," Flynn said. "I hope you don't kick him to the curb because of his wife's issues."

"Yeah, well." I wasn't about to share my feelings for Joe with Flynn. Instead, I decided to deflect. "Kind of a he said/she said situation. Two sides to every story and all that."

Flynn took a step toward me. "Two sides?" he asked quietly. "What are you talking about?"

"According to the private investigator who cornered me the other day, Joe's wife is not only permanently injured, she's heartbroken that he left her. She wants to reconcile or, at a minimum, warn others away from him."

Flynn made a face. "And you believed her?"

I shrugged. "That was the first I'd heard of Joe still being married. After he told me his side of the story, I didn't know what to think. I imagine the truth lies somewhere between the two versions."

"There you go again, little miss know-it-all," Flynn said. He wagged a finger at me. "What did he tell you?"

"I'm not in the mood to go down this road."

He waited a long moment. "Did he tell you she was an addict?"

"Yes."

"That she and her parents colluded to keep the truth from him?"

"He did," I said.

"Did he also tell you that his wife tried to kill him?"

I nodded.

"More than once?"

I shook my head. "What?"

Flynn glanced from side to side again. "The evidence is circumstantial on that second attempt," he said. "But while he was still unconscious after the accident, nurses discovered the wife in Joe's room in the middle of the night. How she'd hobbled in—crutches and all—without anyone noticing is a mystery. But there she was. There's some disagreement about what she was trying to do in there, in the dark, fiddling with his IV port."

"No," I said. "That can't be."

"Believe what you want," he said. "I'm telling you the truth."

"How do you know so much?" I asked.

He glanced eastward. "Got a cousin in the department there. He said that the wife is a real mess and that Joe was lucky to get out when he did."

"She wasn't tried for attempted murder?" I asked. "For the car accident? For sneaking into Joe's room?"

"When you're as rich as her family is, you have resources. Her lawyer got her to plead down to reckless conduct and driving while intoxicated. As for the attempt in the hospital room, she claimed she was simply checking to make sure Joe was all right. Apparently she expressed remorse for the accident and sobbed in court," Flynn added. "A lot."

I shook my head. "How awful for Joe."

"Exactly. Which is why you need to put the guy out of his misery." Flynn gestured in the direction of Joe's office. "Either give him the green light or tell him to take a hike. You owe him that much."

I opened my mouth. He cut me off.

"Joe's a stand-up kind of guy and he's got it bad for you," Flynn said. "Don't mess this up."

Chapter 31

"AND YOU DIDN'T TELL US ANY OF THIS UNTIL now?" Scott asked the next morning when I told my roommates everything that had happened the night before.

We were sitting around our kitchen table with our coffee and the Sunday paper spread out before us. Both the news and the beverages had been long forgotten.

"I didn't even hear the two of you come in," I said. "Too much excitement again." I shook my head. "Plus, I was wiped."

"You could have texted or called. We would have come right home," Bruce said.

"I know you would have," I said. "But I was safe and sound, and honestly, all I wanted was to put my head down and fall asleep. Which"—I held up a finger—"is apparently one of the side effects of the chemicals we inhaled yesterday. As are dizziness and nausea." I made a face. "Believe me, I had a rough night before I fell asleep."

"What sort of health issues are there going forward?"

"Fortunately," I said, "the hospital and hazmat team

believe that because our exposure was short-term, Oscar, Craig, and I will all be fine. We got away from the worst of it quickly, and apparently the fumigation company has tried to eliminate toxic chemicals for its workers' benefit. It could have been worse, but it wasn't."

"I can't believe you were in such a dangerous situation again," Bruce said.

Scott nodded. "And you went there to help us. I feel terrible."

"You shouldn't," I said. "Craig made it clear that he'd intended to target me. He would have made an attempt sooner or later. We were lucky to get out of this one alive. I'm not complaining."

"Craig's probably going away for quite some time."

"Let's hope so," I said. "If I'm called to testify, I'll do so gladly."

"We're so sorry for having introduced you to him in the first place," Bruce said. "When he approached us, we didn't even think to suspect him."

"Of course you didn't," I said. "Why would you?"

Scott frowned. "We just assumed everyone knew we were looking for a contractor, so when he offered his services, we didn't think twice. We should have pushed him harder for details.

"It's okay, guys, really," I said. "There was no way for you to know. There was no way for anyone to know." I shook my head. "None of this was your fault and I don't want to hear another word about it."

"Okay then, what about Joe?" Bruce asked, referring to the conversation with Flynn that I'd related. "Have you talked with him yet?"

"No," I said with a rueful smile. "I spent too much time

emptying my body of toxins last night. But I'm feeling much better and intend to rectify that today."

"When?" Scott asked with a pointed glance at the phone.

"It's too early to call on a Sunday." I rolled my eyes good-naturedly. "I'll wait until after lunch. Besides, I need to figure out what exactly I plan to say beyond 'Hi.'"

"And I imagine Grace would prefer to make this call without us as an audience." Bruce pointed to himself and his partner. To me, he said, "Lucky for you, we're heading to the building in about an hour. You'll have the place to yourself for the rest of the day."

"I promise I'll keep you both updated."

SHORTLY AFTER NOON, WITH MY ROOMMATES out for the day and Bootsie sleeping in my favorite chair, I blew out a breath. Excitement, nervousness, and anticipation combined to ramp up my heart rate. I paced the first floor for a couple of minutes rehearsing what I intended to say when I talked with Joe.

The kitchen phone rang, startling me. Could he have sensed my vibes and taken the initiative?

As I hurried to pick up, I realized the folly of that thought. If Joe called, he would most likely use my cell.

I checked the display before I picked up. No name, just an unfamiliar number. Probably a telemarketer. I decided to ignore it.

Before turning away, I glanced at the number again. Something about the last four digits gave me pause. Slightly familiar. Enough to take a chance and answer?

If this turned out to be one of those scammers trying to convince me that my computer was sending out viruses, or that the IRS was initiating a lawsuit against me, I'd slam the phone in their ear.

"Hello?"

"Oh my goodness. It's so lovely to hear your voice, Grace."

I blinked my confusion at the warm greeting. "Thank you," I stammered. "Who is—" And then it hit me. "Arlene," I said with surprised delight. "How are you?"

"I'm doing wonderfully well," she said. "So very pleased to get your message."

"It's great to hear your voice, too." Arlene's call, coming now after I'd all but given up on hearing from her, required my full attention. I worked to rearrange my brain. "Thank you for returning the call."

She gave a soft, lilting laugh. "I would have gotten back to you sooner, but I just got home yesterday from a cruise with one of my friends from the club," she said. "We didn't land until late last night, though, so I waited until after church this morning to call back."

"I'm so glad you did."

"What's on your mind, honey?" Her tone had sobered. "Not that I don't appreciate hearing from you, but your message took me a little by surprise. I hope you don't have bad news to share?"

Bad news was often a matter of perspective, but I knew what she meant. "Everyone is healthy," I said. "Thanks for asking."

"And you?" she pressed. "How are you?"

We could go back and forth all day with niceties. Time to get to the heart of the matter. "To be honest, Arlene, I'm confused. And I'm hoping you can help me clear a few questions up."

She made a noncommittal noise.

"I don't know if you've heard," I began, then told her

about my discovery regarding my mother's relationship to Bennett.

"How wonderful for you," she said when I finished.

"It is wonderful," I agreed. "Finding out that Bennett is my uncle has been one of the best things that's happened to me since I moved down here to be with my mom."

"Before she died, your mom never told you any of this?" Arlene asked. "About her connection to Marshfield?"

"Not a word," I said. "Did she ever mention it to you?"

"Never. I had no idea."

"I'd like to think that she did tell my dad at some point," I said.

"Oh, I'm sure she did. Your parents were one of the most loving couples I've ever known. Your mother was bereft when your dad died."

Time to ease into it. "You knew them before I was born, didn't you?"

"I sure did. Your mom and I worked together for a few years. We used to double date even before we were married."

"And you and my mom stayed close for a long time, right?"

"Until my husband got that job in Seattle," she said. "Broke my heart to leave all my friends and family, but it turned out to be a great opportunity for all of us."

"When was that?" I asked.

She named the year. I was right. I would have been a sophomore in college.

"So, you knew my mom and dad when they were expecting Liza, is that right?"

Arlene made the same noncommittal noise she'd made earlier.

"You did, right?" I asked again.

"Yes. Yes, I knew them before Liza was born."

Interesting wording. "This is where it gets tricky," I said. I heard her sharp intake of breath.

Despite the fact that I longed for answers, I found it difficult to actually put the question into words. "Do Liza and I have different fathers?"

Arlene remained silent for a long time. Too long. When she finally spoke, she asked, "What's this all about, Grace?"

I told her.

When Arlene and I hung up an hour later, I still wanted to call Joe, but I needed to clear my head. Needed time to assimilate all that Arlene and I had talked about.

I also needed to meet with Bennett. This affected him, too.

I walked into the parlor and lifted my snoozing Bootsie from my chair. I sat down, positioning the little cat on my lap. She stared sleepily at me for a moment, circled twice, then huffed and closed her eyes.

Chapter 32

"WELL, WELL, WELL," FRANCES SAID WHEN I walked in the next morning. "You've certainly had a busy weekend."

No sense wasting time. I threw my purse onto one of the two chairs across from her and flopped into the other. "How much have you heard?"

Her tadpole eyebrows shot up. Clearly, not the reaction she'd expected. Unruffled, she launched into a fairly accurate recitation of the events at the Granite Building that led to Craig's arrest, including the tidbits about Virginia's involvement and her daughter's likely complicity.

She sat forward, head tilted slightly. Eyes sparkling. "Is there more?"

"Depends," I said as I scratched the side of my ear. "Joe Bradley is still married."

"That dirty bird." She sat back, her mouth round. "You've dumped him then, right?"

"There's a lot more to the story than meets the eye. I'll

be happy to share details with you providing you keep everything to yourself."

She crossed her lips as though locking them with a key, but her eyes were wide.

"Good," I said. "I haven't had a chance to talk with him yet. I wanted to, but I had a pressing issue to deal with last night."

The door to Frances's office opened and Bennett strode in. "Look at this," he said with a wide smile. "Two of my favorite people in one place. Today promises to be an excellent day."

I nabbed my purse from the empty chair to allow Bennett to sit. Frances gave him the side-eye. "Uh-oh," she said. "What's going on?"

"I'm glad you asked, Frances," he said. "We need a favor."

She leaned forward, arms on her desk. "Talk to me."

THAT AFTERNOON, BENNETT AND I MADE THE trek to one of the mansion's private rooms. Although referred to as the Guest Hobby Room in the house's original plans, the shape and scope of the enormous space called to mind a grand hotel's lobby rather than a cozy nook designed for reading, sewing, or painting.

For today's event, the staff had stripped canvas coverings from the upholstered pieces and had made the teak, mahogany, and cherry wood furniture gleam. Set in a corner of the second floor, the teal-wallpapered room had two walls of arched windows and a tromp l'oeil ceiling that appeared to soar to the sky.

A circular rug emblazoned with an ornate *M* sat at the room's center, and two long gold sofas faced each other in front of the marble fireplace. An assortment of hard-backed and wing chairs, along with two wood-framed upholstered settees, made up the rest of the room's seating.

"It's been a long time since I've been in here," Bennett said as he strode across to gaze out the window. "I've missed it."

"I'm looking forward to the day we add this stop to our tour."

We'd been eager to open this particular space to visitors, but the corridor connecting it to the public areas was not fire marshal approved for access. Not unless we widened it and installed an additional exit. And we weren't ready to do that.

"That will be a project for another day," he said as he turned to face me. "Are you ready for this?"

I gave a sad laugh. "The fun never stops, does it?"

He closed the distance between us and put his arm around my shoulders, pulling me into a hug. "Almost there," he said into the top of my head. "One more hurdle."

Frances cleared her throat.

We separated as she led Liza, Aunt Belinda, Marshfield attorney Ted Hertel, and a man I assumed was Liza's attorney into the room.

From the look on Aunt Belinda's face, I feared she would swoon from amazement. As she made her way in, I watched as she took in everything: the fascinating ceiling, the opulent artifacts that had been brought back in for today's event, the plethora of portraits and landscapes, and the lush rug beneath her feet. Her fingers grazed Liza's arm as though to steady herself. Her eyes were wide with wonder.

"What have I been telling you, Aunt Belinda? See how close they are?" Liza said in a fake hushed tone loud enough to carry. "Don't tell me there isn't more to this story."

I ignored her as Frances introduced Everett Young. Both he and Ted carried briefcases, and as soon as the social graces were attended to, both men pulled up hard chairs. They sat opposite each other, setting their briefcases on nearby low tables and opening the cases with a quick rat-a-tat of competing clicks.

"Please," Bennett said to my aunt and sister as he gestured toward the sofas, "make yourselves comfortable."

A moment later, we were joined by two staff members from the Birdcage Room, who went from guest to guest taking beverage orders. Two other staffers brought in trays of cheese, fruit, and chocolate, setting them down atop the table between the couches.

Liza and Aunt Belinda sat on the gold couch facing the south windows; I sat facing the door with Bennett on my right and Frances on my left.

"She's not staying, is she?" Liza pointed at Frances. "I don't want her here."

Bennett forced a smile. "Frances stays."

Aunt Belinda patted Liza's leg. "It doesn't matter. Look at this place."

Bennett thanked the staffer who served him coffee. "I take it you approve?" he asked Aunt Belinda. He poured a little cream into his cup. "I hope you've had a chance to look around."

She shook her head as she stirred cream and sugar into her own cup. "Only what I got to see on the way up here. After today, I'll make a point of visiting more often." This delivered with a knowing look to Liza.

Frances jabbed the side of my leg with her pinky finger. I ignored her as I reached for my lemonade. "Please help yourselves," I said to our guests.

Liza had ordered scotch and soda. Frances coffee, and the two attorneys had politely declined.

Everett Young cleared his throat. "Shall we get started then?" he asked.

"No time like the present," Bennett said.

"Good enough," Young said. "I've drawn up a preliminary agreement between you, Mr. Marshfield, and my client Liza Soames." He stood to hand a sheaf of papers to Bennett and a second set to me. "And here's a copy for your attorney." He handed the remaining documents to Ted and positioned himself behind the opposite sofa.

Bennett nodded his thanks and began to read. A moment later, he tapped the page. "Right here," he said.

Young came alert. "A problem?"

"This agreement begins with an erroneous premise," Bennett said.

Young offered a bland smile. "Enlighten me."

"It states that I made Grace my heir because of our blood relationship," Bennett said.

"And?" Young asked. "Are you telling me that isn't true?"

"I don't dispute that Grace will be my sole heir," Bennett said, stressing the word "sole." He grinned at me. "But she doesn't need to wait for me to die. I made her co-owner in all that I possess now."

Young looked taken aback. As did Aunt Belinda and Liza. "I was not aware that you'd taken such a drastic step," Young said. A second later he'd collected himself, and if I could use the word "giddy" to describe his demeanor, I wouldn't be far off.

"Yes, but," Bennett said, "the issue I have is that I didn't make Grace co-owner and heir only because of our blood relationship. I chose to do that because I trust her. There is no law that requires me to share my fortune with family members. If Grace and I were not related, I may have still followed this course."

"Ah, but you didn't," Young said. "You made no such change until after DNA results proved familial ties. There is evidence to back that up. Should you refuse to settle with my client, we are prepared to go to court to prove that what is given to one Marshfield descendent is owed to the other."

"You'll never win," Bennett said easily.

"You can't guarantee that."

Bennett and I returned to reading. I was appalled by the demands, but kept reading, fighting the urge to shout my disdain. Reading over my shoulder, Frances huffed.

Except for Frances's muffled exclamations, the three of us turning pages as we read, and Aunt Belinda and Liza taking sips of their drinks, the room was silent.

When Bennett got to the end of the agreement, he drew in a deep breath and placed the sheaf of papers next to his coffee. He took a sip and placed the china cup back in its saucer with a sharp clink.

"So, Liza." He leaned forward, resting his elbows on his knees. "You believe you're entitled to one-third of my estate, did I read that correctly?"

Her eyes sparked.

"I can answer on behalf of my client," Young said. "Yes, she does."

Bennett flicked a glance up at the man. "She's free to speak for herself."

"Now that you ask," Liza said, squirming forward to sit at the cushion's edge, "I think I'd like to amend that part of the agreement. I didn't know my dear sister had complete control of the Marshfield fortune. That makes my claim to one-third feel like a piddling sum."

"Piddling?" Bennett barked a laugh. "Oh, child, you have no idea."

"I want what my sister has," Liza said. She lifted her scotch and soda in a mock toast to me. "I've only ever aspired to what my sister has."

One of Frances's legs began to bounce. A vein at her temple stood out in sharp relief.

"I understand," Bennett said soothingly. "And I can't blame you. Grace has a great deal more than you could ever hope to attain."

Liza seemed unsure of how to respond.

"However," Bennett continued, "if you are ever to succeed the way Grace has, I'm afraid you'll have to do that on your own." He turned to our lawyer. "Ted?"

Ted got to his feet and solemnly handed one set of documents to Liza and another to her attorney.

As they began to read, Ted said, "This is the agreement my client is offering." He glanced at his watch. "You have one hour to accept before it's withdrawn."

"This is ridiculous." Liza's face flushed red. "This is less than you were willing to give me before. I can't live on twenty-five thousand dollars a year."

"My offer is more than generous, given the circumstances," Bennett said.

"What about living expenses?" Liza slapped the page. "There's no mention of any."

"Grace tells me you refused to move into the apartment we rented for you."

"Of course I refused. I deserve better."

Nearly bursting to chime in, I held myself back. Frances and Aunt Belinda seemed locked in a vicious staring contest—neither willing to back down.

"If you prefer more luxurious accommodations than the ones I originally offered," Bennett said, "you can always get a job."

I smiled.

Liza made an impolite noise.

"Liza," Young said quietly, "please. Allow me."

"No," she said. "This is ludicrous." She threw the document to the floor and got to her feet. "We will see you in court."

"No," Bennett said softly. "You won't."

Visibly rattled by the explosive turn of events, Young begged Liza to calm down. "Please," he said again, "let me handle this."

She threw him a look of disgust. "Fine," she said as she dropped back onto the couch. "But I'm not settling for less than half of the Marshfield millions."

Under my breath I silently corrected: Billions.

Young made an effort to look as though he was studying the agreement before he addressed Bennett again. "First of all, sir, I find it contemptible for you to attempt to coerce my client into signing this agreement within an hour. That's barely adequate time for me to read through it once, let alone prepare a professional recommendation."

Bennett shrugged. "It's very short."

"Yes, I see that," Young said, ignoring Liza's huff. "Fortunately, my client has expressed her preference to reject this insulting offer." He approached Bennett and tried to hand the document back.

Bennett crossed his arms and shook his head.

"May I remind you, sir, of our intent to take this matter to court?" Young said. "Favoring one niece over the other will not play well in the media. We can draw a lawsuit out for a very long time. Is this your best decision for the sunset years of your life?"

I bit the insides of my cheeks. Hard.

"You have the power to make all this go away," Young continued. "If you'll only be reasonable."

Bennett pointed to the agreement in Young's hands. "That is reasonable. More than reasonable." He glanced at his watch. "The clock is ticking."

Young sighed heavily and made his way over to his briefcase. "I suppose we will see you in court then."

Bennett got to his feet. I stood next to him.

Everyone else got up, too.

"One more thing," Bennett said, "before you put that agreement away. Please note that if you insist on filing suit, my attorneys will require Ms. Liza Soames to undergo DNA testing to establish her claim of familial ties."

Young shrugged. "Very well."

"Why should Liza have to do that?" Aunt Belinda said. "If Grace is Mr. Marshfield's niece, then so is Liza. Everyone knows that."

Bennett turned to me and opened his hand.

"Not everyone knows that," I said. "You, for instance."

Aunt Belinda began to sputter. "Your mother was Marshfield's illegitimate child, not me. Or have you forgotten what we talked about?" Her furious glare practically shouted a reminder about my mother's alleged affair.

"I haven't forgotten a thing," I said. "And I refuse to believe you have, either."

Confusion clouded her eyes. Shaking it off, she grabbed Liza's arm. "Let's go. These people don't know what's good for them."

As Young snapped his briefcase shut, I spoke to Liza's back. "Do you know why Mom and Dad couldn't give blood to you that time you were in the hospital?"

She turned to give me a withering glare. "You already told me. We're different blood types. You and I are different blood types. That's no big deal." With a condescending head waggle, she added, "We'll be testing DNA. That's a whole different thing, sis. I would have expected you to know that."

"DNA tests can reveal a lot," I said. "Isn't that right, Aunt Belinda?"

"You're talking nonsense, Grace," Belinda said. "Didn't I warn you about that?"

"You really should take Bennett up on his offer," I said to Liza. "Before time's up."

She gave me a chilly smile. "In your dreams."

She was about to turn away again and I should have let her go, but something in me—some reluctance to cut off her last shot at improving her life—tugged at me. Frances, poking me in my side, may have helped, too.

"Aunt Belinda," I said, "are you going to tell Liza, or should I?"

My aunt's teeth clenched.

"Let's go," Liza said.

I smiled at her. "See you later, 'cuz."

"What is wrong with you?" Aunt Belinda asked.

"Isn't it time to stop pretending?" I asked. "Once Uncle Wade died, you could have come forward. Why didn't you?"

Liza looked to Aunt Belinda, then to me. "What does Uncle Wade have to do with anything?"

"Aunt Belinda?" I said. "Don't you think this is better coming from you?"

"I don't know what you're talking about."

Young tried to interrupt. "I don't see how this discussion is relevant."

Hands fisted, Frances took a step forward. "It's relevant, all right, buddy."

"Good news, Liza," I said with the biggest smile of the day. "Your fondest wish has come true. We aren't sisters after all."

She fixed me with a deadpan smirk. "This is how you think you'll get out of sharing your fortune with me? What a joke."

"Really? Ask Aunt Belinda why there are no photographs of Mom pregnant with you. Why you and I look so very different."

"Nice try," Liza said. Turning to Young, she added, "We're done here."

"My uncle Wade went to prison for five years for drunk driving. Big family secret, by the way. I just found out myself. During that time, your mother"—I pointed to my aunt—"met someone else and had an affair."

"How dare you!" Aunt Belinda shouted.

"Please, correct me if I'm wrong," I said. "Tell me what part of this is untrue."

Again, she started to sputter.

"Do you remember Mom's best friend, Arlene?" I asked.

Aunt Belinda blanched. Liza muttered, "Sort of."

"I talked with her yesterday. She'd been sworn to secrecy, but once I explained all the inconsistencies, she was happy to fill in the blanks. You were born at home by the way, Liza," I said. "Aunt Belinda paid off the midwife to falsify the birth certificate and name Mom and Dad as your parents." I turned to Bennett. "What time is it?"

He checked his watch. "Ten minutes left."

Facing Aunt Belinda, I said, "You begged my parents to take Liza in as their own and then you had the audacity to lie to me and tell me my mother had had an affair?" My voice rose. "How dare you?"

I watched horrified comprehension wash over Liza as she read the truth on Belinda's face. "What is happening here?"

I made a little shooing motion with my hands. "Go ahead," I said. "You want to take us to court? You're subject to a DNA test. Good luck with that."

"But . . . how? What?" Liza couldn't get her words out.

Young stepped between them. "This could all be a ruse to trick you into signing their agreement. Don't fall for it. Let's move forward with our lawsuit. Too much is at stake."

But Aunt Belinda had covered her face with her hands. "I'm sorry," she said.

I didn't know who she was apologizing to.

"Why didn't you come forward after Uncle Wade died?" I asked again. "You and Liza could have had all those years to get to know each other."

She reached out to grab her daughter's arm. "I wanted to tell you."

Liza recoiled. "Don't touch me." With a glare, she curled her lip at me. "How long have you known?"

"Just since yesterday," I said. "Though I had suspicions for a little longer than that. Incidentally," I added as I pointed to Ted, "one of Mr. Hertel's associates is taking a statement from Arlene even as we speak. Just making sure to tie up any loose ends for future reference. And my friend Mr. Tooney—you remember him, Liza?—assured me that he'd be happy to dig deeper into this matter if we feel the need."

Aunt Belinda pulled her face from her hands. "You," she said with venom. "You were always the golden child. My poor Liza got the short end of every opportunity."

"No," I said. "She didn't. But if it helps you to believe that, be my guest."

"Less than two minutes remaining," Bennett said.

Aunt Belinda squared her shoulders. "Sign the agreement," she said to Liza.

"But—"

"Sign it if you know what's good for you." Aunt Belinda motioned to Young to open his briefcase and pull the document back out.

"You can't make me sign this," Liza said. "We can still sue."

"And you'll wind up with nothing," Aunt Belinda said. "Sign it. At least we'll have something to live on."

"Who said anything about 'we'?" Liza asked with a snarl in her throat. She turned to Young. "Give me the pen."

Chapter 33

IT WASN'T THAT I CHICKENED OUT ON CON-
tacting Joe. It was that I couldn't decide precisely how to do
it. He had office hours until five o'clock, and although I tried
several times to come up with a brief yet meaningful text
message, all my attempts at wording came out sounding
lame. And leaving a voicemail or a message with his receptionist felt wrong.

Truth was, I realized as I made my way to the parking
lot adjacent to Joe's medical office, even though Flynn had
corroborated his story, I wanted Joe to know that I'd been
willing to take a leap of faith without it. And I wanted to
tell him so in person.

I found an empty spot in the lot and leaned against the
side of my car to wait. It was five minutes to five. I knew
better than to expect him to pop out the door at the top of
the hour. Patients didn't suddenly disappear when time
was up.

Medical personnel began drifting out at about five fifteen.

A couple of them gave me a curious glance before getting into their cars and driving away. One woman said hello and smiled.

After the departing staffers dwindled and my car and Joe's were the only ones left in the lot, I glanced at my phone. Five twenty-seven.

Maybe I should have called first. What if he planned to catch up on paperwork for the next three hours? I could be in for a long wait.

I walked a few steps one way then another, considering whether I should text him after all, when movement in the greenery fifteen feet away caught my attention.

Giant yews lined the eastern edge of the parking lot. A person, or perhaps a large dog, crouched behind one of them. Now that I looked more closely, I could tell it was a man wearing dark pants, a dark jacket, and a baseball cap. In this late afternoon warmth, he had to be uncomfortable.

I was uncomfortable because it was clear he was watching me.

I took a few steps closer to confirm my suspicion. Yep. The same man who had been taking photos outside the Granite Building the day Virginia had been killed. The man who'd sat near me when I had lunch with Neal Davenport. The man I'd spotted at the bar when I went to dinner with Joe. I'd been so sure it had been Craig following me all this time that I'd forgotten about my mysterious shadow until now.

"Come out of there, you," I called out. "If you think you're being discreet, you're failing miserably."

While I spoke, I pulled my phone out again and navigated to Rodriguez's number.

The man took the long way around the line of yews and emerged at the far left end. I was right. Same guy. He held his phone up at about eye height and made no disguise of taking pictures.

We were about thirty feet apart now. Too far for him to grab me. Nonetheless, I positioned myself behind Joe's car in case I needed cover. Holding up my phone, I wiggled it for emphasis. "Tell me why you're following me and you'd better make it good; otherwise I'm calling the police."

"I'm not following you, honey," he said. "I'm following him." He gestured with his elbow.

I turned to see Joe coming up behind me. No cane today. "Grace?" he said. "What are you doing here?" He pointed at the man snapping pictures. "Who's that?"

"I came to see you," I said before turning back to the man. "Who are you?"

He pulled a business card out of his pocket and tossed it toward us. It fluttered and fell to the ground. I left it there.

"I believe you met my associate, Yolanda," he said. Hoisting the phone again, he aimed. "Say cheese," he said, and clicked. "The two of you get a little closer, okay? You know, snuggle up a bit?" He lowered the phone long enough for me to see his smug grin. "I get paid big bucks to deliver results. I want to keep this gravy train running full speed."

"Get out of here," Joe said. "Get away from me."

"You can't keep me off public property," he said.

"This is private property," Joe said as he advanced on him. "You want to argue the point?"

The man smirked. He made his way to a section of the lot that faced the street and stepped over the concrete divider onto the sidewalk. "Better?" He lifted the phone again and squeezed off more shots. "Come on, smile for the camera."

"I'm sorry, Grace," Joe said. "Is this the guy you saw at dinner the other night?"

Nodding, I came around the car to join him. The two of

us were careful to maintain a respectable distance while the man at the sidewalk grabbed more photos and jeered.

"That's him all right," I said with a rueful laugh. "All this time I thought he was following me." I gave a sad laugh. "I sure sound full of myself, don't I?"

"Not at all, Grace. Completely understandable."

Joe turned to face the guy. Grinning hard through gritted teeth, he pointed to himself. "This a big enough smile for you?" Turning back to me, he sobered. "I have no idea how long this will keep up. Until the divorce is final, at least."

I waved and smiled at the would-be photographer. "Which is my best side? This," I asked, turning to my right, "or this?" I turned to my left.

The guy must not have enjoyed our attention. He pocketed the phone.

Joe rested a hand on the hood of his car. "You came here to see . . . me?" he asked.

"I did." I smiled. "I knew where to find you."

He started toward me, then stopped himself, tilting his head toward the man at the sidewalk. "Are you willing to put up with this guy shadowing us for a little while?"

"This guy and his partner, Yolanda," I said.

"Yes, Yolanda," he said. "How could I forget?" He took a half step closer, his eyes bright and warm. "You know I'd like to kiss you right now," he whispered.

"You know I want you to," I whispered back.

"Hey, you two. A little louder. I can't hear from this distance."

We both glanced back at the investigator. Still watching us, he ran the back of his hand against his forehead and shifted his weight.

Joe turned to me. "What do you say? Are you free for dinner? Or drinks?"

"How about both?" I said with a smile.

"We could probably give him the slip, but that would just play into his game, wouldn't it?"

"It would." I shrugged. "If he intends to be our chaperone, why not invite him along?"

Joe laughed as he dug out his remote and unlocked the car. "We're going to grab dinner now," he shouted to the man.

The guy jerked in surprise. "Smart aleck," he shouted back.

"Not kidding," Joe said. "Feel free to join us. Not at the same table, though. You're on your own for that." Turning to me again, Joe said, "Where do you want to go?"

"Hugo's?"

He gave me a wink and shouted again. "Better get moving, buddy. We're leaving now. Stay close. I'll try not to lose you."

Still looking skeptical, the man trotted over to a compact car parked on the side street. "You better not," he shouted back.

"This ought to be interesting," I said.

"Interesting." Joe shook his head. "That's one word for it, I guess. I'm just sorry to drag you into my troubles."

"Nope." I squinted in the direction of the investigator, who was squeezing behind the wheel of his small car. "No dragging involved. I'm here because I want to be." I met Joe's eyes. "We'll face this together."

He drew in a sharp breath. "Thank you." He swallowed hard, then cleared his throat. "I like the sound of that."

"Me too," I said as I opened the passenger door. "Let's go."

FROM *NEW YORK TIMES* BESTSELLING AUTHOR
JULIE HYZY

ALL THE PRESIDENT'S MENUS

It's an old adage that too many cooks spoil the broth. But when a tour of the White House kitchen by a group of foreign chefs ends in murder, it's Olivia Paras who finds herself in the soup…

Due to a government sequester, entertaining at the White House has been severely curtailed. So executive chef Olivia Paras is delighted to hear that plans are still on to welcome a presidential candidate from the country of Saardisca—the first woman to run for office—and four of that nation's top chefs.

But while leading the chefs on a kitchen tour, pastry chef Marcel passes out suddenly—and later claims he was drugged. When one of the visiting chefs collapses and dies, it's clear someone has infiltrated the White House with ill intent. Could it be an anti-Saardiscan zealot? Is the candidate a target? Are the foreign chefs keeping more than their recipes a secret? Once again, Olivia must make sleuthing the special of the day…

juliehyzy.com
penguin.com